The epic Harbinger of Doom saga continues in *Gods of the Sword*, the exciting sixth volume in the series.

Frem Sorlons' grandmother warned him about the black elves. They're otherworldly, evil imps, devoid of morals or conscience — and they'll kill you, as soon as look at you, she'd say. Until he reached Jutenheim, he never thought he'd meet one outside of her wild stories. He never even thought that they were real. But then one night, the black elves came calling and threatened to take not only Frem's life, but also his immortal soul.

With his parents and older brothers gone, the only things that Ector Eotrus has left are his Dor and his life. But they're coming to take both. The only question is, who will get there first: the Alders or the trolls?

Lord Torbin Malvegil is going to war. War with the Shadow League. War with the Black Hand assassins. And war with the duergar. Each is a war he cannot hope to win. Each is war he cannot survive.

Artol has won most every fight he's been in these last twenty-five years. On the Isle of Evermere, that streak will come crashing to an end. An end from which only the god of lightning can hope to save him.

BOOKS BY GLENN G. THATER

THE HARBINGER OF DOOM SAGA

GATEWAY TO NIFLEHEIM
THE FALLEN ANGLE
KNIGHT ETERNAL
DWELLERS OF THE DEEP
BLOOD, FIRE, AND THORN
GODS OF THE SWORD
THE SHAMBLING DEAD
MASTER OF THE DEAD
SHADOW OF DOOM
WIZARD'S TOLL
VOLUME 11+ (FORTHCOMING)

HARBINGER OF DOOM
(COMBINES *GATEWAY TO NIFLEHEIM* AND *THE FALLEN ANGLE* INTO A SINGLE VOLUME)

THE HERO AND THE FIEND
(A NOVELETTE SET IN THE HARBINGER OF DOOM UNIVERSE)

THE GATEWAY
(A NOVELLA LENGTH VERSION OF *GATEWAY TO NIFLEHEIM*)

THE DEMON KING OF BERGHER
(A SHORT STORY SET IN THE HARBINGER OF DOOM UNIVERSE)

To be notified about my new book releases and any special offers or discounts regarding my books, please join my mailing list here: http://eepurl.com/vwubH

GLENN G. THATER

GODS

OF THE

SWORD

A TALE FROM THE HARBINGER OF DOOM SAGA

Copyright © 2015 by Glenn G. Thater.

GODS OF THE SWORD © 2015 by Glenn G. Thater

ISBN-13: 978-0692597958
ISBN-10: 0692597956

Visit Glenn G. Thater's website at
http://www.glenngthater.com

December 2015 Worldwide Print Edition
Published by Lomion Press

1

A VISIT TO THE WAREHOUSE

Ob and Dolan skulked about the Town of Evermere, seeing what there was to see. It was an odd place. The people behaved strangely, but Ob had traveled about Midgaard more than enough to know that customs varied widely from here to there, such that one man's weird was another's normal. Despite that perspective, he had a bad feeling about Evermere, though he couldn't put his finger on exactly why. He felt that there was something sinister about the place. Just a feeling, but his instincts were rarely wrong.

He and Dolan intended to continue skulking around town until shortly before midnight, when they planned to rejoin Theta and the others at The Dancing Turtle inn for the start of the Running of the Bulls. It was all the townsfolk talked about, but it sounded stupid to Ob. Running down the streets in the middle of the night, chasing a bunch of huge bulls, and then killing them. Odd custom, indeed. And downright dangerous. Stupid dangerous. But it was something to see, and would make for a good story, so Ob didn't want to miss it.

Not long past eleven, while they were snooping in an alley, they spotted Duchess Morgovia, the ruler of Evermere Island. They decided to shadow her and her entourage: several golden armored bodyguards, her scraggly henchman, Slint, and a young woman that Slint pulled along by the arm (a bit too roughly, in Ob's opinion). The Duchess was a beautiful woman, refined, and charming too, but there was something that wasn't quite right about her. Earlier that day, when they dined with her in her villa, she was all smiles and courtesy, but Ob smelled a rat. She didn't ask them the right questions —— the ones any island leader would ask of a vessel that just put to port. Things just didn't add up with her and Ob was determined to get to the bottom of it.

Ob stalked her in near perfect silence and stuck to the shadows, unseen. Dolan was a ghost, making no sound at all, and leaving no track, trace, or trail for even the most skilled bloodhound to follow.

The Duchess's group halted in front of a large building that looked like a warehouse. Slint pounded on the door, and after a while, a man opened it and stepped out. The man was rather nondescript: average in height, slight of build, middle-aged, and balding. They called him Rasker. Dolan and Ob skulked closer so that they could overhear.

"...she was a gift from Lord Rendan," said the Duchess.

"Is she broken?" said Rasker as he looked the woman up and down.

6

"No, she came off the schooner," said the Duchess. "He found her scavenging for food near his estate. A little thief, she is. How she slipped past us, I've no idea. I need you to hold her for me, but don't put her in with the others. She's a pretty thing; they're bound to soil her. I want her unsullied and pristine for tomorrow night's run."

"Aye, Duchess, I will watch over her myself. You can count on old Rasker. If you don't mind my asking, when are they bringing by the other newcomers? I've cleared space for them."

"No need," said the Duchess. "I've decided to surprise them when the Run starts. It will be so much more fun that way, don't you think?"

They all laughed.

"Fine by me," said Rasker. "Saves me the trouble."

The Duchess and her group headed in the direction of The Dancing Turtle. Once the Duchess was out of sight, Rasker grabbed the girl, whose hands were bound behind her back, and dragged her with little effort into an alley on the side of the warehouse. Ob motioned to Dolan who was hiding some yards away, and slunk to the mouth of the alley in time to see Rasker toss the girl into a wooden storage shed propped against the alley wall.

"Just a bit of soiling won't spoil you too much, little one," said Rasker, leering. He growled and dived into the shed.

"Let's go," said Ob as he jumped to his feet. There was no way that he was going to sit back and do nothing while a woman was violated. Ob turned his head to confirm that Dolan was following, but Dolan was already past him, his bow in hand. He moved like lightning. Ob was only halfway to the shed when Dolan reached it, raised his bow, and fired into it at point blank range. Rasker cried out in pain, for the arrow had hit home.

"Shit," said Ob. "We could've just gave him a thrashing," he muttered.

A second later, Dolan fired again, and then again, almost as fast as Ob's eyes could follow. In all his years, he'd never seen anyone as quick with a bow as that.

Just as Ob reached the shed, Dolan stumbled back and reached for his sword, surprise on his face. From out of the shed, leaped Rasker. He had one arrow sticking out of his back, and two shafts in his chest, but seemed unfazed. He bounded across the alley into Dolan, before Dolan could bring his sword to bear. He smashed Dolan to the ground. He straddled him and pounded him with his fists as he spat a string of curses. Dolan blocked the blows as best he could with his hands and forearms. From the sound of it, the punches were powerful, very powerful. Rasker had a strength that belied his modest size.

Ob charged and dived head first into Rasker's side, knocking him off Dolan. Ob scrambled to his feet, axe in hand. Rasker was already up. His pallor was a sickly white, and huge fangs extended from his upper jaw where none had been moments before.

Ob's eyes widened, and for a moment, he froze in shock. He didn't expect this. At a glance, Ob knew what Rasker was. He'd seen his kind

8

before. And he knew enough of them to know that he and Dolan were in the deep stuff.

Rasker focused a withering gaze on Ob. Then he laughed. "What the heck are you? Some kind of deformed dwarf?"

Ob stepped in and swung his axe, but Rasker dodged back. "I'm no stinking dwarf, you scum." Ob swung again and again, but Rasker dodged this way and that — he was too fast, too agile. Despite being quicker with an axe than most any man, Ob could not hit him.

Rasker came in again. Ob swung the axe, but missed. Rasker reached down and grabbed Ob by the belt. He lifted him up, and threw him across the alley. He smashed so hard into the far wall, that the wall's wood planks cracked. Ob slumped down on his rump, back against the wall, dazed — his weapon dropped, his vision blurred, all the breath knocked out of him.

After a moment, Ob's eyes focused. Rasker squatted over him. His fangs were just inches from Ob's face.

"Not enough of you for a good meal," said Rasker, "and probably sour as vinegar, but I'll have a wee taste just the same." He turned Ob's head to the side with one hand — a hand far too powerful to resist. He bared his fangs. He leaned forward to sink his teeth into Ob's neck.

Ob felt and heard a terrific impact against his helmet — a loud clanging sound, and his head was knocked back into the wall. He blinked to clear his vision. An arrow protruded from Rasker's right eye; its tip had gone clear through from the back, and it had impacted Ob's helmet. Ob recognized it as one of the magicked up arrows that old Pipkorn had given to Dolan. Ob tried to push Rasker off, but he growled and stood up on his own, still alive. As Rasker turned, another arrow struck him in the middle of his chest and it pushed him back. Then another caught him in the throat. He lowered his head and charged across the alley. Dolan dived to the side at the last moment and Rasker struck the far wall, caving it in and falling halfway through. Dolan backpedaled, stumbling, obviously hurt. Ob struggled to regain his feet, dazed and battered.

"We've got to run, laddie," shouted Ob.

"No," said Dolan, nocking two arrows at once.

"We can't beat this bastard," said Ob.

Rasker emerged, and flung a dagger underhanded at Dolan, but Dolan dodged it and let his arrows fly. Both struck the man in the upper chest, but he charged again. Dolan's sword was out and Ob dashed toward them both. Rasker ran directly into Dolan's outstretched blade, impaling himself, the sword puncturing clear through him. He grabbed Dolan's throat. He'd planned it. He took the sword thrust on purpose, to get close enough to get his hands on Dolan, so that he could wring the life out of him. He lifted Dolan aloft by the neck and squeezed.

But Ob was there. Rasker seemed to have forgotten him or just didn't consider him a threat. That was a mistake. Ob swung his mithril axe at Rasker's leg with all his strength. The axe sliced through the leg like butter, severing it with that single blow. Rasker howled and fell over, his stump gushing blood, though the color was off, more green than red. Rasker scrambled around and attempted to rise on his remaining foot, but Ob swung his axe in a great arc that ended at the back of Rasker's neck. Greenish-red blood spouted from the wound, Rasker's head half severed. For a moment, Ob figured that was the end of him. He'd fall back dead. But Rasker roared, and growled, and cursed as he tried again to rise. His head nearly cleaved off, yet he had fight in him still.

Ob hit him in the neck again. This axe blow even harder than the last. It decapitated him. Ob couldn't believe it when he saw Rasker's body still thrashing about, his head three feet away. Ob stepped up to the head and crushed it to pulp with a third blow. Rasker's body went limp, but quivered and shook for some moments before all life left it.

"By Odin," said Ob. "That bastard was tough."

"Thanks for the help," said Dolan before he spit a mouthful of blood to the ground. His face was battered and swelling. He bled from cuts around his left eye, from his nose, and from his mouth. "The girl."

Ob dashed to the shed's door and looked in. "She's not moving." Ob pulled her by the feet into the alley, so that he had some light to see by. "There's a lot of blood. The bastard bit her. Those stinking fangs." He knelt down and examined her. "Dead," he said turning back toward Dolan. "He bit her neck. She bled out. She's gone."

Dolan sat on the ground and looked unsteady. "I was trying to do the right thing," said Dolan. "And all I did, was get her killed."

"They was going to kill her anyway, boy. We

did all we could to save her."

"I put maybe ten arrows in him and he kept coming," said Dolan. "What kind of man can do that?"

"Gabe and me ran across a couple of fellows like this one once. Gabe called them blood lords or some such. Tough buggers just like this one. Hopefully, he was the only one of them types hereabouts. If the town is loaded up with them, we're in the deep stuff. Best we get gone before any more unfriendlies show up. We've got to warn the others. I think that that stinking Duchess means to kill us all dead."

"Didn't you hear them before?" said Dolan as he pointed to the warehouse. "They've got other folks locked up in there. We've got to free them now, while we've got the chance, or else they'll end up dead too."

"There could be a whole squadron of them killers in there guarding them, boy. We barely survived the one. We've done our best, and that's all we can do. Come on now, we've got to get out of here while the getting's good."

"You go if you must, Mister Ob. I'm going to try to spring them."

"That will get you killed."

"If it does, it does."

"Dagnabbit. What am I supposed to do? Leave you to your lonesome to get killed?"

Dolan recovered his bow and pulled several arrows from Rasker's corpse. "I'm going in. If I don't make it back, please tell Lord Angle that I did what I thought he would have done, if he was here." He didn't wait for any further words from

Ob. Instead, he gripped the brick wall and heaved himself up, easily scaling the wall up to a second story window. He slowly raised the sash and peered inside; Ob stared after him. Dolan glanced down at Ob, and then slipped inside, silent as stone.

"I ain't no stinking spider," muttered Ob. "Can't get up there if I wanted to, and I don't. Damn fool boy is gonna get himself killed dead." Ob dragged the girl's body back into the shed, and then did the same with Rasker's. At least that way if any unfriendlies came along before Dolan was off, they wouldn't immediately see anything amiss.

Ob scurried to the end of the alley and looked up and down the street to see if anyone was about. It was dark, foggy, and quiet. Off in the distance, toward the docks, he could just make out music and voices, no doubt coming from The Turtle or some other tavern or inn, as there were several of them down there. Then he noticed that the warehouse's front door was slightly ajar. Rasker hadn't closed it up tight before he pulled the girl into the alley.

Ob just couldn't leave Dolan — not with an open door practically inviting him in. He crept to the door, and was taken aback by the stench. An overwhelming stink of unwashed people seeped from inside. Ob peered in, but couldn't see much. He waited for his eyes to better adjust to the darkness and then carefully stepped inside.

From out of the darkness, a figure shuffled toward him. Ob feared it was another blood lord. He had to assume it was. He couldn't take any chances. Those things moved too fast and they were too powerful. He raised his axe, but before he struck his blow, he saw the man's face. Blood streamed from his mouth, dripped from his jaw, and soiled his shirt. Two prominent fangs protruded from his mouth, just as on old Rasker. Dead gods, Ob thought, his mind racing, his heart thumping, he must have gotten Dolan, must have bitten him good and killed him dead. Rage welled up in Ob's gut. He'd kill the bastard, even by his lonesome; somehow, he'd make him pay.

The blood lord moaned or growled and Ob stepped forward to attack when he realized that a sword's tip protruded from the center of the man's upper chest and he was staggering forward in awkward fashion, his eyes glazed over. The blood lord dropped to the floor face first as Dolan pulled his sword from his back.

Ob's axe crashed down on the back of his head, and the blood lord moved no more.

"I feared he got you," said Ob.

"There are people in cages in there," said Dolan as he pointed toward a set of double doors. "Lots of them, locked up tight."

"Any more guards?"

"Not that I saw, but there might be."

They quietly pushed open the doors. Beyond was a large, open warehouse space, filled with iron cages. Typically, six feet tall, the cages varied in length and width. Many stood empty, but some were packed with living men.

Those in some of the cages paid them no heed when they entered. They merely stared down at the floor, their faces expressionless, their spirits broken. Not one of them even looked up to see who had entered. These men wore simple clothes and looked unkempt and badly treated. They numbered thirty, maybe forty.

Other cages held seamen — forty at the least. It was hard to tell how many there were since they were packed in so tight. The seamen didn't look down; they looked defiant and angry. Some of them gripped the bars and stared at Ob and Dolan, hatred in their eyes. A few others lay on the floors of the cages, injured and weak.

Ob and Dolan looked carefully around the room and seeing no other guards, moved to within a few feet of the cages that held the seamen. "We're to spring you out of here," whispered Ob. "How many guards are there?"

The seamen looked to each other, confused. "You're not bloodsuckers?" whispered one.

"You be normal men?" said another.

"Our ship came in today," said Ob. "We didn't know what they were."

A big, scraggly-looking one-eyed man with a gray and black beard stepped toward the bars in one of the cages. The others moved aside. "There's two guards most of the time," said the graybeard, their captain. "A bald one called Rasker, and a tall skinny devil what's called Trern."

"We killed them both," said Ob. "Now let's get you out of them cages. Where do they keep the keys?"

"Are you sure?" said the graybeard. "Them bloodsuckers is mighty hard to keep down. We skewered a bunch of them but good, and up they came again, ready to kill."

"They're dead," said Ob. "We crushed their heads to mush."

The graybeard nodded. "Rasker has the keys in his pocket." The other men crowded up against the bars, hanging on every word.

"I'll get them," said Dolan as he dashed off.

"Who are you boys?" said the graybeard. "How many are with you?"

"We're Lomerian soldiers, from the northern territory."

The graybeard looked at Ob skeptically. "Not many gnomes wear armor for Lomion. They don't like your type, I hear. And your friend has elf ears and a strange look to him. He's no Lomerian and certainly no northerner."

When it became clear that Ob would offer no more, the graybeard said, "No matter, I suppose. You are who you are, and that's your business. Me and mine are out of Tragoss Kell. They call me Captain Graybeard and I'm darned happy to meet you. Is my schooner still in port, or did they sink her, the bastards?"

"We saw your ship when we came in," said Ob. "Looked fine as far as we could tell."

"Thank the gods," said Graybeard. "That gives us a fighting chance." He turned toward his men. "We'll make direct for the ship, boys, as soon as they spring us. Every man for hisself. We heave off at once. No waiting for nobody. So get there fast, or get dead quick in the trying. Whatever happens, don't let them bloodsucking bastards take you alive again."

"How many of them are bloodsuckers?" said Ob.

"All of them," said Graybeard. "The whole darned island as best we can tell, except for a few sorry folk they keep as slaves, like them over yonder," he said as he pointed to the downcast men in the nearby cages. "The bastards got us drunk and happy and then got the drop on us when we wasn't paying heed. Otherwise, we'd have given them what for. The streets would've run red with their blood, not ours — hard to kill or not. They killed twenty of my men. Ten outright, the rest for sport. Hung them upside down, right over there, so that we could see, and drained their blood. Then they drank it. They took the bodies away and I've a sense that they cooked them up. Some kind of stinking inbred cannibals is what they are. They're unnaturally strong — strong like I've never seen. They've kept us rotting in here for near two weeks now. They got plans for us, they say, big plans, some kind of festival. You done got here in good time."

Dolan dashed back into the room. "There is a group of them standing in the alley — five or six. I couldn't get near the keys. They're waiting for someone. They said something about having orders to move the meat to the holding pen."

"You've got to get us out of here!" said Graybeard.

"Please," begged the seamen. "Get us out."

They heard the sound of the warehouse door open and voices talking. "Rasker, you bastard, where are you?" shouted one of the Evermerians. "Why is this door unlocked?"

"A weapon?" whispered Graybeard. "Anything."

Dolan tossed him a dagger; Ob did too.

The seamen secreted the weapons as Ob and Dolan slunk toward the back of the building.

They found a storage room with windows and ducked inside. They pressed their ears up against the door in attempt to hear what was going on.

There was an uproar when the Evermerians found Trern's body. They rushed into the cage area, but after finding all the cages still secure, they concluded that Rasker must have killed Trern, who he had it in for, for years. They never even bothered to ask the prisoners what happened.

"There's nothing we can do to help them," whispered Ob. "You know that, right?"

"I know," said Dolan. "But if they attack the seamen, I'm going in."

Ob shook his head.

"Sounds like they're pulling one man out of the cages at a time," said Ob.

"And chaining them together — hands and feet," said Dolan.

"There's nothing more we can do here," said Ob. "We've got to warn Theta and the others."

They carefully lifted one of the windows open, wincing with its every creak. Once it was open far enough, they slipped through and dashed out into the night.

2

AT JUTENHEIM

Frem Sorlons stood at the prow of The White Rose, gazing through the thick fog at the featureless ocean; the day, cold, a wintry breeze blowing in from the south. They had sailed farther south than Frem ever dreamed he would go; past where he thought the world ended, and then some, and still the ocean went on and on. There seemed no end to the Azure Sea.

He always thought of the south as being warmer — the farther south he went, the warmer it got. That's how it always was. But now he knew better. If you went south for long enough, it started to grow cold again. And they'd sailed far, for it was cold; as cold as the far north.

Frem's squadmates, Par Sevare, and Sergeant Putnam stood beside him holding the ship's rail, Sevare looking paler than usual (and foregoing his beloved chewing tobacco), as the modest swells pushed the ship up and down and occasionally sprayed them with a fine, icy mist. Behind them, weary sailors washed the deck with mops and buckets of seawater.

"Seven days of scrubbing, but they finally got the bloodstains of them sea devils what attacked us off the deck," said Putnam. "That's persistence."

"Father Ginalli's orders," said Sevare. "He wanted the stains gone; so they're gone. The seamen were too afraid to disappoint him. Unfortunately, they didn't get rid of the stench. It isn't much better than it was. It could make a man puke."

"Aye," said Putnam. "Scrubbing with water didn't work. Lye soap did no better. Nothing is gonna get rid of that foulness, short of replacing the deck boards. They're tainted with the stink of them things." Putnam spit over the rail to emphasize his disgust.

"At least Dagon's island is well behind us," said Frem.

"Praise Odin for that," said Putnam.

Frem started. Sevare turned and frowned at Putnam. "Watch your words, sergeant," said Frem. "This be Azathoth country."

"Sorry, Captain. A slip of the tongue is all."

"Keep it sure-footed or else you may end up with your head smashed like old Captain Rascelon," said Frem. "Them wizards are touchy about their religion."

Sevare shook his head but held his tongue.

Putnam went pale. "Aye, I'll be careful. This has been an unlucky voyage, start to end — no need to bring trouble on myself."

"Unlucky would have been if that big lizard thing," Dagon, "had gone for a swim and chased us down," said Frem. "He didn't. I figure that makes us darned lucky."

"Always the optimist, eh Captain?" said Putnam. "That's a good attitude to have, I expect. I've always fretted too much."

"I've noticed," said Frem.

"We've all noticed," said Sevare. "Smooth sailing the rest of the way to Jutenheim would serve us well."

"That's not asking for much, for it won't be long now," said Frem. "We should make landfall later today; tomorrow at the latest."

"What? That soon?" said Sevare. "Why do you think that?"

"I snuck a look at the charts."

"Since when do you read navigational charts, Captain?" said Putnam.

Frem shrugged. "Just something I picked up somewhere."

"How many more secret skills you got up your sleeve?" said Putnam.

Sevare eyed Frem suspiciously.

"And there it is," said Frem. "Even closer than I thought."

"Land ho," shouted the lookout from the crow's nest.

The fog surrounding the ship cleared and a large land mass came into view. It was close — less than two miles away. A rocky coastline with treacherous cliffs that rose straight up hundreds of feet above the water that crashed into its base. The cliffs were made of huge columns of black basalt — old stone, from Midgaard's youth. Atop the cliffs were trees, tall and stately, their tops lost in the mist. Every once in a while the mist parted just enough for the men on The Rose to catch a glimpse of white-tipped mountains that loomed in the background, far inland. Those were no common hills, but high peaks, as great as any in

21

Midgaard.

"Reefs ahead," shouted the lookout.

The first mate turned the rudder hard to port even as he shouted to the crew to adjust the sails. Quick reactions notwithstanding, the hull scraped against a submerged reef, and for a moment, threatened to run aground. What small leaks sprung from the collision were quickly dealt with. On Captain du Mace's orders they turned south and followed the coast, though they could approach no closer than a mile out, and in most places two to three miles out, due to continuous reefs that would have torn the ship apart had they attempted to breach them.

At last they sighted Jutenheim's only port. A wide channel, formed in some forgotten epoch when immense sections of cliff sheared off and fell outward into the sea, led to it. That rock fall and a lava flow from deep within the ground created a peninsula upon which sat the island's only large settlement. Shallowest where it met the water, the rock sloped up as it went inland. Some of Jutenheim's buildings resided only a few feet above sea level at the seaward end of the peninsula; others, on the landward side, existed high on the cliff face, accessible only via uneven stone steps that wound their way up. Some of those were built right into the cliff face and on terraces of stone.

"Now that's a sight," said Lord Ezerhauten as he approached the others. "Stone buildings every one —— walls, walks, and roofs. Nary a bit thatch or planking in view."

"I thought this place more fable than truth,"

said Frem. "Yet there it be. Finally, we come to the end of this journey."

"At least the town is right there, so we've no trek to make this time," said Putnam. "Maybe we'll wrap this mission up quick and get gone home. I miss civilization."

"I miss sleeping in a bed what doesn't move," said Frem.

"The town is not where we're going," said Sevare.

The others turned toward the wizard, surprise on their faces.

"What do you mean?" said Frem. "We're headed to an old temple in Jutenheim, and that is Jutenheim, isn't it?"

"It's not as simple as that," said Sevare. "The town is called Jutenheim, but the whole island is also called Jutenheim. We're to find an old temple deep in the interior, far from the town. It is only there that Lord Korrgonn can open his portal to Nifleheim."

"The interior?" said Putnam. "What do you mean? Atop the cliffs?"

"Legend says there is a huge valley on the other side of the cliffs," said Sevare. "It extends for dozens of leagues, maybe more. Somewhere in that expanse is the temple that we seek."

"Somewhere in that expanse?" said Putnam. "Oh, that's just wonderful."

"Do the wizards have a map showing where it is?" said Frem.

"Not that I'm aware of," said Sevare. "Hopefully, the locals will be able to point us in the right direction. If not, we'll have to search until we find it."

"And you didn't think to tell us this before now?" said Ezerhauten.

"Ginalli's orders," said Sevare. "He said no one else was to know."

"Ginalli's orders?" said Ezerhauten. "You work for me, mister — not the priest. Did you forget that?"

"What difference does it make whether you found out we're headed to the interior now or a ten day ago?" said Sevare.

Ezerhauten moved very close to Sevare, menace on his face. "From now on, you tell me everything you know as soon as you know it, mister. You got it?"

Sevare stared at him for a few moments before responding. "Aye, commander," he said. Then he stared at the deck for a moment, as if contemplating whether to say more, then turned, and walked away.

"Wizard," said Ezerhauten. Sevare stopped and looked his way. "Don't cross me. Don't even think about crossing me." Sevare made no response and continued on his way.

"Your wizard friend may cause us some trouble," said Ezerhauten. "I'm counting on you men keeping him in line. He needs to remember where his loyalties lie."

"It's the religion what's making him all weird," said Putnam. "A bit of it can do a man some good and see him through troubled times, but too much can clog up the brain and turn it to mush. He'll be back to his old self once we get done with this mission and get him clear of the Leaguers."

"I don't care about his beliefs," said Ezerhauten. "I only care that he follows my orders, and that he's loyal to the company. Right now, it seems, his loyalties are with Ginalli. I can't have that. We can't have that. Frem — can you keep him in line or not?"

"Yes, and it won't be as big a problem as getting over those cliffs. How are we supposed to do that?"

"There's got to be a way," said Ezerhauten. "They must have a stair or hoist or some steep path."

"And if they don't, we climb?" said Putnam.

"I don't climb mountains," said Frem.

"I don't either," said Ezerhauten. "But we may just have to learn."

The port was larger than it appeared at first, with several protected coves that housed berths for many ships of varying sizes. The docks bustled with activity, ships coming and going, loading and unloading. More than a few were of exotic design, from lands that even Ezerhauten and his well-traveled band had never visited, and a few that they had never even heard of. It was nothing in size compared to the ports of Lomion City or Tragoss Mor, but it was a substantial port nonetheless.

The locals seemed unconcerned about security. It soon became apparent why. Everyone in Jutenheim — men, women, and all but the smallest children, openly carried weapons. Swords, shields, spears, daggers, axes, and bows. Most of them wore armor as well, leathers more often than not, even just going about their daily toils. Heavy coats of fur protected them from the cold. And the people were large. The average male was at least six feet tall, the women, only a couple of inches shorter. On average, that made them taller, and a good deal broader, than Lomerians, who were amongst the largest folk in the known world. They were even a match or perhaps more so, in physique to northerners, such as the Eotrus and their kin, and in fact, resembled them in many ways, save for the Jutens' lighter hair.

Unlike most places, Jutenheim was a free port. No harbormaster accosted The Rose asking after their business and demanding fees or tariffs for this or that. Nonetheless, a strange contingent greeted them as they tied off their ship to its berth: an ancient crone, a boy, and a wolf. They were waiting for them in the very spot that the captain chose to park the ship, as if they knew The Rose was coming. The crone, all wrinkles and stringy gray hair that reached near to her knees. Tall she was, even for a Juten — maybe six feet or more in height, if she had stood straight, but she was withered and stooped, her back, humped. She carried a long wooden staff in one hand, similar to what wizards sometimes bore, though it had no jewels or other riches adorning its surface, only runes, carved all around it, with a polished and faceted shard of obsidian mounted atop its end. The boy was but ten or eleven, though his height and breadth were more than most grown men. His wolf was similarly large. The crone called for The Rose's headman.

Ginalli stepped down to speak with her,

perhaps out of respect, but more likely out of curiosity, though he only did so after securing Ezerhauten by his side. Frem, Putnam, and Sevare followed on their heels.

"The Angel of Death would have words with you," said the boy, his childish voice belying his size.

"What words?" said Ginalli as his eyes darted this way and that, a nervous sound on his voice. He would not look the woman in the eyes and seemed at once to regret stepping down to speak with her.

"Words of warning," said the boy. "And words of wisdom, as is her wont. If you would hear them."

"Speak your name, headman," said the crone, her voice grating to the ears, her accent, heavy.

"Speak yours," said Ginalli.

"Any name I once had is long forgotten, though sadly so," said the crone. "The Angel of Death, they call me, for the future I often see — — the signs, the portents, the omens."

"A seer," whispered Ezerhauten in Ginalli's ear. "She reads the bones, like the witch-women of the northlands," he said pointing to the leather bag that hung from her rope belt.

"I am Father Ginalli of Azathoth."

"A priest of Azathoth, you say?" she cackled. She coughed up a wad of phlegm and spat it to the ground. "Ho, ho, a rare visitor indeed, though little more welcome than the plague, methinks. Bring us no olden demons here, Ginalli. Bring us no evils from the Dawn Age, for we've plenty of our own, we have. Wotan be our god, and Donar

27

his son. We put our stock in them, and them only, we do. We suffer no false gods here. So if you've come to proselytize our people, disappointed you will be. Come you to grow your flock, priest? Be that your purpose?"

"Not at all," said Ginalli. "Though our purpose is our own."

"Speak your purpose, Ginalli, and tell me true. Why come you to Jutenheim with these men, with this ship and what it carries?"

"It is a private matter and of no concern to you, old woman."

She sneered. "All that happens on Jutenheim be of concern to me. Gave you a chance, I did. But no matter. Hold your tongue until you choke of it, priest. For I know your purpose. I know what you seek; I know why you seek it. I have long known that you would come. I have been waiting for you."

"You know nothing, old woman," said Ginalli shaking his head. "We are Lomerians, not backwards inbreds to be frightened by an old woman of the bones. Put on no performance for me, for it will profit you nothing. If you—"

"She foretold your coming," said the boy. "She foretold it when my grandfather was a boy younger than I am now. The Rose,' she said, will bring an ancient evil to Jutenheim. The priest, the company of steel, the red demon of Fozramgar, wizards great and small, and the lord of chaos to rule them all. They will come and Jutenheim will weep for it, for death and doom will follow them."

Ginalli and the others wore surprised looks.

"Do you know what you carry on your ship,

priest?" said the crone. "Do you know?"

Ginalli made no answer.

"A creature," she said. "A thing not of Midgaard. An alien thing of power — great and terrible power, as old as the sea, as secret as the dark, as slippery as the serpent. A puppet master, it be, ho, ho. Pull he your strings, Ginalli? Pull he your strings?"

"Korrgonn, the son of Azathoth travels with us," said Ginalli. "Speak no blasphemies of him, or you will regret it."

"Ha, ha!" said the crone, hopping from one foot to the other. "You know not! You know not. Foolish priest. A comeuppance will there be. Oh yes, a reckoning. A reckoning the like of which Midgaard has not seen in an age!"

"Your babbling makes no sense to me," said Ginalli. "Speak plainly or begone."

She paused her cavorting and stared Ginalli in the eye. "As plain as I can, I'll speak it, for I see that you're dim as well as daft. When comes the Harbinger of Doom — then you will know fear, priest. Your blood will run cold. Your feet will root to the earth when his sword and his hammer seek your life. You will regret your path, then, priest, your petty part in this game of gods and demons. But then, it will be too late. Hold on to your soul, priest. Hold on tight, ha, ha!"

Ginalli stepped closer to the woman, as if to intimidate her by his bearing and presence. He failed.

"What do you know of the Harbinger of Doom?"

"I know that he is the one man in all Midgaard

that can hope to stand against the creature that you've brought to Jutenheim."

"How can we defeat him?"

She smiled an evil looking smile, her teeth yellow and stained. "Of that I would tell you nothing, if even I had something to tell, and I do not. But one thing more I will say. One boon will I grant you, though you do not deserve it and are too dim to heed it. To survive what is coming, you must run, and never stop running. You must abandon your path. You must throw down your mission. Cast out your demons, Ginalli, and be a man again. Throw down your false idol and run, priest. Then only may you live out your span in peace."

"You're a mad old witch," said Ginalli. "Your words are as feeble as your body. I've borne your insults too long already. Get you gone now, or suffer Azathoth's wrath."

"Azathoth," she said. "Ha, ha. I fear not the dead, priest. Not yet, anyway. There be yet time. Ha, ha!"

She, the boy, and the wolf turned and walked toward the boardwalk at the pier's inland end. Ginalli and his companions crossed back over the gangway onto the ship. Ginalli stopped and whispered in Ezerhauten's ear. "The witch is a minion of the Harbinger. Kill her. And waste no time about it."

Ezerhauten put his hand to his sword hilt and looked down the pier. After but a moment, he grabbed Ginalli by the elbow. "Look," he said.

Ginalli turned. They had a clear view of the pier. Two hundred feet to shore, only a few empty dinghies docked in the shallower water between The Rose and the strand. There was no sign of the crone, or the boy, or the wolf.

"They could not have reached the boardwalk so fast, could they?" said Ginalli.

"At a run, not even the wolf, methinks," said Ezerhauten.

"Then where?" said Ginalli.

Ezerhauten shook his head.

"This be an evil portent, indeed," said Ginalli. "We must waste no time in this place, for now we know that the Harbinger has a foothold here. Send a man into town and find us a guide to bring us inland. The best there is. Of sound reputation — reliable. I will meet with him myself. We must leave for the cliffs at dawn. Make it so."

"I will," said Ezerhauten.

3

A PENNY FOR LITTLE TUG

Little Tug manned the longboat's tiller as his men rowed toward shore. After four trips hauling barrels of water and other supplies to the outer edge of Evermere's bay where The Black Falcon lay anchored, they were beat, and despite the chill air, their shirts were soaked through, their faces red.

Tug looked forward to meeting up with Captain Slaayde and the others at The Dancing Turtle inn for some good food and drink. Just as much, he looked forward to a night in a soft, warm bed that didn't move with the waves. If he was really lucky, he might even get to take a hot bath, not that they'd have a tub big enough for him to fit comfortably, but he was used to that. He worried that the festival he'd heard about might get noisy and keep him awake. After all they'd been through on that voyage, he deserved at least one quiet night ashore, didn't he? He doubted that he'd get it. If the beer was cold and the bed was soft and warm and didn't have any bugs, he supposed that that would be good enough. Such was a seaman's lot.

They eased the longboat up to its berth just as they'd done before. Four sailors climbed up the ladder to the pier deck to tie off the boat; the other two remained in the longboat with Tug to secure it from that end. Six men were all he was allowed to bring, much to the unhappiness of the rest of the crew. They could have no more men ashore than could fit safe and secure in a single longboat, per the captain's orders.

Three fancy dressed Evermerians awaited the seamen on the pier deck, which was odd, since the pier, in fact, much of the dock ward, had been deserted all evening. Two of the Evermerians were young men, not yet twenty; black haired, fair skinned, and obviously brothers. One stood on each side of a tiny wisp of a girl, perhaps eight years old, but likely even younger. Her hair was blonde and long, reaching past her waist. She sat atop a barrel, her legs crossed. She waved and smiled at the seamen as they made the deck.

"Hello there," said the girl, loud enough to get the men's attention. "My name is Penny. These are my beloveds, Moby and Toby. We've come to play with you. We've been waiting."

"Sorry, darling," said seaman Gurt, "but we've got a date with a barrel of beer and a side of beef."

"We're hungry too," said the girl, "and thirsty, and we're not waiting for you to eat dinner. That won't do at all. That's why we came down here instead of waiting for the Bulls' Run."

"We got no food for yous," said one of the sailors, "so be off home with you. Skedaddle."

"What do you mean?" said the girl. "You've got plenty of meat."

"We've got no meat, girl," said the seaman. "And no other food neither. So scram."

"You can't fool me," said Penny with a

mischievous smile on her face, and a singsong quality to her voice. "There's plenty of meat on you, and I'm going to eat it all up. It's too bad that you're so dirty and smelly — I'll probably have to hold my nose, but that's okay. When I'm hungry I'll eat almost anyone."

The two young men moved to block the sailors' path.

"We're hungry," said Moby.

"What is this?" said one of the seamen. "We've no time for your games. It's late already."

"We're thirsty," said Toby.

"What are you about?" said another seaman. "Are you kids drunk or nuts?"

"We're not letting you leave," said Penny in a cold, severe voice.

"Move aside, or we'll move you," said seaman Gurt, his hand on his sword's hilt.

The whites of both brothers' eyes turned black. Without further warning, they vaulted toward the seamen. Their teeth instantly grew to fangs; their nails to claws.

"I can't wait to drink your blood, hee hee," said the girl. "Every drop for me!"

The brothers moved like lightning. The closest two seamen never had a chance. Razor-sharp claws raked their throats; the cuts expertly placed to sever the jugular. Blood spurted everywhere. Their bodies had barely fallen to the deck in their death throes when the brothers lunged at the other seamen. They expected their prey to scream in terror, to freeze, or to flee in a panic. That's what prey always did. And they encouraged such behavior, growling and slavering, and slowing their movements, intentionally giving the prey time to react, because their reactions were often entertaining and sometimes led to a wild chase that relieved the endless boredom of Evermere, at least for a short time. A mini little Bulls' Run, just for them.

If the prey had the chance, they'd beg for mercy. They'd plead for their lives. Then they would do the dance: threats of torture, pleadings and promises, insults and humiliation, vows of servitude or retribution. The words and the order of things always differed, but the game usually played out much the same. It was always fun. And it always ended in the lovely screaming and the beautiful torture that lasted however long they wanted. Or rather, however long Penny wanted. And then the sweet reward: the blood, the meat, the souls. Penny usually left them a generous share. Not always. But usually. That's how things went, for more years than they could remember.

That night was different. The men of The Black Falcon were no ordinary sailors, no common prey. They didn't panic or pee themselves. And they didn't run.

Their cutlasses and dirks were out in a flash. And desperate battle was joined — hack and slash, fangs and fists. The deadly skill and experience of the seamen pitted against the uncanny strength, speed, and preternatural resilience of the Evermerians. The brothers didn't expect such resistance, but they liked it. They reveled in it. Except when taking a ship outright, they hadn't had such fun in decades.

The last two seamen made the pier deck. When they saw two of their comrades already down, they pulled their weapons and rushed forward to aid their fellows. Tug climbed up the ladder behind them, Old Fogey (his huge battle hammer) in one hand.

"Odin's ass," Tug said eyeing the carnage. "More stinking monsters. They're everywhere on this trip."

"Oh, a big one!" squeaked Penny in delight as she spotted Tug. She clapped her hands in joy; her smile ear to ear.

"Take the one on the right," shouted Tug to his men as he moved to the left to aid seaman Gurt.

Gurt was a knife master — one of the best in the crew. He'd dueled a dozen men in his time and lived to tell the tales. Despite the Evermerian's speed, he held his own and slashed Moby multiple times about his hands and arms.

As Tug barreled forward, Moby decided he'd toyed with his food long enough. He didn't mind taking a few slashes, but he'd little interest in getting pounded by Tug's big hammer. And so, he let Gurt stab him in the chest. That brought him in close. That brought him to a spot from which he couldn't get away. Moby grabbed Gurt about the neck. He leaned in. Gurt squirmed almost out of his grasp, but not far enough. His fangs clamped down on the seaman's shoulder. It wasn't the neck bite that Moby wanted, but it would do. Now all he had to do was knock Gurt down, leaving him free to deal with Tug. But as Moby pulled back, Gurt held him fast and with unexpected strength. Moby strained and pushed.

After a few moments, he was able to break Gurt's grip and fling him down. As Moby started to turn, Old Fogey slammed down onto the top of his head. A battle hammer blow to the head would kill any normal person, but Evermerians had hard heads. Very hard heads. A single such blow, even a powerful one, even one thrown by a great warrior, a hero, would do them little harm, perhaps none at all. Yet that single strike from Old Fogey crushed Moby's head to pulp. His body flopped lifeless to the deck.

Penny screamed — a high-pitched wail that nearly popped the seamen's eardrums. No human throat could make such a sound.

Then she saw Toby getting slashed to pieces by the other three sailors. A powerful cutlass stroke cut one of his arms off at the elbow. His beautiful arm. She stood up, atop the barrel. Tears ran down her face. Her shock quickly turned to anger. She hadn't expected this. Her beloveds, dead and dying. She couldn't believe it.

She expected to make a merry feast of the interlopers. One that she didn't have to share with anyone save for her beloveds. She wasn't used to food fighting back. At least not like Tug and company did. They had deadly skill. But so did she. And she'd had many more years to practice than they had. She would show them. She would make them pay for what they'd done.

Her face changed. Like the brothers, her eyes went black and her teeth became fangs — but hers grew longer and thicker. They glistened and dripped with saliva. Her ears lengthened. They grew pointy. Her beautiful face took on a grayish cast. All this in a mere moment.

A tiny thing was she, not even close to five feet tall. Nowhere near a hundred pounds. Had she not that evil look about her, Tug may not have had the heart to battle her at all. She looked so much like the baker's daughter — the one from Shield Street. That one always smiled at him and gave him extra rolls when he bought bread in the morning. She even had her eyes (before they went all black). And the same golden hair.

But Penny was no sweet little girl. She was no person at all, as far as Tug could tell. She was some kind of monster; some kind of thing, just like the brothers. Tug knew how to deal with such things.

Penny leaped at him from atop the barrel, covering the fifteen feet between them in a single, impossible bound. Had he froze in a panic or surprise, she would have landed on him, her teeth at his throat.

But Little Tug didn't freeze. Despite the speed at which she came, Tug swung Old Fogey at just the right angle and at just the right moment to catch her mid-leap. Few warriors in all Midgaard could've made that strike, but Tug did, veteran as he was of hundred melees and skirmishes at sea and on land over the previous two decades.

The hammer slammed into Penny's shoulder, upper chest, and the side of her head. The power of that blow knocked her through the air, and sent her tumbling across the pier and over the side into the water.

The battle between Toby and the other seamen still raged. One man was down, unmoving on the pier deck, his throat torn out. Toby fought on, displaying wounds that would've killed any normal man five times over, though his face showed his desperation. He was like a wounded animal that was cornered. He knew he couldn't win the fight, but he was going to do as much damage as he could before death took him.

Tug wanted to aid his comrades, but witnessing the superhuman resiliency of the Evermerians, he knew that the girl was still alive. He knew that at any moment, he'd see her hand reach up and grab onto the rail's edge. It was impossible. No one could've survived that hammer blow, but he knew that she did. He had to keep telling himself that she wasn't a little girl. She wasn't human. She was something else. He didn't know what, and it didn't matter. She needed killing, and when she showed her face again, he'd finish her. He turned from one side to the other, looking for any sign of her. He couldn't afford to have her sneak up on him. Not with the claws she had.

Tug didn't expect the girl to catapult out of the water, rising ten feet above the pier and landing on her feet. But that's just what she did. Her arm and shoulder were mangled and hung limp. Blood streamed down the side of her face. Her jaw was wrenched into an unnatural angle, either broken or dislocated, or both. Tears streamed down her face. She sobbed, in terrible pain, though her eyes were hard and cold as the sea.

Tug wouldn't let his eyes go soft. She was a

monster, he told himself. A monster. And monsters needed killing.

She raced toward Tug, this time too fast for him to bring Old Fogey to bear. She ducked under his blow and grabbed him about the belt. She lifted Tug from his feet — all five hundred pounds of him, and bodyslammed him to the deck, landing atop him. Her hands were at his throat. She struggled to envelop his huge neck with her small hands. She squeezed his throat with a force beyond any that Tug had felt before. Try as he might, he couldn't dislodge her hands, though he held her aloft with ease.

His meaty hand went to her throat and with all his might, he leveraged himself and rolled to the side, ending up atop her, pressing down with all his weight on her torso. For all her strength, her mass was so slight that he was able to manhandle her. They struggled. Not for moments, but for minutes, squeezing and snarling. Adrenaline alone kept Tug going, for he was far past exhaustion. Penny seemed to have no end of energy. Tug finally dislodged one of her hands and punched her in the gut over and over — blows that would have a splintered a man's ribs and ruptured his innards. All to no effect. Punches to the side of her head were equally ineffective.

Finally, Tug reached the dagger sheathed at his side, pulled it out, and rammed it through the girl's neck. Its tip came out the other side. Her grip loosened and Tug was able to knock her hands away and quickly withdrew the dagger. Down came the blade again. This time through her forehead, pinning her head to the pier. Her body quivered for some moments and then went limp. Tug checked her as best he could. Dead.

The battle nearby was long over as well. Seaman Gurt sat on the pier, shaking. His sword was lodged through Toby's heart and had him pinned to the ground, just as Tug had pinned Penny. Toby's limbs thrashed back and forth. He strained to pull the sword from his chest, but he could not. The other seamen were down.

Tug hauled himself to his feet and walked over to Toby, Old Fogey dragging behind him.

"Don't kill me, please," said Toby. "Mercy."

"Mercy is for men, not for monsters," said Tug. "Say hello to Old Fogey," he said as he slammed the hammer down on Toby's head, blasting it to mush.

4

DARMOD AND SONS

Near to dusk, Ginalli, Par Keld, Ezerhauten, Frem, Sevare, Putnam, and four other Pointmen arrived at a seaman's inn called The Grasping Grond — a stout stone edifice just a few blocks up from the water's edge with walls some three feet thick. The square outside the inn featured a central fountain with a stone statue of a grond (a man-sized, hairy, long-limbed beast with fingers and toes similar to a human's) hanging one-handed from a tree limb.

"He's late," said Ginalli. "I wanted someone reliable."

"It wasn't an easy task," said Putnam. "Most of the locals don't speak much Lomerian, if any at all. The one we're meeting with comes highly recommended."

A mountain of a man, taller even than Frem and just as broad soon approached their table. Two young men that resembled the first followed behind him.

"One of you is called Putnam?" said the big man in a deep voice with a strong Juten accent.

"That be me," said Putnam.

"I be Darmod Rikenguard," said the man. "I hear you're looking to hire a guide. You want someone to take you to the top of the cliffs for a looksee or are you planning on going down into the valley?"

Ginalli motioned for Putnam to keep quiet. "I'm going down into the valley," said Ginalli.

Darmod shifted his gaze from Putnam to Ginalli. "You the headman?"

Ginalli nodded.

"Just you going?" said Darmod, "or all these men too?"

"These and more," said Ginalli. He motioned for Darmod to take a seat. He did. The two young men remained standing behind him.

"It's not often what folks want to do that," said Darmod. "Lots of folks want to look from the cliff top, to see what there is to see, but not many got the stones to head down into the valley. Why do you want to? Sightseeing, exploring, treasure hunting, or something else?"

"My purpose is not your concern," said Ginalli.

"How well do you know the paths over the cliffs and through the valley beyond?" said Ezerhauten. Ginalli scowled at Ezerhauten as he asked his question.

"My sons and I know those ways better than any men alive."

"Quite a boast," said Par Keld.

"Truth is no boast," said Darmod.

"How many times have you traveled the valley?" said Ezerhauten.

"Ten times or thereabouts over the past thirty years."

"Pfft," went Keld.

"That's not very often," said Ginalli.

"It's about nine more times than anyone else,

except for my sons who've gone with me the last two times."

"When was your last trip?" said Ezerhauten.

"Four years ago."

"Pfft," went Keld again. "Four years is a long time. He probably doesn't even remember the way."

Ezerhauten spoke again. "Why has—"

Ginalli raised a hand and cut off Ezerhauten's question. "What is your price to guide us?" he said.

"The interior is a dangerous place," said Darmod. "Even I do not travel there lightly. I would know your purpose."

"You'll ask no more questions in that regard, or I will find another guide," said Ginalli.

Darmod and his sons laughed. "There are no other guides for where you're headed, and a guide you most certainly need. There are a few what will take your coin, lead you down into the valley, and strand you on your own. I trust you'll see little value in hiring one of them no goods. Now if you just want to go up top for a looksee, there are a hundred men what will bring you up there fair and square. But for traveling inland, there is only Darmod and sons; nobody else. Only we have braved those ways and come back again. Warriors or not," he said, looking them up and down, "those wilds would not suffer you long. If you go on your own, none of you would return, of that you can be certain. I cannot guide you, if I do not know where you want to go or what it is that you seek. The lands beyond the cliffs are vast and dangerous. Men who do not know the secret ways are unlikely to last a day out there. It is a dangerous place. So I ask you again, what is your purpose in this journey?"

Ginalli wouldn't budge.

"You'll know when we're safely down on the valley floor," said Ezerhauten. "Then and only then."

"Treasure hunters then, I suppose," said Darmod, "Don't matter to me. If there's treasure to be found, it's yours for the taking. I just get paid my fee is all. Half up front. Half when I bring you back."

"Done," said Ginalli, who made ready to get up, the business concluded.

"How much?" said Ezerhauten.

"Five thousand pieces of silver, or the like in gold, or stones. Half up front, as I said. The rest when I bring you back, regardless of whether you find what you're looking for out there."

"You're mad," said Ginalli. "No one would pay that."

Darmod stood up. "You will, if you want a guide. The interior is more dangerous than you would believe until you see it with your own eyes; I don't risk my life or my sons' lightly. Ask around after other guides. You won't find any what you can trust. Then come back to me. When you do, my price will be six thousand silver. And even then, I'll need some idea of where you want to get to in order to prepare the proper supplies."

"I'll not pay such a price," said Ginalli. "I will find another guide. Good day to you."

Without a further word, Darmod and his sons were off.

45

"Did you see the look on his face?" said Keld. "He disrespects us. That man is no good. No good at all. Very unreliable," he said as he looked accusingly at Putnam.

Ginalli turned to Putnam. "What other guides did you find?"

"Like the big man said, lots will take us up the cliff," said Putnam, "but few will enter the valley, and all those are of ill repute save for Darmod. There is another possibility, though. One man told me that there is an old temple, way up on the cliffs, where live some monks. He said they've been to the valley and could guide us, if we paid their price."

"A temple?" said Ginalli, nearly leaping from his seat. "We're looking for a temple, you fool."

"Could it be the right one?" said Ezerhauten. "I thought it was inland?"

"I don't know," said Ginalli. "Legend says that the one we're looking for is deep within Jutenheim. But maybe atop the cliffs is deep enough. If that is the correct temple, we won't need to venture into their accursed valley at all."

"I'll hire us a guide to bring us to that temple," said Putnam. "Head up there at dawn?"

"At dawn," said Ginalli.

The group finished their drinks and prepared to leave. Two tall Jutens blocked the exit, a steel crossbar across the door.

"Stand aside," said Frem as he reached the door.

"It's too late, night has fallen," said one of the men. "Didn't you hear the call?"

Frem looked confused and looked to Putnam

who shrugged.

"What call? And so what if it's night?" said Frem. "Is there a curfew in this town?"

The guard shook his head. "You come in on a ship today?"

"Aye," said Frem.

"Old Fortis called out sundown in fifteen, a while back," said the guard. "That's when near half the folk got up and left. Didn't you notice?"

"I saw folks leave," said Frem. "What of it? Explain yourself."

"It's not safe to be out after dark in these parts," said the guard.

"Spirits roam the streets at night," said the other guard in little more than a whisper. "Spirits of the dead. They'll suck out your souls and leave nothing but bones behind."

"And there are imp about," said the first guard. "The black elves of Svartleheim, from deep under the cliffs. They roam about after dark, looking for the sick or injured to waylay or for small children to steal. They're dark wizards, they are. Their hearts are made of black stone, solid and cold as the cliffs."

"They're demons, they are," whispered the other guard.

"They rule the night, them creatures. The daytime is ours, but the night belongs to them. You don't want to go out there. Not if you value you lives."

"And not if you value your souls."

Frem turned around to see bewildered looks on his companions' faces.

"Superstitious primitives," muttered Keld.

Old Fortis came waddling over, all five hundred pounds of him. "Is there some trouble here? Something wrong?"

"Your man says it's not safe to go outside," said Ginalli.

"That it's not, your lordship. When night falls, we lock up tight in Jutenheim. I didn't realize this was your first night here or I would have made certain to explain things to you."

"I suppose that there are rooms we can rent in this establishment?" said Ginalli.

"Of course," said Old Fortis. "The Grond is one of the best inns in town. I think I've rooms for each of you, and then some if you're agreeable to double up. I'd be happy to extend you a discount, considering you're new here and got caught unawares."

Ginalli smiled a knowing smile. "No doubt you are."

"Just what do you take us for?" said Par Keld. "Bar the door, tell us it's not safe outside, and then take our money to let us stay? Nice try, but we're no fools."

"Now tell your men to stand aside," said Ginalli, "or I'll tell mine to move them."

Fortis looked surprised and then his face grew dark, and his voice grew cold. "We bar our doors to keep folks safe, not to keep them prisoners. And we don't care much for threats; not much at all. You want out, then get out. When the spirits suck out your souls, don't come running back here, for my door will be locked up tight and will not open again until the sun shines on it."

The guards removed the crossbar and opened

the door to the night air, chill and foggy, the square deserted.

The group stepped out into the night. There were no moons out that night, and the stars were trapped behind the clouds. The moment that the Grond's door closed behind them, the group was plunged into near complete darkness. There were no street lamps lit. No lights in windows — all the shades down and shutters tightly closed. From them, no light escaped. There was little hope to find their way safely from the square, little less back to the ship.

Ginalli thumped the butt of his staff to the ground and the stone upon its top began to glow. It grew brighter and soon they could see as well as if they carried a torch. Par Keld and Sevare did the same trick with their staffs.

"What if they were telling the truth?" said Ezerhauten.

"Then I trust that your men can handle a few little elves," said Ginalli. "Let's get back to the ship. Sergeant —— at first light, you find us that guide. I want us up there by midday at the latest."

5

RUNNING OF THE BULLS

Just outside The Dancing Turtle, Duchess Morgovia shouted at Par Tanch, Theta, and their companions. "Run, bulls, run," she said while the entire throng of slavering Evermerians (blood lords, one and all) looked on. "That way lies the sea," she said as she pointed in the direction of the docks. "That way lies your ship. Your only escape. Your only chance. Make for it now if you want to live. Run! Run, bulls, run!"

"Run bulls! Run!" shouted the crowd.

"Moo!" shouted others, laughing.

Glimador, Guj, and Bertha looked back to Theta for some direction, terror on their faces, as the crowd parted around them.

"That way lies only death," said Artol to Theta.

"Into the inn," said Theta.

Two hulking Evermerians stood between Theta, Artol, and the inn's door. Artol pivoted, and elbowed one. Its teeth and jaw shattered. It dropped.

Theta shouldered the one closest to him, knocking the man back two steps. Theta's falchion was out in a flash. With a wave of his hand, almost too fast to see, his stroke entered the Evermerian's shoulder and exited at the opposite hip: he cut him in two.

Artol opened the door of The Turtle. The inside stood deserted. The others needed no prodding. Sir Glimador Malvegil, Par Tanch, Captain Slaayde, Bertha Smallbutt, Guj, and Ravel scurried back toward the inn's door as fast as they could. The Evermerians didn't try to stop them, but they pushed and shoved them at every opportunity, laughing, and taunting. Twice, they knocked down both Bertha and Ravel. Slaayde fell as he tried to help Bertha up.

"Not that way," shouted several Evermerians within the crowd. "Run for the sea! It's your only chance. Run for your ship, bulls. Give us a merry chase. Run for your lives," they repeated over and again. The Duchess tried to push her way through the crowd toward the group, but she made little headway, the Evermerians oblivious of her in their frenzy.

If the crowd had surged forward and swarmed them at that moment, it would've been the end. Only Theta and Artol would have had a chance to make it inside. The rest would have been torn apart. But the crowd didn't attack. They just stood there, slavering, howling, and taunting. They wanted no quick and easy kill. They wanted a chase. They wanted sport. That gave the group the moments they needed to get inside, to whatever little protection the building might provide.

Ravel was the last one in. Just as he passed the threshold, a dainty hand surged forward and grabbed him by the back of his neck. The Duchess.

One-handed, she wrenched Ravel from his feet and pulled him back outside. Artol lunged to aid him, but wasn't quick enough. The Duchess's teeth sank into Ravel's neck in an explosion of blood. He screamed and extended a pleading hand toward his comrades, even as Artol slammed the door shut. Theta lowered the crossbar into place.

"What are you doing?" shouted Bertha. "Open the door. We've got to help him. He's not dead, for Odin's sake. Don't you hear him? He's screaming. He's not dead. We can still save him. Do something!" she said, eyeing Theta.

"There are too many," said Artol.

"Dead gods, what do we do?" said Tanch.

"We've got to move," said Artol.

"Out the back, and fast," said Theta. "Stop for nothing."

"They'll kill us all," said Tanch as he backpedaled.

"We've got to go," said Slaayde as he pulled Bertha along by the arm.

"Ravel," she yelled, tears streaming down her face as she struggled against Slaayde's grip. "He's your friend," she shouted at Slaayde.

"We've got to go," said Slaayde.

The group was halfway across the taproom when the inn's front door burst open with a loud, splintering sound. In streamed a group of Evermerians. Most of those in front were covered in blood. They slowed to lick it from their hands; to lick it from each other's faces and clothes; their appetites wet for the slaughter. A command from the Duchess held them back.

The taproom went eerily quiet despite the throng of Evermerians that crowded the door. The only sounds came from outside: the yells, taunts, and catcalls of the Evermerians as they chased down their prey (the seamen they captured off the schooner, and the human slaves that the Evermerians called 'Bulls'), and the shrieks and pleadings of those whom they caught. Those sounds grew more distant by the moment. Both sides eyed each other, the tension growing.

Glimador stood near the back of the taproom. His fingers moved in subtle motions this way and that as he murmured ancient elvish words taught him by his mother. With those words, he called forth eldritch energy from the grand weave of magic. That energy, wild and chaotic as it was, bent to his powerful will and did his bidding.

"Run," shouted Slaayde.

"Yes, run," cried the Duchess, her face bathed in red, bits of Ravel's torn flesh hanging from her hands. "Give us a merry chase, will you? You're good for that much, aren't you?" She turned to her subjects. "Have your fun with them my lovelies, but do not dare kill them. We're going to drain them, slowly. We're going to carve delectable pieces off of them night after night until the festival is over. Only then shall we let death take them. A just punishment for harming members of our family, and spoiling our Bulls Run, wouldn't you say? But hear me well; you will leave the wizard for me. He is mine and mine alone. I have plans for you, Par Sinch," she said, her eyes wide and wild. "Oh what beautiful plans I have for you."

She motioned to her fellows, and eight Evermerians armed with swords, claws, and wicked teeth surged forward to engage Theta and Artol who stood at the van. The warriors met the frenzied charge with icy stares and grim resolve. Two gods of the sword, two giants among men, against a cadre of superhuman creatures of the night. The battle: steel and strength, honor and courage, against the soulless darkness, the heartless offspring of the nether realms.

"Take off their heads," yelled Artol, as he smashed his battle hammer down atop the skull of one of his attackers.

Glimador's spell completed, there appeared a shimmering blue barrier across the inn's open door. The energy of that sorcery crackled and sparked as it spread across the inn's front wall, covering and sealing every window. Evermerians broke the glass and pressed against the translucent barrier, seeking entry. They pushed, then they clawed, and they pounded, at last using every ounce of their preternatural strength, but the mystical barrier held them back. The press of numbers availed them naught, for no matter their efforts, the barrier would not yield. They howled and they raged, but the barrier dampened much of the sound. Most importantly, it kept them out, but it also kept their fellows in.

The Duchess's movements were calm and controlled despite the mania that ruled her face. Her concentration on her prey, she ignored the battling swordsmen around her and was oblivious of Glimador's spell. She sauntered forward, her festival dress a ruin of blood and gore.

Guj stepped toward the Duchess, his massive axe in hand. He howled some battle cry and swung the weapon with all his considerable might. The Duchess stepped in, faster than anyone should be able to move, and caught the weapon's haft in her hand, stopping the blow cold. She twisted her arm and wrenched the axe from Guj's hand. Her fist shot out and crashed into Guj's jaw. He reeled back, but she grabbed him with one hand and then punched him with the other. Before Guj could even raise his hands to defend himself, he was struck by four punishing blows that knocked him senseless. The Duchess lifted the 250-pound lugron into the air, twirled around, and threw him across the room. He spun around and around and crashed into Theta and the Evermerians that he battled. The whole group went down in a heap.

As the Duchess turned her attention toward the others, Slaayde's saber slid between the ribs of her upper chest. The steel blade pierced her heart, and its tip exited her back. The Duchess's eyes went wide and she groaned in pain. Her knees buckled for a moment, but then she caught herself and did not fall. Her hand shot out and clamped down on Slaayde's throat; his air, instantly cut off.

Slaayde strained against her with both hands. He tried to pull away, but her grip was too strong. He tried to peel her fingers back one at a time, but they wouldn't budge, not one of them. She held him in a death grip from which he quickly realized he could not escape. He couldn't draw a single breath. His eyes started to glaze over.

Just then, Bertha clobbered the Duchess over the head with a bar stool. "Get off him, you bitch." The stool shattered but the Duchess remained standing. She staggered forward and lost her grip on Slaayde. Blood streamed down her forehead, but this time, it was her own. She stuck out her tongue — it stretched out, impossibly long, and she lapped up her own blood as it dripped down her nose and cheeks.

"I was saving you for tomorrow, cow," she said as she grabbed Bertha and pulled her close. Bertha, for all her fury was powerless to resist that iron grip. She beat her fists against the Duchess's chest — all to no effect. "But now I think I'll drink you dry today." The Duchess's mouth opened wide. Her fangs twinkled in the inn's dim light. She bit down hard on Bertha's neck as the quartermaster screamed.

Slaayde looked up, his head throbbing, his neck so stiff he could barely take a breath. He saw Bertha's blind dagger thrust. By some boon of the gods, the blade sunk directly into the Duchess's left eye. Then he saw the spurt of blood that shot from Bertha's throat. She was hurt. It looked bad.

"No!" he yelled.

The Duchess howled in pain and fury, grabbed Bertha's wrist (the one that held the blade) and crushed it, the bones splintering within her inhuman grasp. She dropped Bertha and staggered backward, clutching at her face, the wound forever marring her ageless beauty. "No!" she screamed. "My eye, my face."

Bertha fell back limp in a faint. Slaayde caught her as he tried to rise, but was knocked back down by her weight. He immediately applied pressure to the puncture wounds at her neck, trying to staunch the bleeding.

The Duchess had had enough of that fight, and turned and made for the exit. Only when she reached the magically barred door, did she realize that she was trapped. "Attend me," she shouted to her minions. Those who lurked around the door drew close to her and those few that still fought with Theta and Artol withdrew to her side. Some surrounded her protectively, while others sought to break down the mystical barrier.

Around Theta lay several bodies, two with their heads severed, and two others with their necks twisted 180 degrees around. Two more Evermerians lay dead at Artol's feet. Artol's armor was battered and slashed in several locations, but the plate and mail held.

The Duchess had only six or seven of her fellows left; the rest were trapped beyond the barrier.

"Let's finish them," said Artol to Theta.

"Best we get clear before that barrier falls," said Theta. He and Artol backed toward the kitchen door, Theta dragging Guj by the collar. "Glimador," said Theta. "Will your spell hold on its own?"

"No," said Glimador. "I must remain to keep it up."

"I can make it hold," said Tanch.

"Then do it," said Theta. "Slaayde, pick her up, we've got to go now. Out the back."

"Get off of me," said Guj as he struggled to pull himself to his feet. Blood streamed from his nose and mouth, and his eyes teared.

"We've got to go, my love," said Slaayde as he pulled Bertha up while trying to maintain pressure on her throat. "We've got to get out of here now." She was barely conscious; hurt seemingly more from shock than from the wound itself. Her eyes pleaded for help. She moaned in pain and tears ran freely down her face.

"It burns," she muttered.

Slaayde wrapped a cloth about her shoulder and neck and pulled it as tight as he dared.

"Move," said Artol. We'll hold them here until you get clear."

"I can fight," said Guj.

"Then help the others," said Theta. "There may be more of those things in the kitchens."

Guj, Bertha, and Slaayde crashed through the kitchen door, searching for the back exit, Bertha supported between the two men. The heat within the kitchen was oppressive and washed over them like a wave. The smell of meat, spices, and vinegar filled the air. The place was bathed in a bluish light from oil lamps of exotic vintage. The kitchen was cluttered but clean — more than such a place was wont to be. Rows of huge pots or, to be fair, vats, simmered on wood burning stoves, one after another after another. There was enough food bubbling in those cauldrons to feed hundreds.

The room was deserted save for the inn's proprietor who sat on a stool in a back corner, guarding a door that presumably was the inn's rear exit. His cooks and serving maids were all outside for the running of the bulls.

The group had caught only a glimpse of the proprietor earlier in the evening. Then he appeared a jovial, bald man of impressive girth. Though still just as wide, his skin now had a distinctly gray pallor and tusk-like fangs extended from his upper jaw, one of them oddly bent and twisted, as if from some old injury. Long claws lived at the ends of his fingers. He wore butcher's coveralls and a belt that held several large cleavers and knives. He lifted an opaque jug to his mouth while keeping an eye on the group, and took a long swig. Thick red liquid that looked like blood, dribbled down his chin.

"Well, well, got by the others, did you?" he said as he stood up. "Think something of yourselves for that, do you? You shouldn't. Most of them are just children. Not much experience or skill, and even less discipline. I'm not like that. I've been around for a long time. I've dealt with your kind before —— uppity bulls what think they can escape us. What think they're something more than food. You're not. When I'm done with you, you'll take your rightful places in the meat locker. We'll make a merry feast of you. You'll not get by me."

Guj and Slaayde looked at each other. "He's more your size, don't you think?" said Slaayde.

The proprietor charged toward them. Guj pulled a hammer and a dagger from his belt and moved a couple of steps forward. Halfway to where Guj stood, the proprietor snatched up one

59

of the huge, bubbling pots in his bare hands, spun around, and flung it with terrific speed at Guj. The lugron dived to the side with nary a moment to spare, as did Slaayde and Bertha. Boiling stew exploded in all directions, burning whatever bare skin it touched.

Just as Guj was getting up, a second pot crashed above his head, drenching him in scalding liquid. Luckily, his armor and heavy clothing shielded him from much of it. Then another cauldron hit the same spot, and then another. Guj tried to scurry clear on his knees. Then the proprietor crashed into him, crushing him to the floor. Guj howled as his face hit the hot stew that puddled on the floorboards. Both he and the Evermerian twisted and turned, trying to make their feet, hampered by the hot stew and slippery floor.

Guj's dagger sank into the proprietor's side even as the Evermerian's cleaver sliced into Guj's shoulder. Then began a furious series of strikes: hammer and blade against razor sharp cleavers. Parry and slash, strike and bash, the battle raged for several moments, neither opponent able to beat down the other's defenses, though each scored several wicked hits that drew blood.

Glimador slipped through the kitchen door, Tanch just behind him.

"Fry him!" shouted Slaayde from behind a table, his hands still applying pressure to Bertha's wounds. She'd fallen unconscious again.

Tanch quickly sized up the situation. He mouthed strange, foreign words, harsh and deep, and then a cone of blue fire emerged from his hand. It raged toward the proprietor, and enveloped him (though it left Guj untouched). The Evermerian screamed — a pitiable, bloodcurdling wail that went on and on as the mystical fire consumed his fleash. That fire hovered about his head and refused to go out. The proprietor staggered this way and that, and knocked over more pots, large and small. At some point, he found a pot of water and dumped it over his head, dousing the blue flames that assailed him.

His face was a ruin, a horror: both eyes gone, the flesh of his cheeks melted and sloughed down, his teeth exposed and blackened. Once the flames were gone, he no longer cried out, though through clenched jaw he growled like a cornered animal. Such injuries were not survivable. Yet the Evermerian still lived, still stood, and had some fight still left in him.

Glimador was on him. He slashed the proprietor across the chest with his sword, once and then again, to no discernable effect. Shockingly, the Evermerian still held one of his cleavers and swung it with uncanny speed despite his grievous injuries. Glimador dodged the blow and chopped down with his sword even as the Evermerian raised the cleaver for another strike. Glimador's slash severed his forearm. Another strike took the Evermerian in the throat. The sword stuck in his neck and Glimador had to dive to the side to avoid the claws that now flailed this way and that. Glimador snuck behind him, and brought his dagger down with all his strength into the top of the Evermerian's skull. The proprietor fell to his knees, blood streaming down from the top of his head. He raised his hand to grasp the dagger but had no strength left. He collapsed face forward to the floor and moved no more.

The sounds of a desperate melee issued from the taproom. Glimador retrieved his weapons and headed in that direction.

"Stop," said Slaayde. "If those two can't handle them, you'll be of little help. We need to get out of here while we can. I need your help with Bertha. I can't carry her alone."

"Guj can help you," said Glimador as he looked toward the lugron. Guj was on his knees, though slumped over. Blood pooled on the floor beneath him, mixing with the spilled stew. The lugron's eyes were open, but it was clear enough that he was dead, a cleaver lodged in his chest. Glimador moved to Slaayde's side and together they hefted Bertha to her feet and carried her between them. They and Tanch moved as fast as they could to the back door that the proprietor had been guarding.

Only it wasn't the exit. It was another room — dark, frigid, and it smelled of death. Waves of cold air poured from the room. The light from the kitchen allowed them to see only a few feet inside. The floor was wet. There were dark shadows barely visible in the distance, as if drapes or tapestries hung from the ceiling. They dared not step inside until Tanch grabbed the nearest lamp from the kitchen, stepped into the doorway, and raised it high.

The light revealed a slaughterhouse. Pigs, sheep, and goats hung from the ceiling on hooks, their throats cut open, buckets of blood beneath them. Rows upon rows of them. And to their horror, they saw that interspersed between the animals, hung the bodies of men. Pale or blue, dead and drained — in preparation, no doubt, for the proprietor's stew pots. Blocks of ice were stacked here and there, no doubt, brought down from the island's mountains. The floor was slick with a mixture of slushy water and blood.

"Dead gods," said Tanch. "They really are cannibals."

"Let's find a way out, now," said Glimador.

"We ate that stew," said Tanch. "Gods forgive us. I'm going to be sick. I want to be sick," he said holding his stomach.

They moved through the room as fast as they dared given the darkness, the slick floor, and the potential for more Evermerians skulking about.

"There's no way out," said Tanch. "There's no door, no windows, nothing."

"Not even a hatch in the floor or ceiling," said Glimador.

"Back to the kitchen," said Slaayde. "There has to be another way out through there. No inn has only a front entrance."

As they approached the door that led back to the kitchen, they saw Theta and Artol dashing through the kitchen, a tide of howling Evermerians hot on their heels.

"Oh shit," said Glimador. "The barrier fell."

"They're all coming this way," said Tanch. "We'll be trapped." Theta and Artol raced into the meat locker, and promptly slipped and fell on the slick floor as Glimador slammed the heavy iron door shut behind them. Artol careened into Tanch, knocking him over and sending the lamp flying. Nary a moment later, the Evermerians crashed against the door. They pounded on it, howling. Glimador set the deadbolt just as Tanch's fallen lamp sputtered out, plunging them into darkness. Utter and complete darkness, for not even a glimmer of light shown through the door due to the tightness of its seal.

"Shit," was said all around.

"I saw a crossbar," said Slaayde.

"I've got it," said Glimador. He fumbled with it for some moments trying to set it in place in the darkness as the Evermerians pounded on the door, howling, laughing, and cursing taunts.

"Get that lamp lit," said Artol.

"It's in pieces," said Tanch. "I can't get it to work. We're doomed."

A light appeared in Theta's hand, brighter than was the lamp. The illumination came from a short metal rod that glowed as if white hot, yet he held it freely in his hand. It gave off as much light as several candles.

"Will it hold?" said Slaayde looking at the door and then at Theta's light and back again.

"For a while, it seems," said Artol. "You a wizard, too, Theta?"

Theta shook his head.

"But you've got quite a bag of tricks," said Artol.

"Let's move," said Theta as he turned his head, looking around. "We cannot linger here."

"There's no way out," said Slaayde. "We're stuck here."

"It's a tomb," said Tanch shaking his head and

wringing his hands. "Our Tomb."

"We searched high and low," said Glimador. "There's no way out of this room, save through the door we came in."

The pounding on the door grew louder. The metal strained and threatened to buckle.

"Can you put up that barrier again?" said Theta. "And reinforce it, as before?"

"Yes," said Glimador and Tanch. "But it won't hold forever."

"Do it," said Theta.

"Why bother?" said Tanch. "There's no help coming. It's just delaying the inevitable."

"Where life yet remains, there is always a chance," said Theta.

"Hope?" said Tanch. "Is that what you mean?"

"No," said Theta. "Hope is not a strategy."

Glimador set to work invoking his sorcery. Tanch stood by to aid him.

"Why a crossbar on the inside of a meat locker?" said Glimador.

"Who cares?" said Tanch. "Just set the spell, quickly."

"What of Guj?" said Artol.

"Dead," said Slaayde. "What happened back there?"

"They came at us again," said Artol. "But we gave them what for. Theta took off the Duchess's arm with that falchion of his. Just as we had them, the barrier fell and they poured in on us like a wave. There was no stopping them and no holding them. We had to turn tail."

"A strategic withdrawal," said Theta.

"The door is caving in," said Artol. "Make

ready."

"I have it," said Glimador as he completed his spell. The shimmering blue barrier appeared and spread across the full area of the door, just as it had in the taproom. Tanch added his words and the barrier brightened and pulsed.

"It will hold now, for a time," said Tanch. "Not only the barrier, but the door itself. So long as the magic remains, they'll not be able to tear the door asunder."

"Did you kill her?" said Slaayde to Theta.

"Any normal woman would be dead from the wounds she took," said Artol. "Yet she still stood when last we saw her, cursing us all the while."

"They heal like lighting," said Theta. "They kept fighting when they should've been dead. Arms cut off, thrusts to the chest, throats cut open, and yet they kept coming. She's still out there, for certain."

"They're going to break through that door eventually, magic or no," said Artol. "Unless they decide to wait us out."

"What do we do?" said Slaayde. "Bertha needs tending to. We can't stay here."

"Go up to the door and yell at them," said Theta. "Taunt them. Threaten them. Make as much noise as you can."

"What do you plan?" said Artol.

"To make a hole," said Theta. He passed another of the illuminating metal rods to Glimador. "Ready your hammer," he said to Artol. Theta pulled out the massive battle hammer that he wore strapped to his leg, hefted it in both hands, and walked to the back wall, Artol following.

Tanch, Glimador, and Slaayde started yelling and returning the Evermerians' taunts.

With a grunt, Theta swung his hammer at the stout masonry wall and blasted several bricks to bits. The wall was thick. Artol took position opposite Theta and put his own hammer to work. A few mighty strokes each and they were through the two and half foot thick wall, with a hole large enough for them to squeeze through.

Theta slipped under, looked around for a moment, and waved the others through. They found themselves in a warehouse; no one was about. They ran to the far side, found a door, and slipped out into the night. They crossed the street and stopped in a shadowed area to get their bearings.

"They're gonna find that hole, and quick," said Artol. "We may only have a few minutes before they're on us again."

"Which way?" said Tanch.

"Three blocks east," said Theta. "Then turn south and make for the docks. If we're lucky, the way will be clear."

"They'll have people waiting for us at the longboat," said Artol.

"We could head to the villa," said Glimador. "Ambush her on her return."

"No. There's no victory to be had here," said Theta. "Only death or escape. It's an island. We make for the ship. We'll fight our way through. There's no other way."

"What if The Falcon is taken?" said Tanch.

"Then you may yet have a warrior's death,"

said Theta.

"They'll not take The Falcon," said Slaayde. "Not my ship. Not my crew. They won't even get out there because Tug will hold the docks," he said, his eyes red and watery. "He'll be there waiting for us."

"Can you manage her?" said Artol to Slaayde and Glimador.

"For a while at least," said Glimador.

"I don't understand why she's still out of it," said Slaayde. "She didn't lose enough blood for that."

"The bite may have been poisoned," said Theta. "But we can't deal with that now; we've got to move."

"What are they?" said Glimador.

"Stinking spawn of hell," said Slaayde. "Just like everyone else I've met since you bastards first boarded my ship."

They all looked to Theta.

"I don't know what they are," he said. "No more talk. Let's go."

6

NOW YOU WILL BE QUEEN

Marissa Harringgold's shocked scream rattled Dor Lomion's windows; her chamber's door did little to muffle it. Luckily, her father, the Duke, had foreseen her reaction and directed the servants and guards to keep their distance. Marissa balled up her fists and her whole head shook. The Duke actually stepped back from her, for fear of attack.

"Are you mad?" she shouted. "He's a monster. He's out of his mind."

"He's the prince," said the Duke as he took a seat in the plush armchair in the bedchamber's sitting area. "The heir to the granite throne." Harringgold needed a brandy for that conversation. He didn't have one. He couldn't carry a tumbler down from the drawing room without Marissa suspecting that something was awry and without the servants' beginning to gossip. He couldn't have that, since he wanted to tell her in his own time and he hated gossip.

He wanted to talk to her where she felt most comfortable — where she felt strong and safe. Her chambers were that place. The furniture, linens, draperies, all to her taste — light, airy, and sophisticated, let playful. Her perfume in the air. All her little things carefully arrayed in their proper places, just as she liked them. When she came of age, she'd thrown out most of the décor from when she was a child. She needed to make the rooms, her space. But he was happy that she had kept nearly all the exotic toys and artwork that he'd bought her over the years from parts foreign. So he did without the brandy. That made a very hard conversation even harder for him, but that was how it had to be.

"He's a disgusting beast," said Marissa. "The way he carries on—"

"I'm sorry," said the Duke shaking his head. His hand fidgeted; he didn't even have his pipe; he'd left it at his desk. He couldn't look into his little girl's eyes. If he did, he wouldn't be able to hold back tears, for the pain and guilt of hurting her. He couldn't let her see that. He couldn't bear to do anything that hurt her. And yet, here they were.

"Besides, I'm to marry Jude Eotrus, if he's not...so the whole idea is quite impossible. It can't even be considered. How could you?" she said, tears in her eyes.

"If you marry Cartegian, you would be queen, someday. Much more comes along with that than being the wife of the brother of a Marcher Lord."

"I...would like to be queen, I suppose, but not if I have to marry him. I'd rather be dead than marry that beast. He's revolting."

"I'm sorry my love; I know that it's hard for you to hear this, but more than likely, Jude is not coming back."

"He's not dead," she said, tears rolling down her cheeks. "I would know if he were. I don't want to be queen. I want Jude."

"Before, you wanted Claradon."

"He's a fool," she spat. "He could have married me. We could have had a life together. We should have. Instead, he became a monk. A monk! I am the Archduke's daughter and he tossed me aside to become a monk."

"A Caradonian Knight, not a monk," said the Duke, his voice soft to try to calm her.

"They are monks by another name, father," said Marissa, "as you well know, for they cannot marry, so they are monks all the same. And it was his choice to join up with them. Nobody made him; nobody pressured him. Most everyone tried to talk him out of it, even Sir Gabriel, but he wouldn't listen, he didn't care. I tried to talk to him, but he didn't even pay attention to me. My opinion didn't matter, not at all. He didn't care what his choice meant for me."

"And it was his choice, and his choice alone. The idiot! I don't even want to think about him; I don't want to see his face; I don't even want to hear his name. Not ever! We could have had a life together, children, but he gave it up, for what? For nothing, the fool. Aargh! I hate him!"

"Is it Jude that you truly love, or is it still Claradon?"

She looked like she'd been struck; her mouth hung open. "I love him; Jude; I do. I don't know; I think I do. It's not the same as it was with Claradon. It's not the same at all."

"If Jude doesn't return, then what will you do? Is there another young man that you would consider?"

"I don't know. How can I even think of that

now?"

"I know it's hard, but you must. We must at least discuss it. These things must be planned."

"There are other young men of station," said Marissa. "I heard that Lord Baldin's son is very handsome."

"He is, but alas, he does not fancy women — or so they say."

"Oh, I see," she said raising her eyebrows. "I had no idea. There is Lord Mardot's eldest son, the one who did so well in the tourney last season. He is—"

"Engaged to Dalria Karenteen of Dyvers."

"No? That witch! He'll be sorry for that match, I'm certain. She's vile and devious and always has been, even as a child. What about Lord Portfrey's sons? I don't know them well, but—"

"One is to wed one of the Kandars next spring. The other is more than five years younger than you and dumb as a rock."

Marissa stared down at her hands. She looked defeated. "There is Ector Eotrus."

"A fine young man he is, but he's the third in line to his Dor. That makes him not a suitable match for the Archduke's daughter."

She nodded. "There must be others of appropriate age and station. There must be. Are there not? What other options do I have, father?" she said, her voice quaking.

"You could be queen."

She shook her head. More tears rolled down her cheeks. "Why? Why would you do this to me? Why make me be with that thing? He'll kill me. Father, he'll kill me."

"The king says that he is gentle, despite his afflictions. He has assured me of that."

"The king is a drunk. You can't trust what he says."

"He knows his son. He says that Cartegian will treat you well."

"I see that it's all arranged," she said bitterly. "All planned; probably for years, if I know you. You probably have the guest list completed, and the invitations prepared and ready to go out. I can't even do that — not even that! And if he doesn't treat me well? If he harms me? Beats me?"

"If he harms you, I will put a stop to it."

"That gives me little comfort, father," she said. "There will be little that you can do once I am his wife. I'll have to endure whatever he does to me and you know it. Whatever perversions, whatever horrors that beast can dream up. Unless he near kills me, but falls short of it, then maybe you'll be able to act, if even then."

The Duke's eyes betrayed his sadness, his guilt. "The realm needs a queen. A woman of virtue and values; a woman of strength and smarts. Alas, there are few that could be trusted to fill that role with the fate of the realm at risk. The strength and stability that you would bring to Cartegian, to the throne, could save us all. You could save Lomion. You could save the Republic. It's a weighty burden for anyone, but one that I believe you have the strength to bear."

"All I wanted was a handsome knight," she said, her voice now slower, calmer, resolved. A man respected and kind, that could share the wonders of the City with me, and the quiet of the country. A man that would give me many children and that would be a good father and a loyal husband. That's all I wanted. Why was that too much to ask? Even for the Archduke's daughter? Why was it too much? Why was it so impossible? Why can't I have what I want?"

"Now, you will have the realm. Now you will be queen."

7

HERE I SIT

Ob and Dolan limped from shadow to shadow, headed for the longboat, making the best time that they could. They heard yelling and howling behind them from many voices. Something was up. Something big. They dashed across the boardwalk and onto the pier where they had docked the longboat. It was still there.

"Tug is by the boat," said Dolan as he peered into the distance. "He's been in a fight," he said as they started down the long pier. "I see bodies on the deck."

That was news to Ob. His vision was better than most people's, but the far end of the pier was dark and still a goodly ways away. He could barely even see the outline of the longboat. When they drew close, he saw Tug sitting like a grim statue. The huge seaman was perched atop a barrel and leaned on Old Fogey, the hammer's head resting on the pier boards between his legs. The torn dead were strewn around him, seaman and Evermerian alike.

"Have you seen Slaayde?" said Tug.

"Not for hours," said Ob. "We've been snooping about, reconnoitering and such."

Tug nodded. "My men are all dead," he said as if it wasn't obvious. "Except for Gurt the Knife.

He's in bad shape," he said, gesturing toward the longboat where the wounded seaman laid. "Are them islanders all monsters? The whole bunch?"

"So it seems," said Ob. "Bloodsuckers, top to bottom."

"That's it then," said Tug. "No warm bed tonight. Forget about a bath."

The howling grew louder. They heard the pounding of many feet headed toward the docks.

"Don't worry, old friend," said Tug as he patted Old Fogey's haft. "There are more coming. We're not yet done for the night."

"Did they jump you?" said Ob.

"There were three of them at first," said Tug. "One was just a child. Then came another — a big one, older, tougher than the others. He knew how to fight. Then three more showed up, howling for blood — more animal than men. I gave them all what for; me and Old Fogey did," he said patting the haft of his hammer again and pointing toward the carnage. What was left of the Evermerians was unrecognizable; every one of their heads was crushed to pulp.

"You done good, Tug," said Ob. "Real Good. But now we best shove off, afore any more come calling."

Tug shook his head. "Here I sit until my Captain's return, or death takes me."

"What? Death will take you right quick, if you don't get off your duff and get in the boat," said Ob. "They'll be on us in a minute. We need to get our behinds out of here. Dying here won't help nobody."

Tug didn't move; he didn't react at all.

"We've got wounded here," said Ob. "Your man's hurt bad. Dolan is hurt too. We can't stay here. We've got to push off. Get us out a ways — — out there, maybe fifty yards, maybe more. If the others show up, we'll row straight back in and get them — don't you worry."

"Hogwash," said Tug. "There will be no rowing back. When that lot comes howling down the strand, if we're out there, we'll have to turn tail. No choice we'd have. So I'll just sit here and wait. Me and Old Fogey. And don't get any ideas about taking the longboat. I'll need it for when the captain returns."

"Then what are we supposed to do?" said Ob.

Tug turned and stared menacingly at the gnome. "Whatever you want, so long as you don't go near my boat."

"Here they come," said Dolan. "Sounds like the whole town. They're chasing somebody."

"No doubt Mister Fancy Pants is behind it all," said Ob.

"It's the men from the schooner," said Dolan.

"How many?" said Ob.

"Twenty at least. Most are running for the schooner." He paused, watching. "The blooders are jumping them, biting them, tearing them apart. There are hundreds of them. Hundreds. The whole town."

"Tug!" said Ob. "We've got to go. We can't fight that lot."

Tug shook his head and didn't budge from the barrel.

"The blooders are waiting for them, two piers over from the schooner," said Dolan.

"A trap, heh?" said Ob. "It figgers."

When the main group of seamen, nearly a dozen strong, closed on the schooner, the Evermerians sprang their trap. A dozen of their kind leaped from the shadows and set upon the sailors, claws and fangs; no mercy or reprieve. They howled in glee as they tore, drank, and killed their prey.

Another wave of seamen sprinted down the hill to the docks; they saw what happened to their fellows, turned off the boardwalk, and ran down the nearest piers. Five chose Tug's pier by chance, it seemed, since it's unlikely that they saw the longboat from where they were. Five Evermerians howled at their heels.

Dolan raised his bow as they closed.

One seaman tripped on something, stumbled, and went down. An Evermerian pounced on him, biting and slashing. The man never had a chance.

A few moments later, another Evermerian leaped forward and caught the heel of the nearest sprinting seaman, tripped him, and sent him crashing to the deck. The Evermerian leaped onto his back; his mouth opened abnormally wide and revealed his spike-like fangs. Before the seaman could react, the Evermerian bit down on the back on his neck, those fangs sinking deep, puncturing muscle and bone alike.

As the remaining seamen approached the end of the pier, Dolan let loose an arrow that struck their nearest pursuer in the throat. He fell, writhing, to the deck.

Tug stood in the middle of the pier as the seamen passed him, and pulled up, for they'd reached the far edge. Nothing but frigid black water lay beyond. Old Fogey was perched on Tug's shoulder ready for action. Brass knuckles were affixed to each of his hands.

The next Evermerian veered toward Tug. He was moving fast. Old Fogey was faster. Tug caught him in the side of the head. His skull shattered like a melon; his neck broke; what was left of his head flopped over. The force of that blow was so great that it sent his body sailing over the side of the pier. The last Evermerian came on and leaped at Tug's throat, claws first. Tug twisted and spun, avoiding the direct impact. He grabbed the Evermerian by the collar and bodyslammed him to the deck with such force that the deck boards splintered. Tug straddled him and punched him in the face. Stunned, the Evermerian put up no defense. That first blow cracked his skull and knocked him out. The second blow staved in the side of his head, finishing him. Tug scooped up the body, lifted it over his head, and dumped it into the bay.

The Evermerian that Dolan had shot was up and loping forward, slavering and fuming. It either hadn't seen what Tug had done to his comrades, or didn't care, for he displayed no fear at all.

Dolan put a second arrow in his chest. That one didn't even slow him. The third arrow took him in the middle of his forehead. He fell straight back like a falling tree and moved no more.

Tug stepped up and crushed his head with Old Fogey for good measure.

The three sailors spotted the longboat and made for it, pushing past Ob in their frenzy to escape.

"Into the boat before they swarm us," shouted Ob.

Dolan put his bow over his shoulder and moved toward the longboat as the seamen untied the lines.

"Let's go, giant," said Dolan. "We can't do any more here, and you're about to lose your boat."

Tug's eyes searched the docks for any sign of his captain. He saw only the Evermerians and their prey. A few seamen had made it into the water and swam frantically from the shore or from piers. The bay was large and deserted save for a few wrecks. The swimmers had nowhere to go, save for a cold death. A few more were fighting here or there for their lives. Most were already down and being eaten.

"I'm sorry, captain," said Tug.

Tug hauled himself over the side and into the longboat, and they set off. They'd rowed only a few strokes when they spotted a desperate battle at the end of a nearby pier. A clutch of four sailors were fighting two Evermerians. A dozen other cannibals looked on from only a few feet away. One of the seamen was Captain Graybeard. He'd procured a sword from somewhere and was holding the Evermerians back, hacking and slashing with surprising skill and an agility that belied his years. His men all had knives, but the shorter weapons were ineffective at keeping the Evermerians at bay. Ob and group rowed toward that pier, hoping to pick up the men if they swam for it. Ob and the sailors shouted for them to jump into the water, but their attention was focused on

80

their attackers.

Captain Graybeard's slash took one Evermerian in the throat. As the Evermerian's hands clutched its neck, Graybeard stabbed him in the heart, then kicked him, and pulled the sword free. The Evermerian turned to flee, but Graybeard slashed again and nearly cut off his head, severing his spine. The Evermerian dropped. Another sprang in, and the Captain's quick upward thrust took him through the mouth, up into the brain. He fell dead immediately, the sword stuck in his skull. The Evermerians swarmed forward and Graybeard leaped into the water even as claws shredded his shirt in attempt to stop him. Two of Graybeard's fellows followed him into the water; hungry claws and teeth pulled down the third.

Minutes later, Tug and the others had Graybeard and one of his men in the longboat, the other was lost amid the frigid waves.

"Let's get farther out," said Ob. "If those things decide to go swimming en masse or if they pull a boat out of somewhere, we'll be in the deep stuff."

"Where's your ship?" said Graybeard as he looked around the darkened bay.

"At the far edge of the bay," said Ob pointing. "But we've got people still ashore."

"Pray Odin that death takes them quick," said Graybeard.

8

ON TROLLS

Ector Eotrus and Sir Sarbek, Dor Eotrus's acting Castellan, stood in the alchemy laboratory awaiting the Leren's preliminary report on his examination of the body of the troll that they'd brought back from the field.

"I've never seen anything quite like it," said Leren Sverdes, House Eotrus's venerable alchemist and physician, as he stood before the ponderous, stone examination table, a troll's corpse atop it. Sverdes was hard of hearing and spoke about twice as loudly as most folks, perhaps to hear himself the better, or perhaps, just to be annoying. As was usual, the pockets of his gray smock bulged with all manner of tools and instruments. That day though, his clothes were smeared with troll's blood from the examination that he just concluded. His assistants, similarly attired, but two-thirds of a century younger than he, carried the troll's organs, one by one, in bowls to another table that held, amongst an abundance of curious instruments, a scale, to weigh them, and recorded their readings in a leather bound log book. The troll's corpse wasn't rotted as yet; it was too recently dead, but it stank. The whole room stank. The hallway leading to the room, and most of the pathway from outside the citadel to the alchemy laboratory was tainted with more than a hint of the dead thing's stench.

"Its sternum is twice as thick as a man's," said Sverdes as he sharply rapped his knuckles against it. He spoke through a damp cloth mask that he wore to lessen the oppressive odor. "And its bones are made of harder stuff than ours are. To make a clean cut through it, I had to sharpen the blade on my best bone saw, and even then, it was hard going."

"Beneath its sternum, I found two hearts, one on each side of its chest. That's a first for me. Nothing else I've seen in nature has two hearts. But it only gets stranger from there. This smelly bugger has got two livers; a multi-chambered stomach (more like a cow's than a man's), four separate lungs, and a couple of other organs that I can't yet identify. Four lungs —— did you ever hear of such a thing? Its muscle tissue is thicker and denser than anything I've seen before, suggesting great strength. Its sinews and tendons are long and highly flexible, suggesting great agility. Its claws are near as hard and strong as iron. Taken together, these features make the troll incredibly robust. They must be darned hard to kill."

"Hard to kill, yes," said Sarbek, "but we killed our share of them up Mindletown way. Don't forget about its ability to heal. Cut it open, and it heals up straightaway and right as rain."

"I can't find any evidence of that," said Sverdes, "but since it's dead, perhaps that's to be expected."

"What else?" said Sarbek.

"Its eyes resemble those of cats. Hard to say what meaning that has, but I'm guessing that they see well in the dark. Most strangely, is the bone and bone marrow," he said pointing to its midsection. "Its stomachs are full of it and not much else."

"You're telling me them things eat bones?" said Sarbek.

"Its teeth are made for it," said Sverdes. "Thick and wide and perfect for biting through bones or whatnot and grinding them down. And it all fits with the legends."

"You mean about the touch of a troll turning a man's bones to jelly?" said Ector. "I've always thought that a fairy tale and a silly one at that."

"A tale to scare the misbehaving whelps," said Sarbek. "Never put much stock in it."

"Like most legends," said Sverdes, "there appears to be some truth to it. From the dried and caked blood beneath its claws, I'd say that sometime within the last day, this thing killed something, maybe a person, or a large animal. It cut them open with its claws, extracted some of the bones, and ate them, or parts of them, sucking out the marrow along the way. Why it didn't eat the flesh too, I can't say that I understand. Maybe the marrow is a delicacy to it, and it comes back and eats the flesh later. Who knows?"

"It's a stinking monster," said Sarbek. "Who knows why it does anything?"

"It's an animal, not a monster," said Ector. "Same as a bear or a lion. Father always said that calling something a monster just makes it something to fear, something unknown. That gives it a power over you. I'm not going to give it that. It's an animal and nothing more."

Sarbek nodded; a sad look on his face.

"Wise words, young master Ector," said Sverdes, "but I'm afraid that you too are incorrect. It's no animal. As you see, it wore a loincloth —— stitched from dried deerskin. It's not something any Lomerian would wear — so it didn't steal it. It (or one of its kind) made it. That means that they know how to skin animals and prepare the hides, and how to sew. Those skills require an intelligence that's far beyond any animal. Perhaps even more telling, it wore bracelets of forged metal."

"Stolen," said Sarbek. "They must be. It picked up some shiny baubles, is all."

"That's what I suspected as well," said Sverdes, "but it wore one on each wrist, both of the same design. Somewhat crude in workmanship, but I've seen worse on sale in the bazaar. They made these themselves."

"If that's true, then they have metalsmiths," said Sarbek. "And that means they could have armor and weapons. Oh, boy —— that's all we need."

"It means that they have intelligence," said Sverdes. "Great intelligence. Maybe on par with us. They could be capable of anything. You must always keep that in mind when you deal with these things."

"I'd rather that they were monsters," said Sarbek.

"As would I," said Sverdes. "There's more."

Sverdes displayed one of the bracelets before Sarbek. Look at the inside face of the bracelet," he said pointing to some odd markings etched there.

"Some kind of runes?" said Sarbek.

"They are Thurisaz — troll runes," said Sverdes. "Many such marking have been uncovered in caves, crypts, and old, long-abandoned places. We always thought that ancient peoples drew the runes, but perhaps that was wrong. Perhaps it was always the trolls themselves."

"What do the symbols mean?" said Ector.

"Some say the runes can invoke demons from the nether world. Many wizards maintain that the runes can be used for divination and prophesy, and they even speculate that the trolls themselves have the ability to see the future. But now that we suspect that it's the trolls that draw the runes, the theories about what they mean may well be useless."

"For what man could know the mind of a troll?" said Sarbek.

"Aye," said Sverdes. "How many of them are there? Do we know?"

"Enough to cause panic and wreak havoc," said Sarbek. "None of our towns or villages are safe."

"But as far as we know, there are not enough of them to threaten the Dor," said Ector.

"Pray Odin that you are right," said Sverdes. "A troop of these would be hard to stop, even for our best." The alchemist lowered his voice to normal speaking levels — a whisper for him. "The organs, as I explained — they have more of them than any other creature that I've seen. So many differences between the troll and everything else in nature is very strange, very unlikely."

"What are you saying?" said Sarbek.

"I'm saying that either this thing, call it a troll or whatever name you like, is of some line of creatures long died out, the last race of its kind, or else, it's not of Midgaard at all."

"Not of Midgaard?" said Ector. "You mean to say it's something conjured by magic? By some wizard? Something called up from the nether realms? Haven't we had enough of that business of late?"

"Perhaps," said Sverdes. "It's just too different from everything else found in nature. It shouldn't exist. Yet it does."

"Why are all these things happening now?" said Ector. "One crazy thing after another? The gateway in the Vermion. Jude being taken captive. That messenger that attacked the Dor. And all the rest. Why now?"

"Things are stirring again in Midgaard, young master," said Sverdes. "Old things. Dark things. Things out of legend. Evils from the bowels of Midgaard. Things from the Dawn Age. There have been hints of this for some time. For a couple of years at least. Signs, portents. Omens. Perhaps these trolls crawled out of some mountain cave for the first time in centuries. Or perhaps they've been called up from hell itself. Who knows?"

***

"You know that they are still out there?" said Ector to Sarbek as they walked through the central tower's imposing corridors, four guardsmen trailing them. "They didn't chase us all the way here only to turn around and head back to their lair."

"We have to put them down," said Sarbek. "Every last one. Tough work it will be if they don't face us for a standup fight. But it has to be done, and quickly. With the Dor and the Outer Dor on lockdown, all trade and travel is held up. We can't keep the people boxed in here too long. We'll have riots on our hands."

"That's all we need," said Ector.

9

A CRAZY, A TROLL, A CAT, AND A KILLER

"**F**ather, you're wearing a groove in the carpet," said Gallick Morfin from where he sat atop his cot reading a book under the soft yellow light of an oil lamp.

"You know it's how I think," said Baron Morfin as he paced back and forth in the large cell they shared. A cell in the dungeon below old Tammanian Hall, the high seat of government in Lomion City. "I want to try to pop the door hinge again. I think that if we pull up at the same time, and I twist it just right, we might get it. We have to try. I can't wait any longer. I can't stand it in here."

"They'll put us in a real cell if we try to bust out again. No light, no bed, and rats. Rats. Do you want that, because I sure don't? We've got to be patient."

"We're prisoners here, son. We're in a cell. A cell. It might be decorated all nice and comfy, but it's a cell just the same. A lousy dungeon. It's where we put criminals. Criminals! Not me! I'm a High Councilman, for Odin's sake; a lord of Lomion; the patriarch of a Noble House. And they lock me up down here? Just for speaking my mind and thwarting their stupidity? Two months! And my son too. I will see the Vizier dead for this, the no good traitor. I'll hang him from the city gates for the crows to pick at."

"Please, father, calm down. If the guards come—"

"I'm through being calm and I'm through being patient. One way or another, we're getting out of here today, whether our friend comes through or not. If he doesn't, we'll get out on our own or we'll die trying. No Morfin has ever rotted in a dungeon before. Never. Not in all the centuries of our House. Never. I'd rather be dead than be a prisoner. Every day we languish here and do nothing, we disgrace ourselves and our House, and all our line back unto the beginning. I'd rather be dead."

"Do you want me dead too?"

The Baron paused and took a breath. "I don't want either of us dead, son. I just want us free. We need to get out of here. We need to bring the Vizier to justice."

"Once the Freedom Council makes its move, we'll be freed. They'll get us out. I want out of here just as much as you do, but I'd much rather wait another day, another week, or even another month, and get out clean, than get killed today in the trying."

There was a sound from out in the hallway, beyond the locked door.

"Someone is coming," said Gallick.

"Too early for lunch," said Morfin. "It's either our boy or one of the Vizier's cronies.

A man spoke loudly in the corridor, his voice

90

shrill. "Open the doors, open the gate, don't make me late, I've got a date. Don't call it torture, it's just clean fun, cut off their heads and bake them in the sun. They've got it coming, you know, ho, ho. Don't we all; don't we all?"

Morfin and Gallick looked at each other and shook their heads.

A burly guard opened the door. Prince Cartegian capered about behind him, drooling. Other guards stood behind the prince. Usually, when the guards needed to enter the cell, three or four of them would go in, no more than that, but when the king's son came to visit, things were different. To insure the prince's safety, six men went with him — the dungeon's full duty compliment of guards.

The prince pushed his way to the front and stared at the prisoners for some few moments. Then he began to dance and twirl around, holding the hand and waist of an imaginary dance partner as he sang his tune.

"They've had it coming for so very long,

My troll and my cat, for you, I sing this merry song.

Your time has come at long, long last.

I'll pluck out your eyes and make you cry;

I'll cut off your heads and make you dead.

Dearest troll, dearest cat, today you meet your ends."

"Alright, traitors," said the keyman. "Get up against the wall and put your hands in the manacles. Do it quick and give us no trouble this time."

"He's going to kill us," said Gallick, his hand on

the bloodstained bandage on his right shoulder. Several other bandages were bound about his body. His father suffered similarly.

"He always says that, but he hasn't yet," said the keyman. "I wouldn't worry about it. Now get to the wall."

Neither Gallick nor the Baron moved an inch. "He means it this time," said Gallick. "You can't allow this —— the council will hold you responsible. They'll have your head — all of your heads — on a platter. You have to protect us from him. You have a duty."

The keyman looked uncertain and eyed Cartegian.

"I'm only planning to take out one of their eyes," said Cartegian, waving a large spoon. "Or possibly two, if the spirit so moves me. I'll pluck them out with this," he said, indicating the spoon. "They come out so much cleaner that way than with a knife, don't you agree? But never fear, beloved cat," he said, gesturing toward Gallick, "between you two, you have four eyes, so you'll have plenty left over once I'm done, should you need them." He turned toward the guards. "Eyeballs are so tasty with bread and jam, and with frogs legs on the side. Raw, of course. That's the only way to eat them, the eyeballs, I mean. The only civilized way, that is."

Some of the guards smiled in anticipation. Others went pale and looked disgusted.

"I'm sure that the good prince will use restraint in whatever penance he inflicts on you," said the keyman. "Against the wall, now, or we'll do it the hard way."

Morfin and Gallick held their ground.

With a nod from the keyman, the guards surged toward the Morfins, clubs raised (they carried no blades, for none were allowed in the dungeons, save for as instruments of torture, and even then, only upon their imminent usage). Cartegian capered to the side to let the guards pass.

There was a clicking sound and one of the rear guards yowled, clutched his back, and dropped to his knees. His face was filled with shock and anguish. A moment later, before anyone reacted, another click — the sound of a crossbow firing — and a second guard was hit in the back. "Aargh," he yelled and staggered toward one of the cots even as his club dropped from his hand. The other guards turned toward whatever threat lay behind them. A shadowy figure with a sword charged them.

The Morfins were on the nearest guards in an instant, jumping them from behind while they were distracted. Baron Morfin grabbed one guard about the head and neck, and squeezed. He didn't let go until the man slumped to the floor, unmoving. Gallick wrestled with the keyman, pitting strength against strength.

The swordsman's blade sliced by once and then again, and the guards that stood against him went down, sliced open and bleeding badly. So quick was the swordsman that they never had the chance to swing their clubs.

Gallick and the keyman squeezed each other's throats, grunting and straining, both held in a death grip.

A blade appeared in Cartegian's hand and he plunged it into the keyman's back. That took all the fight out of him. Gallick pushed him away and scrambled to his feet, ready to fight, but the melee was already over.

The man Morfin fought lay unmoving, as did one of the swordsman's opponents — his throat sliced open, blood pooling about him. The other guards gasped and groaned, cursed and moaned: they were injured but conscious.

The Morfins looked each other up and down but saw no injuries. Both were unscathed.

Gallick turned toward Cartegian. "Thank you, my lord," he said.

Cartegian stood tall, his eyes clear. "You're welcome," he said in a distinctly normal voice, uncharacteristic for him. "I only wish that I could have freed you sooner."

"So do we," said the baron.

"And we thank you as well," Gallick said to the tall swordsman who wore a black mask tied about his head, obscuring his face.

The man's only reply was a nod.

"Masks are the realm of assassins," said the baron, not restraining his disdain for that olden profession.

"That they are," said the swordsman showing a wide, toothy grin.

"I've little use for The Black Hand," said the baron.

"As do I," said the swordsman, to which the baron seemed surprised.

"They'll be after you now," said the baron to Cartegian. "What are you going to do?"

"No one knows I'm here," said Cartegian. "I made certain of that. In fact, right now, I'm taking a bit of a nap in my chambers."

"They know," said Gallick pointing to the injured guards.

The swordsman stepped over to the keyman.

"No, please," said the man, anticipating the swordsman's intent. Before he said another word, the swordsman's blade entered his chest once and then again. The keyman spit up some blood, but never spoke again.

"Stop," said Gallick. "You can't just murder them. I won't allow it." He tried to step forward, but his father's hand gripped him tightly about the upper arm and held him back. That grip was iron.

"It must be done," whispered the baron. "The prince's involvement in this cannot be known."

Despite their pleadings and calls for help, the swordsman quickly killed each of the guards without hesitation. When he was done, he went back and checked each one for any signs of life. There would be no witnesses.

Through it all, Gallick's face wore a look of anger and disgust. He stared at the floor and shook his head.

"Is this what we've come to, father? In league with murderers? Killing unarmed, helpless men? Is that what we do now?"

"It had to be done," said the baron.

"The League has brought this upon us," said Cartegian in a commanding voice with a sharp edge to it. "No one has felt the League's bite more than the Tenzivels. They've driven us to this. Now we do what we must to preserve the Republic."

Gallick stared at him, listening to his words. Words that sunk in. "Who is he anyway?" he said of the swordsman. "One of The Black Hand?"

The swordsman chuckled.

"Much worse," said Cartegian. "Best you don't know. Best you don't ask."

"He's Dark Sendarth," said the baron.

Gallick's expression turned to surprise. No denials came from the prince or the swordsman. "Dead gods!" he said. "Odin, preserve us."

10

WHEN THE BLACK ELVES COME CALLING

After Ginalli and his group left The Grasping Grond to head back to their ship, they heard an eerie, otherworldly wailing the like of which none of them had heard before. It grew louder by the moment. Something was headed in their direction. Something strange. Something unnatural. Something dangerous.

"Weapons ready," said Ezerhauten. As one, the soldiers pulled their swords. "Eyes sharp, and stay together."

While they were still in the square outside The Grond, from down a side street came the thing that wailed.

"Douse the lights," whispered Ezerhauten as he and then the others crouched down. "Be still, be silent."

The wailer was a floating, disembodied skull that glowed an eerie white. It was large; nearly twice the size of a man's skull, with teeth long and pointy. Its lower jaw moved up and down as it screamed a sound so horrid as to still the blood of a brave man. But a glance told the men that this was no living being. It could be naught but a thing of magic, conjured by a dark wizard for some fell purpose, or an undead creature that somehow crept up from the nether realms in search of blood and souls.

It had almost passed them by when it stopped. It turned its head in their direction. Red light shone in the empty sockets where its eyes should have been. Then it wailed again. Louder that time. So loud that it pained the men's ears. It began to move toward them.

"A skull demon of Ratismar!" cried Keld. "See how it taunts us?"

"To the ship," said Ginalli. "Let's fly."

They stood, and moved with speed away from the glowing skull. The wizards reignited the lights atop their staffs to brighten their way. They stopped when they passed the edge of the square and turned onto the street that led to the docks.

"It's not following," said Putnam. "It turned back to its course. In no mood for a chase, I guess."

"Frem, I want you to follow it," said Ezerhauten. "Take Putnam and Sevare. Learn what you can, but don't get dead."

"Is that wise?" said Keld. "The demon's power is far beyond them."

"Then perhaps you should go after it?" said Ezerhauten.

"My place is at Father Ginalli's side, safeguarding him," said Keld without missing a beat. "How dare you try to divert me from my duty. You overstep your bounds, mercenary."

Ezerhauten shook his head. "Frem, get moving."

Two more blocks did the skull travel, yowling

98

all the while, before finally it went quiet. Then it floated for another block, but this time, in silence, before halting near a three story building. The skull flew unsteadily over a low wall and into the building's small rear yard. Frem and his men moved after it as quietly as they could, which was quiet indeed, despite their armor. Long years in the skulking business had taught them how. Nevertheless, they stayed well back from the skull, for they had no wish for it to turn its gaze on them again.

When the Pointmen reached the wall, they looked over it and through the tall hedge beyond as they best they could. The skull was at the rear of the building, right up against the wall, some ten yards from their position. Suddenly, it dropped to the ground, its glow extinguished.

Just enough starlight shown through the clouds at that moment to reveal the truth. The skull creature was no monster at all, no demon from Keld's imagination, and no thing that crept from the grave. It was a fraud. Hogwash and horsefeathers. It was a costume. Three small beings clad in black operated the skull, which they held aloft via a black pole. The creatures doffed their black robes, which they wore over tight fitting gray and black shirts and breeches. Their heads were bald and large for their bodies. Their skin, dark. Their size, small as that of a young child. Their oddest features though, were their large eyes, and overlong, spindly limbs.

"Black elves out of Svartleheim," whispered Frem, surprise on his face. "I never thought I'd see them with my own eyes. Look at them — right out of the faerie stories, big eyes and all."

Putnam mouthed a quick prayer and made a religious gesture with his hand, imploring the Aesir's blessing and protection.

The svarts studied the building's back wall for some moments. They found handholds in the stone (handholds far too small for a man to use) and began to scale the wall. Up and up they went, seemingly with little strain or struggle, though one of them carried a sizeable bundle strapped to its back.

They reached a third floor window of what was clearly a grand manor house of a wealthy family, and two together raised the sash, quiet as could be. Those two slunk in. The one with the bundle followed behind them.

"What are they about?" said Putnam. "Burglars, are they? Or cutthroats?"

"Worse, I fear," said Frem, "if the stories my grandmother told me hold any truth. But let's wait and see."

After a few moments, a flash of light shone in the third floor room. Sevare jerked back and fell on his rump. Putnam and Frem grabbed at him.

"What happened?" said Frem. "Did something hit you?"

"They threw a powerful spell up there," said Sevare. "Never felt anything like it. It caused a disturbance in the magical weave, and a wave of energy flew out in all directions. It felt like a horse ran into me. You didn't feel it? Not anything?"

"No," said Frem and Putnam.

A moment later, the black elves crawled out the window and carefully closed it behind them.

They climbed down the wall together, much more slowly than they had gone up; the one with the bundle was in the middle, the others aiding it. The bundle seemed larger, and the svarts struggled with it.

"Loot?" said Sevare.

"No, the bundle is moving," said Putnam. "Like it's trying to wriggle free. What the heck?"

"Dead gods," said Frem. "It's just like in grandma's old stories. They've stolen a baby; pulled it right from its crib." He turned toward Putnam, a look of horror on his face, his eyes wide. "They left behind an imp," he muttered.

"There could be a cat in that bundle," said Sevare. "Or anything."

"It's no cat," said Frem. "It's a baby. Few men have seen this. Perhaps no others yet living."

"What do we do?" said Putnam, as he and Sevare looked to Frem.

"We stop them," said Frem.

"But they're black elves," said Putnam. "They've got dark powers. Magic and such. They can probably roast us alive or turn us into something...unnatural."

"We shouldn't get involved," said Sevare. "It's none of our business, and our orders were to follow them, not to fight them."

"I'll not let those things take a child," said Frem. "We jump them when they come over the hedge. We'll take them alive, if we can, in case I'm wrong about this and they're just burglars. Keep down and keep quiet."

The bushes rustled as the svarts crawled through them. Frem popped up from where he crouched behind the wall. He swatted the nearest svart about the head with an open hand. The slap was hard and loud and sent the svart tumbling to the ground. It rolled over the wall and fell, landing at Putnam's feet. The other svarts cried out in alarm. Then one spoke. To the end of his days, Frem never forgot the sound of its voice; that strange, inhuman quality; the menace in its defiant tone. "The night is ours, volsung!" it spat. "Begone with you."

The one with the bundle stumbled back into the bushes. His companion (the one who spoke) raised his tiny hand and pointed it at Sevare, who stood closest to him, even as Sevare pointed his own hand at the elf. A sizzling sound erupted from near the elf, and the sound of a lightning bolt came from near Sevare. Magic flew from unerringly each hand. The svart and Sevare were both blasted backward and crumbled to the ground. Frem didn't wait to see the outcome of that. He stepped onto the wall and crashed through the bushes, charging after the svart with the bundle.

A woman's cry rang out from above. A glance informed Frem that lantern light shone from the manor's third floor room. Frem knew that the mother had sensed her child's danger via whatever strange intuition mothers have about their children. She'd gone to check on it. And Frem felt certain that in its crib, she found not her beloved babe, but an imp, a creature born of darkness and bathed in malice and human blood.

Frem ran as hard as he could. The black elf was fast. Faster than Frem by a goodly ways, but it was burdened by the bundle. Weighed down by an infant that no doubt weighed near as much as the svart itself. As he ran, Frem thought of his own little girl, his beloved Coriana, and he ran the faster. He'd die before he let the svart steal that child. Over the manor's far wall and into the street beyond they ran. Frem was certain he heard the baby crying. Crying in terror. He was convinced of it.

As he drew close, Frem bent low and reached forward as far as he could. At first, his fingers clutched only air, but then, he grabbed ahold of the svart about its upper arm. He clamped down on it with a grip that he would not loose so long as life remained in him. He wrenched the svart around. It spun and twirled in the air as Frem ground to a halt. Frem straddled the elf the moment that it thumped to the ground. He punched it in the face —— the kind of punch only a huge man like Frem could throw. He felt a thud and looked down to see the creature's black dagger and the dent it had made in his breastplate. Had he not been wearing his armor, the blade would have sunk into his left lung, maybe even into his heart. He punched the thing again (that time, harder still), though it still reeled from the first blow. The svart went still. Knocked out or dead. He knocked the elfin blade away, and kept a knee pressed on the creature's thigh as he pulled the fallen bundle from its shoulder. He unwrapped it; his heart pounding in his chest. And he saw: a human baby. Frem had been right. The moment the baby's eyes locked on Frem's, the child began to cry. And Frem smiled.

11

A MESSAGE FOR THE REGENT

Captain Kralan of the Myrdonians pulled his horse alongside Brock Alder and Rom Alder (the elder male of House Alder and brother to Mother Alder herself), as they rode near the head of the brigade, a thousand soldiers lined up behind them.

"Our scouts report that the outer town is partly evacuated, the gates are closed, and the walls are heavily manned."

"They've been tipped off," said Rom. "And they mean to fight. This adventure will be much harder than we had hoped."

"Let's ride up for a parlay," said Brock.

"You will not talk your way past those walls, nephew," said Rom. "Blood will spill afore we set foot inside."

"The blood shall be theirs," said Brock. "We have the weight of law behind us. The writ issued by the High Council appoints me as legal regent of Dor Eotrus. I will take my rightful place."

Rom shook his head, but said nothing more.

***

"Sir Sarbek," said a guardsman as he dashed toward him, panting from having run all the way from the main gate. "A troop of soldiers approaches from the south."

"Who and how many?" said Sarbek.

"Lomerian regulars, by the look of it. A few companies at the least. Perhaps a full brigade."

Sarbek looked surprised.

"A coincidence?" said Ector.

"When's the last time a brigade of Lomerian regulars came calling on Dor Eotrus?"

"Never, as far as I know," said Ector.

"Aye, so it's no coincidence. They've got wind of the trolls somehow. There may have been other attacks farther south."

"Then they're here to help," said Ector. "We should let them in, shouldn't we?"

"No. Let's not be hasty about such things. If they were really coming to help us, we'd have gotten ravens, and we haven't. So something is not right about this. Let's go talk to them. Once we sort them out, we can decide what to do."

A short while later, Sarbek, Ector and Malcolm Eotrus, and Sir Indigo stood atop the wall above the south gate of the Outer Dor, which was some thirty feet above the ground beyond. Men were hauling stones and placing them in piles supported on dunnage beams that spanned from parapet to parapet to avoid overloading the slab. Other men were setting up hearths to heat water or oil. They were preparing for a siege. But not one initiated by the soldiers that marched toward them. They feared an attack by the trolls that had destroyed Mindletown and nearly wiped out Ector's patrol.

The brigade marched toward the gate, the lead men only two hundred yards away and closing fast. Aligned in orderly rows, their helmets enameled red, they were a sea of gray and red tabards embossed with the standard of the Lomerian guard — a white tower on a field of green. Most were on foot, and wore armor of chain links. Squadron after squadron marched in step, disciplined, and with purpose. Beyond them, in the distance, wagons aplenty burst with supplies and equipment, including ladders of great length — fit for a siege. Amongst the troop were several squadrons of heavy cavalry, barded and adorned. At the fore of the troop, a squadron of Myrdonian Knights that looked regal in their emerald green armor, their weapons finished to match. Amongst the vanguard rode Brock Alder, soldiers in Alder livery clustered about him. Beside him came Rom Alder and Dirk Alder (eldest son of Bartol Alder), adorned in gleaming blue armor of unusual design. Then came several Alder bannermen — named men, admired and feared for their exploits.

"They demand that we open the gates forthwith," said Indigo, "but they will not reveal their purpose. They're carrying Alder standards as well as those of the Lomerian guard. That means that the chancellor sent them."

"Any mention of trolls?" said Sarbek.

"No," said Indigo. "Bald Boddrick rides with them."

"The Backbreaker?" said Sarbek as he peered out at the troop of soldiers. "I see him, even from

106

here. Big as a bear and twice as ugly."

"We should go down and speak with them," said Ector.

"Should we now?" said Sarbek. "Those men out there haven't happened by to ask after our health, you know. Boddrick is one of the Chancellor's chief bullyboys. If he's called him into action, he's planning trouble. That means Boddrick's whole gang of cronies will be with him: Sentry of Allendale, Black Grint, Bithel the Piper. Maybe even Gar Pullman. Those are killers, every one. They're here for a knife fight, not tea and biscuits. If they're not hunting trolls, then they're after us. Why they might be looking for a fight with the Eotrus is what I'm wanting to know. And if so, why come with only one brigade? It's an insult, it is. Best we speak with them from on high," he said. "You agree?"

"Aye," said Ector, weakly, his face pale. "It would seem wiser, all things considered."

Sarbek turned toward the watch captain of the gate. "Get every crossbowman and archer you can find atop these ramparts as fast as you can muster them."

The watch captain dashed off.

Sarbek moved to the centermost section of the wall, leaned forward, and stared down at the five men on horseback that waited before the gate.

"Guardsmen only," said Sarbek to the others. Then he spoke to the horsemen. "You men, go tell whichever Alder is in charge back there to get his butt up here and speak his peace. Otherwise, the gate stays closed."

The soldiers stared up at Sarbek for several

moments, taken aback, uncertain of what to do. After conferring for a few moments amongst themselves, they turned their horses and rode back to the main troop. Several minutes later, they returned with two others.

One was forty or so, slight, and finely dressed with a broad brimmed hat. The large man at his side wore the heavy armor of a knight, but to which order he belonged was not clear. The five soldiers lined up behind them; one carried the Lomerian standard, another, that of House Alder.

Sarbek looked them over and then turned toward the Eotrus brothers. "The dandy is an Alder for certain. I don't know his face, but I imagine he's one of the younger sons, or an older grandson or nephew. The knight is likely his bodyguard or one of their bannermen. Let me do the talking. Agreed?"

The Eotrus brothers nodded.

"Who goes there?" shouted Sarbek.

"I am Brock of Alder," he said. "Duly appointed emissary of the crown. To whom do I speak?"

"Sir Sarbek du Martegran, acting castellan of Dor Eotrus, and Knight Captain of the Odions."

The guards behind Brock glanced at each other at the mention of the Odion Knights, no doubt because they were the most feared militant order in the realm. Each Odion, it was said, was a match for five normal knights.

Brock stared at Sarbek, as if expecting him to call for the gate to be opened, or at least to say something more. But Sarbek just stood there staring down at him. After a time, Brock spoke again. "The gate, sir," he said, pointing to it.

"Speak your peace from where you sit," said Sarbek.

Brock's brow furrowed; a look of disdain on his face. "I bear a writ from the High Council in Lomion City," he said. "To be read to the Eotrus brothers and the Dor's castellan."

"We're listening, Mr. Alder," said Sarbek. "So read it."

If looks could kill, the stare that Brock leveled on Sarbek would have left him as little more than dust. Brock handed a scroll to the lead herald; he unfurled it and began to read it aloud on Brock's behalf.

"For heinous crimes, various and sundry, including but not limited to: assaulting a duly appointed officer of the realm, resisting arrest, and murder most foul, Claradon Eotrus, son of Aradon, is hereby declared and confirmed before all goodly citizens of the realm, and before the gods themselves, an outlaw of the State."

Gasps of alarm and disbelief came from all along the wall.

The soldier continued. "He shall be arrested on sight by any and all loyal and true agents of the realm, and executed outright if he dares to resist this just and lawful writ. Furthermore, all Eotrus holdings, property, livestock, currency, and all other items of value and consideration are hereby and irrevocably forfeited, in their entirety, to the crown."

"And furthermore, Mr. Brock Alder, sixth son of Mother Alder, Matriarch of that storied and honorable House, is hereby appointed sole and supreme Regent of Dor Eotrus, commander of all

Eotrus forces, and sovereign of its people, until such time as the Council sees fit to appoint a permanent regent or confer the title of Dor Lord upon an appropriate person in good standing with the crown."

"As such, all Eotrus forces are ordered to stand down and to submit to the command of the new Regent immediately. Failure to do so will result in charges of treason and summary execution upon the Regent's discretion."

The soldier rolled up the scroll and handed it back to Brock, who placed it inside his coat, a smug look on his face.

"Now Sir Sarbek," said Brock. "Open the gates. As is customary, I will provide you with copies of the warrants for Claradon Eotrus's arrest, as well as those that have been issued for his cohorts: the gnome, Ob A. Faz; the hedge wizard, Par Tanch Trinagal; and the foreign knight, Theta."

"What have you done with Claradon?" shouted Ector.

"No one has done anything to him," said Brock. "As far as I know, he remains on the run from the law —— an outlaw, as the writ said. Now, open the gates. I will not ask again."

Sarbek stared down at Brock, his jaw set, his eyes hard and cold.

"What do we do?" said Malcolm quietly.

"We're not handing them the Dor," said Ector.

"If we don't let them in, the bastards will lock us all up for treason," said Malcolm.

"Give me that," said Sarbek to Indigo. In one fluid motion, he snatched the heavy crossbow from Indigo's hands, pointed it toward Brock, and fired.

The bolt flew true. Brock's eyes widened, though he had no time to react. The bolt struck him amidst the forehead and blasted out the back of his head. There were gasps of alarm from the men on the wall and from the regent's group. Brock teetered on his horse, mouth agape, for a few seconds before his body tumbled over and fell to the dirt. The horses reared, the soldiers spitting curses.

"Dead gods," said Ector, his eyes wide, his mouth open. "You killed him."

"Darned right, I killed him, the bastard," said Sarbek.

Brock's soldiers turned their horses in a panic and bolted. The big knight with him stared up at the wall, his visor down, his identity unknown by the Eotrus. Eotrus crossbowmen stared back, their weapons pointed at him.

"Do we take him?" said Indigo.

"No need," said Sarbek. "The message has been sent and received."

Rom Alder stepped down from his horse, picked up his nephew's body, and draped it over Brock's horse. He took his time about it. He moved slowly, deliberately. Once back on his horse he stared up at Sarbek and the others, though he said nothing.

"That one has too much faith in his armor, I think," said Indigo. "My bow can pierce it. You have only to give me leave."

"No," said Sarbek. "There's still a chance that it will end here. That chance goes away if we keep shooting. Let him go."

"Why did you kill him?" said Malcolm. "The Chancellor will not let this go."

"You heard him," said Sarbek. "They carry a legal writ to take the Dor; to take everything that you own, everything that's yours by right, everything that your family has worked for, for centuries, even your good name. And they wouldn't have stopped there. They would have arrested you and everyone close to you too. Maybe even killed you."

"What will they do to us now?" said Ector.

"What more can they do than that?" said Sarbek.

"They can send an army, instead of a single brigade," said Ector.

"Let them come," said Sarbek. "Let them come with an entire corps. If we're lucky, the Chancellor will lead it himself. If we kill that bastard, maybe the Republic will get back on track. Not killing him when he had the chance, was the biggest mistake your brother ever made. The biggest."

"Maybe without the Alder leading them, they'll withdraw," said Malcolm.

"I doubt that," said Indigo. "They had to know that we wouldn't turn over the Dor to them. They must have reinforcements on the way."

"Who knows what's in the minds of an Alder?" said Sarbek. "Plotters and schemers, every one, going back generations. They can't be trusted except to be untrustworthy."

"What about the trolls?" said Ector. "Most of the soldiers out there are not Alder men — they're Lomerian regulars. Shouldn't we warn them?"

"They'll never believe us," said Indigo.

"Especially not after Sarbek's 'message'."

"But we should warn them all the same," said Ector

"There are not enough trolls out there to menace a whole brigade," said Sarbek. "Not by a long ways."

"We don't know how many there are," said Ector. "What if more come? That's what we have been expecting, and planning for, since we got back, isn't it? That's why we've been moving people into the citadel and bolstering the guard, preparing our defenses."

"Aye," said Sarbek.

"Then we should warn them," said Ector.

Sarbek stared at the Alder troops for several moments before responding. "To Helheim with them," he said. "Every one of them what the trolls kill is one less that we will have to deal with and vice versa. Let them wipe each other out. Better for us."

"I don't think father would approve," said Ector.

"Maybe not," said Sarbek. "But staying put and letting it play out may be the best way to keep the Dor in Eotrus hands."

"Saving them from the trolls would be a help too, don't you think?" said Ector.

"I'm sorry, boy, but it wouldn't," said Sarbek. "By the time the Alders got done twisting the story, they'd say we sent the trolls down on them. They'd say the trolls were working for us. And then we'd probably be accused of conjuring them up by witchcraft or some such. In any case, there would be no credit coming our way, I'm certain of that. Let the trolls have them, I say, and shed no tears over them."

"You're a hard man, Sir Sarbek," said Ector.

"It's a hard life," said Sarbek. "Especially up here in the north. You've come to know that more than most in recent times. Best we worry after our own and not these usurpers."

"What will they do now?" said Malcolm as they watched Rom Alder ride back to the troop with Brock's body.

"Depends on who is in charge," said Sarbek. "Boddrick will have his say, so will whatever Knight Captain commands that Myrdonian squadron. There will be a captain over the regulars as well. Which of them, or some other, is actually next in line of command, we don't know. More than likely, they'll debate things for a time back in their camp, trying to sort things out, come up with a strategy. But if whoever is in command is a strong leader, he might come at us straight away, any minute now——"

"With everything they have," said Indigo. "Out for blood and vengeance."

"He'll be hoping for a quick breach of a gate," said Sarbek. "To catch us with our pants down. If he doesn't get that, he'll pull back and wait for reinforcements. If they don't come right at us, that means that they've got a cautious man in charge — a thinker. A man like that will prepare a siege, and only come at us in his good time, when he has the men to do it, if he comes at us at all; he may try to starve us out."

"Or else, maybe they've got a fool for a leader or maybe two or more men what don't agree, so they won't do anything for fear of a fatal mistake," said Indigo. "They know they're outnumbered here and that we have a strong position. If they've any sense at all, they'll siege us and wait for more men."

"Is there a chance that they'll just pull out?" said Ector.

"Only if they're led by a coward," said Sarbek. "Which is possible."

"They won't pull out," said Indigo. "That one," he said, pointing at Rom, "will come at us, one way or another. Not just a bodyguard, I think."

"But they don't have enough men to be a threat," said Malcolm.

"Not to the citadel," said Sarbek. "But the Outer Dor is vulnerable. We don't have the manpower to fully cover these walls —— not without our bannermen. But I'll not cede the Outer Dor to the Alders or to the trolls. It's the lifeblood of our community."

"Then let's get everything we have out here," said Ector, "leaving a reserve only on the main walls and within the citadel. We can fall back there if necessary."

Sarbek looked surprised. "Your father would've advised much the same. I will make it so."

12

THE CHANGELING

Frem heard the family moving about inside the manor house, and he heard their whispers. He pounded on the door, but they would not open it.

"We have your boy," said Frem. "The black elves took him, but we snatched him back and caught the elves. Open the door."

After several minutes of this, with no response, Frem heard a woman's voice. She argued with her husband. Finally, the man answered Frem.

"Go away," said the man. "You're mistaken. My children are all safe. If what you say be true, they took a child from another house. Look elsewhere."

"We saw it ourselves," said Frem. "They took the child from the third floor window at the back of the house. A boy, several months old, with blue eyes and black hair."

Frem heard the wife gasp. "Open it," she yelled. "Open it. Let them in."

"What are you talking about?" said Rothmar, her husband. "Ragnar is in your arms. He's right there."

"I don't know," said the woman. "I don't know. Just open the door. I have to see." She was insistent and would not back down. Eventually, Rothmar gave up and opened the door. He stood in his nightshirt and bare feet. Even so, he was tall enough to look Frem straight in the eyes. Chiseled and mustached, with muscles on muscles. He held a sword ready to thrust and a big shield of ornate make. He braced himself against a rush.

"Make no false move or you die," said Rothmar.

Frem held the baby before him; the child's little face clear to see.

"What trickery is this?" said Rothmar, a confused expression on his face. "My son is in Helda's arms, though this baby could be his twin."

Helda placed the baby she held in a basinet and ran toward Frem. She looked at the child for but a moment and then snatched him from Frem's arms, weeping and wailing.

"Do not move from that spot," said Rothmar to Frem. He backed up, pushing Helda away from the entry, his other children looking on from the stairs. One son, a boy of twelve, stood at the bottom step, holding a sword. The younger ones behind him. Rothmar backed up to the basinet, still braced for a fight. He looked into the basinet. "Aargh!" he said, shook his head, and rapidly blinked his eyes. Then he peered closer. "Ragnar. It is my Ragnar, but for a moment..."

"For a moment, it wasn't," said Helda. "I saw the same when I picked him up in his room minutes ago."

"But not when you looked at the child he brought?" said Rothmar.

"No," said Helda.

"What did you see in his room?" said Rothmar. "Tell me true."

"I don't know. It was only for a moment; just a moment. I don't know. By Wotan, I don't know."

"Tell me what you saw, woman," said Rothmar raising his voice. "Exactly what you saw."

Her body shook, as if she were fighting against herself to get the words out. "He had the look of...of an imp, like in the stories. The eyes, those eyes! And the strange, gray skin. I don't know; it was just for a moment. I don't know. I don't know what I saw. What could this mean? Has someone bewitched us?"

Rothmar's jaw hung open. He was uncertain, confused. He turned his gaze on Frem. Frem quickly told him all that they saw in the garden.

Rothmar and Frem stepped outside to look at the elves. All three were hogtied and gagged, one still unconscious. Putnam stood over them, sword in hand, his face pale. Sevare sat on the stoop, his head down.

"They are black elves, indeed," said Rothmar to his family when he stepped back inside. He engaged the oldest boy to keep the other children inside, for they all wanted to look upon the black elves, creatures they'd never seen afore, but had heard of in a hundred legends.

"We don't know that the elves switched our boy for an imp, even if these men speak true," said Rothmar.

"You saw, you saw," said Helda, cringing as she looked to the basinet.

"Perhaps the spell they laid makes our boy look like an imp for but a moment when anyone looks upon him for the first time. Perhaps this other child is the true imp. I'll not take a child from our home and cast it aside for one brought to my door by a stranger."

"Dear gods, dear gods," cried Helda as she clutched Ragnar to her chest. "What do we do? Do you speak true?" she said looking to Frem.

Frem nodded.

"Rothmar, what can we do?" said Helda.

"We must call for the Angel of Death," said Rothmar.

The crone came down the walk, her boy, and her wolf beside her, Rothmar's eldest son leading the way.

"You came off The Rose," she said to Frem. "What mischief have you wrought here?"

Frem didn't answer.

She stepped close and inspected him. "Look into my eyes," she said.

Frem did, unafraid.

She stared up at him for some moments, and then patted him on the arm. "Some hope there is, I see. Some hope, indeed. Good man. Now where are these elves and this imp I hear tell of?"

They showed her first to the shed in the yard where they'd put the elves, Putnam still guarding them.

"Black elves, you said," spoke the crone. "Black elves these be. There be no doubt. A wonder to catch such creatures. You men must know your trade well. Did any escape you?"

"None," said Putnam. "Of that we're certain." He held one hand to his belly and looked as if he was about to puke.

"Certain enough to bet your life, soldier?" said

119

the crone.

"I'll not bet my life on anything," said Putnam, "but I'm certain, all the same."

"Good. But bet your life, you have, whether you know it or not. Best cover their eyes, or mayhaps they'll beguile you with their elf magic, or worse, pluck out your soul," she said, cackling. "Souls are funny things, you know. Everyone gets one easy enough, but once you lose it, it's darned hard to get it back. Elf magic is strong. Beware it; shun it. Oh, and covering over their heads should do wonders for your unsettled stomach," she said patting Putnam on the shoulder. "Watch them close until we decide on proper course."

They led the crone inside. She looked with interest upon the baby in Helda's arms. Then she looked upon the one in the basinet. When she did, she jumped back and gasped, despite herself. "Dark magic there be on this child. Elf magic. But I must know more."

She laid some strange paraphernalia on the table and began to chant, her words unintelligible. From a leather bag, she pulled a fist full of small bleached bones and cast them onto the table. She bent over and looked closely, nearly touching her face to the bones. Then she pulled a holy symbol (a strange, bent cross) from beneath her shirt. She held it over the bones and said more words. Then she touched it to the forehead of the baby that clung to Helda. It cried. She studied the child's reaction for a moment, and then moved on to the other babe. She repeated her words and held the token to the child's forehead. When she did, it yowled a high-pitched wail and immediately appeared no longer as little Ragnar, but as a tiny black elf baby, an imp. The crone held the token to the imp's head as it thrashed about in the basinet trying to escape her touch. She said more words, some in a language or languages that Frem knew not, but others of her words were in Old High Lomerian. She called on the Norns, on Wotan, the All-Father, and on Donar, his son. She spoke also the names of Baldr, Vindler, and Cyo. When at last she pulled the token from the child's head, it changed back. It looked again as little Ragnar, face and body. It lay there panting and gasping for breath. An exact twin to the baby Helda held.

"A changeling, it be," said the crone. "The magic that made it so is dark and strong. I cannot break it."

"What does this mean?" said Helda.

"It means the child at your bosom is your own, and this one is not," said the crone. "But know that already you did. That's why you're holding the right one. A mother always knows, though sometimes she cannot admit the truth even to herself." She turned to Rothmar. "You owe these men a weighty debt, blacksmith. For without their intervention this night, your true son would be gone forevermore. You would never have known the truth, not unless you had the courage to bring the imp to me and then do what must be done. Few have such courage, even after the imp has brought ruin to their household. The truth is often too painful to face."

"What must be done?" said Helda.

"The imp must die," said the crone. "And at

121

once. I would have already killed it myself, but the elves would smell its stain upon your home, and they would not rest until you all suffered for it."

"Black elf or no, it is but a child," said Frem. "An innocent."

"A child of Loki," said the crone, "is never innocent. It's a changeling. A doppelganger. Had this imp remained in this household, it would have worked its dark magic, its curses and hexes, upon every member of this family. One by one the other children would have died by illness or accident. The family business would have fallen to ruin, as would this very house. Its wood would rot. Its walls, infested with vermin. Lice in every bed; worms in the food, the wine turned to vinegar. And all love would be lost between the parents. That's what this 'child' would have sown here. I have seen this before, and alas, I will see it again."

"And the elves?" said Frem.

"They too must die," said the crone. "If allowed to return to their lairs, they will tell all that they know. We will be blamed for the death of their imp, and rightly so. The elves will seek vengeance on this family, on me, and on you and your ship."

"Then just let them all go, the imp too," said Helda. "Then there will be no need for vengeance. They'll leave us all alone."

"You think so, do you?" said the crone. "You've done nothing to them so far, I trust, yet they took your child, and did their best to destroy your family. I ask you, have you wronged the elves in any way? Any insult? Think carefully — all of you. You children too," she said pointing at the children on the stairs. "Anything? Any slight, however, unlikely?"

Rothmar looked to each member of his clan and elicited a response from each. None admitted any encounter with the elves. None had done them any wrong by word or deed

"You see?" said the crone. "Yet they inflict this evil on you. There is no appeasing them. If we do not kill the imp, if we let it go, the elves will place it with another family to work its evil. Or mayhaps, they'll return here another night to take your Ragnar. I will not abide that. Nor will I allow such a plague on any other family of Jutenheim. The imp must die. But with its death, and that of the three captured, at least, there will be some uncertainty amongst the elves. The elves will know nothing of your involvement (indicating Frem) or mine. And they may not know which house these creatures went to tonight. It may end here."

"If it doesn't?" said Rothmar. "If they come back?"

"Then you must fight them off, blacksmith," said the crone. "With courage, skill, and whatever aid the All-Father sees fit to send you. Though I think he's helped you much already," she said gesturing toward Frem. "And if you survive that struggle, should it come, you must flee Jutenheim at once with all your brood, never to return."

"This is our home," said Helda. "We know nowhere else."

"Then take your chances and stay, come what may," said the crone. "Perhaps it's best that you do stay, at least for now, for if you flee at once, they will surmise why. The reach of the black elves

123

is long. They may be able to follow you wherever you go, or else alert others of their kind. Best you stay for now, and hope their kin knew nothing of which home they planned to visit this night."

"We should question them," said Frem. "Find out why they choose this house, and this boy. Find out what their true purpose is."

"You would know the mind of a black elf?" said the crone laughing. "Go and question a bear or a lion. See what good it does you."

"Animals don't speak," said Frem. "The elves do."

"Black elves speak nothing but lies," said the crone. "I wish to speak to them more than anyone else here. More than I can say. I've thought of little else since Rothmar's boy showed up at my door. What secrets I could learn. What truths I could glean. But I will not speak with them. For if I do, they will use their dark magic on us. Even I may not be able to counter it. It may kill us all or twist our minds. And if not, still we cannot trust a single word that they say. They are tricksters, one and all. Born liars. True spawn of Loki. I will debate this no further."

"This soldier," she said pointing to Frem, "and the one who guards the elves, and you, Rothmar, will go with me to the base of the cliffs, north of town. There we will drown the elves in the sea and cast their bodies into the water. With luck, the sharks will take their fill of them. But if their kin find any trace of them, they'll find no wound inflicted by sword or dagger on them. They may conclude that they fell from the rocks and drowned in the night. That may temper their anger and stay their vengeance. It's our best chance. So that is what we will do."

Frem carried one of the elves in a burlap bag as they trudged over the rocks near the water's edge. The clouds had cleared. The stars and a sliver of a moon gave them just enough light to see by. Rothmar and Putnam each carried an elf in a sack akin to Frem's. The crone walked beside Frem, her footing sure, despite her age. She held the little bundle that the elves had carried, the imp wriggling within it. The crone's wolf walked before them all. In the distance behind them, the crone's boy, her great-great-grandson, waited with the ponies. They walked as far along the rocky coast, and thus, as far away from Jutenheim, as the landscape allowed, which wasn't far, perhaps one mile and a half, but no more than two.

"Your conscience troubles you, Frem Sorlons?" said the crone.

"To kill a man in battle is one thing," said Frem. "To drown him — to murder him in cold blood, is another. And to kill a child is unforgivable."

"Not a child, a changeling," said the crone. "A thing of evil, created for but one purpose, to do evil for evil's sake. And they are not men. They are black elves of Svartleheim. Ancient enemies of mankind. I warned you of what would happen if they lived."

"I don't doubt your warnings," said Frem. "But I do doubt that any child is a thing of evil from birth."

"Do you? Then take in a panther from the

mountains as a pet. Raise it alongside your children. Let it play with them each day; let it sleep beside them each night. Teach it the same values you teach your children, as best you can teach, and as best it can learn. Your children will love it. You will love it. It will be a member of your family, nearly as important and beloved and any other. And still, one day, that panther will bite one of your children on the back of the neck and kill it, or else rip its face off, or disembowel it with its claws — all your love of it notwithstanding. Do you agree that the panther would do this?"

"Yes, probably," said Frem. "For they are wild animals. Hunters, killers."

"And yet if it happened to you and yours, you'd ask, 'why?' Why has our beloved friend and pet killed our child? The answer is simple and is just as you've said: it's a panther, and that's its nature —— despite all your nurture. Similarly, the black elves do their evil, because they are black elves — it's their nature. This imp would have been the death of the blacksmith's family. They don't deserve that. No family does. Let not your heart be troubled, for we are doing the right thing. And in any case, we are doing the only thing that we can do and hope to keep the elves at bay." She stopped and grabbed Frem by the arm. She looked into his eyes. "Sometimes, Frem Sorlons, one must do something that appears to be wrong, or is wrong, yet serves a greater purpose. I think you know of what I speak."

Frem nodded but would offer no more.

13

THE SCHOONER

The luck of the Vanyar was with Theta's group, for the run to the docks was uneventful. Theta led them several blocks east, well past the cordon the Evermerians set to contain the "Bulls." That permitted them free passage south, toward the docks, through streets dark and deserted. The schooner lay on the eastern edge of the port, whereas The Falcon's longboat was berthed more toward the west.

The docks were a scene of carnage and mayhem. The group saw a clutch of men from the schooner get ambushed by a contingent of Evermerians that laughed and howled as they pounced on them. The seamen fought tooth and nail, but unarmed, they had no chance. The Evermerians tore them to pieces. Some seamen ran to the water, waded in, and swam for it, which was merely choosing a different death, for the waters were frigid and there was nowhere to swim to. Others breathed their last along the strand, fighting for all they were worth. Brave men they were, but far outmatched. Some few dived through windows of nearby buildings, seeking any refuge or escape.

One last wave of men ran down the main thoroughfare. There were several dozen of them, all dressed in rags. These were the original prey meant for the Bulls Run. What their origin was, who knows? The crew of the schooner and the Eotrus party just happened to arrive at the right time to get thrown into the mix. It was behind this third group of men that the main swarm of Evermerians came. Hundreds strong. They crashed into the ragmen, clawing them, and pulling them down. Most put up little or no fight. The screams and roars of the slaughter were deafening.

Theta's group made it to the schooner unseen, the Evermerians fully occupied with their other prey.

"There are no longboats or dinghies," said Glimador. "What do we do?"

"We take the schooner," said Theta. "Get Bertha below deck and get the sail up. Slaayde, we need you for that."

"There's no time," said Slaayde. "They'll be all over us."

"I will hold them back," said Theta.

"Are you serious?" said Slaayde.

"Get the darned sail up now," said Theta in an icy tone.

"You're a madman," said Slaayde as he and Glimador hefted Bertha into the schooner. "You'll be the death of us all!"

Artol cut the mooring lines.

"She's low in the water," said Slaayde. "Something's not right." The boat did not sway at all with their entry or movements. It didn't respond to the surf. It was bottomed out. Stuck in the sand. They weren't going anywhere in that ship.

Glimador opened the door to below decks. There stood the Duchess's henchman, Slint, grinning. Behind him, more of his fellows. Many more.

Glimador tried to slam the door shut, but the Evermerian was too strong and pushed him back. They swarmed like ants onto the deck — a score or more of them, and still more below. Glimador backed off, sword out. Slaayde tried to drag Bertha clear.

"Thought to escape, did you, bull?" said Slint. "That's not going to happen. This isn't our first festival, you know. We've been doing this a long time. A very, very long time. We know all the tricks, bull. There's no escape from Evermere. Not for you, or any bull or cow. Not even for us. Not for anyone."

"Now pray give us a bit of a chase and a good fight, will you? We missed the main run all holed up here. Somehow, I don't think you lot will disappoint us," he said with an evil grin.

Glimador backed away.

"There are some big ones here, boys," said Slint. "We're going to eat good tonight."

Tanch stood in shock some feet away, his hands opening and closing. He backed up against the gunwale; he could go no farther.

The Evermerians, leering and drooling, began to move forward, slowly, savoring the moment.

Artol and Theta simultaneously vaulted into their midst, weapons humming. Theta's hammer was in his right hand, his falchion in his left. For Artol, it was sword and dagger. Slint's face was full of shock. He brought both hands up to catch Theta's hammer blow. Those hands, though more powerful than the combined strength of two, perhaps three, normal men, were no hindrance to the hammer at all. The hammer crashed through his guard and blasted down through his head and neck with incredible force, reducing them to nothing but pulp before lodging in his chest. The other Evermerians gasped in shock. No force that they had ever seen could do that to a man. In that brief moment of hesitation, which lasted no more than two, perhaps three seconds, Theta killed three more, and Artol felled two.

Then began a dance of death unlike any that Evermere had ever seen. Theta moved like lightning, twisting and spinning, hacking and slashing; brute force backed by preternatural skill only hinted at in the wildest legends from the Age of Heroes. With him, there was no wasted motion. Every blow crushed or cut off a head or limb. Every step put him in position to do the same again. His armor unerringly turned aside every claw, punch, or blade that struck him.

Artol grunted and spun, constantly moving in attempt to keep the bloodthirsty horde at bay. He alternately swung his sword in great arcs and then in tight downward strokes to slice off arms or heads, as they came at him.

Steps away, Glimador's sword whirled, hummed, and spun with speed and finesse, the envy of most that were called sword masters. He fought at the perimeter of the main melee, taking care to let no Evermerian have his back.

Slaayde, for all his skill and grit, could do

nothing in such a fight. His saber was too light a weapon to sever heads, and he'd already learned that anything short of that would not stop an Evermerian. Had Bertha not been with him, perhaps he would have fled. But while she yet lived, he would not abandon her. Not even if it meant his very life. He couldn't carry her alone from the ship, so while the Evermerians were occupied with the others, he dragged her to the far corner of the deck. He put the gunwale to his back, his saber poised in one hand, his dirk in the other — ready for his last stand.

Tanch didn't know what to do. For all he'd been through of late, he wasn't a soldier; he wasn't some kind of battle mage, some warrior wizard. He wasn't one of the great sorcerers like Talbon of Montrose or Grandmaster Pipkorn. He was just Par Tanch — little more than a trumped up hedge wizard that carried a few useful spells and a magic ring that he didn't even understand. He couldn't believe what was happening around him; it had to be a nightmare. The melee was too wild. Too frantic. Though he suspected, he didn't fully grasp what his opponents were, but he knew that they were nothing natural. They were inhuman. Creatures of the dark. Stalkers of the night. Monsters. Monsters that preyed on humankind.

Everything, everyone was moving too fast. Only at the battle of the gateway in the Vermion had he seen combat that remotely resembled what he saw on that ship. For all his fears and uncertainty, he wanted to help, to do his part. He wanted to throw a spell that could turn the tide and send those creatures screaming to Nifleheim or whatever hell claimed them. More so, he wanted to save himself and his companions. He thought of throwing his Spheres of Power spell, as he called it, but it only targeted one or two opponents and everyone was moving so fast, he couldn't be sure that he wouldn't hit Theta or Artol or Glimador. He considered the Scorched Earth spell, the one that he used on the docks of Tragoss Mor; the one that had killed all those men; that had burned them. He never wanted to use that magic again. It made him feel like a murderer, like a monster. He swore that he wouldn't. Even if he dared, that sorcery did not distinguish friend from foe. Any within its range would burn. So long as the others fought on, he could not throw that magic. But there was more magic that he knew, and even more that the Ring of Talidousen hinted at and whispered of to him, but he couldn't focus, he couldn't think, not with all that went on around him.

Then an Evermerian leaped at him. Tanch instinctively swung his quarterstaff and struck the man in the side of the head before his claws could tear into him. The Evermerian staggered. Tanch brought the staff up again and slammed it down on his head. The man fell to his knees. Then he hit him again. Then again. And he kept hitting him. After a while, Tanch realized that the man was dead. But the battle still raged about him.

Slaayde braced himself as an Evermerian stalked toward him, leering, saliva dripping from his mouth in anticipation of his meal. He rushed forward. Slaayde thrust with his sword. The blade sank deep into the middle of the Evermerian's chest. Slaayde sidestepped as his opponent barreled forward, unfazed by the blow, and tried to tackle him. Slaayde spun clear, but a single claw caught the side of his face and tore his cheek open to the bone. Slaayde punched the Evermerian with one hand and buried his dirk into his ear with the other — the blow so hard it pierced his skull and sank into his brain. The Evermerian dropped straight down. Slaayde sensed movement behind him and spun. A large clawed hand grabbed him about the throat and lifted him off his feet. The Evermerian thrust its other clawed hand at his belly to eviscerate him, but Slaayde deflected the blow with his knee. Ignoring the terrible pressure on his throat, he gouged his fingers into the Evermerian's eyes with every ounce of the strength and ferocity that he could muster. The Evermerian screamed and dropped him. It took a few seconds for Slaayde to get his bearings, for his head spun, dizzy from lack of blood flow to his brain, and his eyes teared, making it hard to see. When he could focus again, the Evermerian stood before him fuming and raging, one eye dangling out of its socket, its clawed hands opening and closing in rage. It stepped forward, Slaayde now completely unarmed. And then Tanch's quarterstaff blasted into the back of the Evermerian's head. He staggered and Tanch hit him again. That gave Slaayde enough time to retrieve his dirk. As the Evermerian turned and staggered toward Tanch, Slaayde buried his dirk into the base of his neck, killing him.

Artol swung his weapons wildly, desperately.

He wanted nothing more than to run for it, to escape, but that was impossible. Each opponent he faced was his match or more so in speed, and perhaps even in strength. And there were lots of them. There were too many of them. Only the great length of his sword and the long reach of his arms had thus far kept them at bay. His vast skill at arms and his Dyvers steel armor had kept him alive.

The Evermerians were fast and powerful, far, far beyond normal men. They had a resistance to pain and injury that was beyond belief. That and their claws, fangs, and ruthlessness made them terrible opponents. Despite all that, in truth, they had little skill in battle. Their movements were wild and uncontrolled, their defenses poor to non-existent; their attacks, clumsy. Such weaknesses didn't matter when they faced normal folk. But they did against a man like Artol. His skills aside, it was only their weaknesses that allowed him to survive against their press of numbers. And Artol knew it.

For Artol, there was no winning that battle. It was only a matter of time before they slashed his throat or took him from his feet. And then he'd be finished. He knew it. There was no escape. All he could hope for was a quick death. A warrior's death in battle to secure his place in Valhalla beside his forefathers.

He tried to get to the poop deck, to limit how many could get at him at once, but they blocked him at every turn. His sword ran red with blood and gore, the deck boards slick with it beneath his feet. His energy was fading fast. His sword felt heavier with every stroke.

An Evermerian dived into his lower leg from behind and tried to bite him. He struggled to kick the man off even as two more dived at him from the front. He couldn't step back, overbalanced, and fell onto his back, the bloodsuckers atop him. He pushed one back with one hand, but couldn't get a hold on the other, its spittle dripping onto his face. Just as it surged toward his throat, fangs first, something blasted into it, and knocked it off him. Explosions rang out all around. Evermerians screamed. Another blast disintegrated the head of the second Evermerian atop him and pelted him with gore. Artol stayed down, laying as flat as he could, as more balls of fiery energy passed over him and exploded around him. There seemed no end to them, the explosions lasting a minute or more. It was Tanch's magic; the wizard had saved him. How that quirky character carried that much power in him, Artol didn't understand. But after what happened on the docks of Tragoss Mor, nothing the wizard did shocked him. As soon as it seemed safe, Artol scrambled to his feet. The area immediately around him was clear, save for the bodies of the dead.

Theta was still fighting a ways away. He was a juggernaut of death and destruction. None could stand against him for more than a moment. One Evermerian dived into his leg to try to take him down. Theta kicked him off, sending the man flying over the side into the water. He splattered the heads of two other Evermerians with a single swing of his hammer. His falchion took off the head of another and the leg of yet another. His movements never slowed, the strength of his blows never diminished.

And thus, Angle Theta taught the Evermerians fear. Their numbers thinned, and they withdrew from him.

Artol watched in amazement as the Evermerians fled. Theta's skill and Tanch's magic were too much for them. They dived off the boat into the water, or jumped onto the pier and ran for the boardwalk, a dozen of them, perhaps more. They fled for their lives.

Theta stood halfway across the deck. His armor was drenched in blood. His helmet was off. His shield was torn from his back. His cloak was ripped to shreds, his armor dented and gouged, but he still stood. He still held both his weapons. Blood ran ankle deep at his feet, the Evermerians piled in heaps about him, some still twitching and gurgling, but most forever still. No fewer than twenty lay dead or dying about him.

Artol couldn't believe his eyes. No man could fight like that. No mortal ever had. No mortal ever could. What Theta was, Artol dared not even contemplate. He fought like the gods themselves.

And then Artol noticed Theta's hammer as if for the first time. The enormous size of the thing; too weighty for even Artol to wield — a weapon for a giant, not a man; the esoteric runes inscribed on its side — ancient characters and symbology of the Aesir, the gods. And then the thought occurred to him. It was a mad thought, but could it be true? Could that hammer be storied Mjolnir itself? And Theta its master? Dead gods, the implications of that were too incredible to be true. On the face of it, the very idea was madness. But looking at him amid that killing field, seeing what he could do, what he had done, it all started to fit together. His profound knowledge, his superhuman strength, his stature, his charisma, the hints at his vast age and his mysterious origins. The fact that creatures of Nifleheim seemed to know him, to fear him, to seek his death. It all fit. It was impossible, but it was true. Theta was no knight-errant from some foreign land across the sea that no one had ever heard of. He was from much farther away than that. He was from Asgard itself, the home of the gods. He'd come down from the heavens to save all of Midgaard from Korrgonn and his ilk, to seal the pathways to Nifleheim forever. The more Artol thought about it, the more that he knew it to be true. Theta was the god of thunder, the son of Odin all-father himself: Thor, prince of Asgard.

The battle wasn't over yet. The docks had gone quiet. There was no sound but the surf. Artol moved a few feet to where he had a view of the boardwalk. He saw Tanch in the back of the schooner, Slaayde by his side, battered but alive. The Evermerians were on the boardwalk. Lined up. Looking at them. Staring at the schooner. All of them. Thousands of them. All with fangs and claws, and superhuman strength and speed, and appetites only sated by the flesh and blood of the living. Their feasting on their other prey suspended, the entire throng stood silent and motionless as statues.

From somewhere far back in the crowd, one voice spoke out. "Kill them! Kill them all!"

bellowed the Duchess. And en masse, the Evermerian horde surged forward, the fires of Helheim alight in their eyes.

14

THE FREEDOM COUNCIL

"What has happened?" said Duke Harringgold as the guards closed the doors to his drawing room, leaving him and Lord Torbin Malvegil alone inside. Malvegil looked tired, sweaty, and disheveled, and strangely, he wore the garb of an upscale merchant. "Are you in disguise?"

"I am," said Malvegil. "Quite a bit has happened since we last exchanged messages," he said as he pulled out the missive that directed him to report to Lomion City. "Did you send this?"

Harringgold's face went red and his jaw stiffened as he read it. "No," he said. "I think I need a brandy for this. Join me?"

"If it's a good vintage," said Malvegil with a forced smile.

"Barsen's Reserve, twenty years old."

Malvegil raised an eyebrow. "That will do."

"A gift from my brother for my last birthday."

Harringgold poured them each a glass and they settled down in the adjoining sitting room. The outside wall of the room was sloped inward, the ceiling high, the wall almost entirely made of glass. The glass itself, a wonder in its size and clarity, crafted by Lomion's finest glaziers, their skills unsurpassed anywhere in the known world. High in the central tower of Dor Lomion, the great windows afforded a grand view of the eastern and southern sections of the city.

Harringgold took a generous sip from his tumbler. "Have they moved against you?"

"Once on the road coming here from my Dor," said Malvegil. "Again when we entered the city, not an hour ago. Your man, Fischer, helped us good and proper when they gave us trouble near the south gate. The Black Hand both times. They're down three assassins, and I lost three good soldiers."

"So they've unleashed The Hand," said Harringgold. "We feared that this was coming, and yet, I'm surprised. I didn't think it would be this soon. And I didn't think it would be against you."

"In case you forgot, they did try to kill me the last time I was here too," said Malvegil. "My back is still sore from that blade, and I've hardly taken off my chainmail since."

"We were never certain that it was The Hand."

"Now we are," said Malvegil.

"That makes all the difference. If they would murder a Dor Lord in broad daylight by Lomion City's gates, it tells us that the League has reached the point that they'll stop at nothing to achieve their ends," said the Duke.

"I've reached that point as well," said Malvegil. "The difference between us, is that they're afraid of me, and I'm not afraid of them. I'll come at them direct, not through the shadows."

"If you do, they'll kill you, and anyone that stands with you. You won't—"

"Have you been paying attention? They're trying to kill me already. They're trying pretty hard, in fact."

"You won't have a chance if you move against them. No chance at all. The League has grown more powerful than you know."

"Yet I've survived them thus far."

"You've been lucky."

Malvegil leaned back in his chair and paused a moment before he spoke again. "I'm going to war," he said.

The Duke raised his eyebrows. "With who? The League has no army of its own; it uses ours: the Lomerian Guard. Will you fight our own men?"

"If they follow the League's orders, I will."

"They do, but not knowingly. It's all through deception and lies. The League's proxies control much of the city, much of the country."

"They don't control me or mine. The Malvegils will bleed them. I will put them down and The Hand too."

"The Hand too? You might as well declare war on the wind or the rain. I hope that you're just blowing off steam, old friend. If you act directly against the League, the Council will declare you a rebel and march against you."

"I've called my banners," said Malvegil. "Let the League come."

"They control twenty brigades for every one of yours. You cannot win. You cannot even survive."

"I still say, let them come."

"And they will. They will not back down to threats or intimidation. They've declared your nephew a rebel," said Harringgold. "Do you know that?"

"Claradon?"

"Aye. Even now, a brigade led by a troop of Myrdonians under Alder command marches on Dor Eotrus. They mean to install a regent."

"What? They're really doing it? Marching on a Dor?"

"Aye. This is for real, my friend. Go carefully."

"A single brigade, you say? Does the chancellor think Eotrus walls are made of parchment and their men cowards? Ector will wipe them out to the last man. He'll hang their commander from the front gate."

"Ector is untested boy," said Harringgold. "We don't know what he'll do. He doesn't have many advisors left up there, so I can't predict how this will play out. But Barusa hopes that he'll back down and let the Regent take control of Eotrus holdings. But if he doesn't back down, then Barusa hopes that Ector will attack the Regent's troops; maybe even wipe them out as you say. That's why he's only sending one brigade. Their deaths will be all the excuse Barusa needs to send a full corps against the Eotrus and yet have the support of the Council and many of the people as well. He needs that support to justify his actions. Once the Eotrus campaign is wrapped up, he'll feel empowered to move against all his enemies. Perhaps one at a time, or if he thinks he's strong enough, against all of us at once. If the Eotrus fight, it's the beginning of the end; the start of a civil war. A war that will tear the Republic apart."

"And if they don't fight?" said Malvegil.

"In the end, it will be the same, but we'll have a lot more time to prepare; to build our defenses. Eventually, they'll come for us, one way or another. That has always been their plan; I'm certain of it."

"They're afraid," said Malvegil. "You only kill the enemy that you fear can harm you."

"Apparently, you're quite frightening to them," said the Duke. "Happily, their fear of me is not so great."

"Keep your guard up all the same."

"I always do. You've sent men to check on your Dor?"

"As soon as we figured out what was what, I contacted Landolyn. All is well at home."

"Contacted her?" said Harringgold. "Ravens, you mean? You're still using them?"

"We do, for routes that are still secure," said Malvegil. "But this time, I used different means, which brings me to the other news that I bear. News of an even greater danger to the realm than the League, if you can believe it."

Harringgold's eyes locked on Malvegil. "I pray that you are joking."

"No joke," said Malvegil. He then related all that transpired when the svart king and his retinue visited Dor Malvegil and told of the fall of Thoonbarrow to the duergar. Toward the end of the discussion, Malvegil brought in the Seer Stone that the svart king had gifted him, and showed it to the Duke, but warned him not to get too close to it. "If things were as they should be, this stone would go to the king," said Malvegil. "If not he, then the High Council. Neither can be trusted with it. So it goes to you, Archduke, like it or not. It must stay here in Dor Lomion, locked behind your walls, gates, and doors. Guarded by your guards, but only those you trust the most."

"Does it work, truly?" said the Duke.

"Aye. I've seen the image of a man a hundred leagues away through its surface, and he spoke to me just as we're speaking now. And it was with this, that I contacted my wife after the Hand assassin struck."

"That is a wonder," said Harringgold as he stared at the intricate swirling designs of the stone's surface. "The stories I've heard say that only a true seer can operate such a device."

"She's in your antechamber now with Fischer and my guardsmen. A svart."

"A svart? In all my days I never thought to see one of them."

"Well, now you have one of your very own. At least until this crisis is over. Treat her kindly. We'll be able to communicate between us (you here at Dor Lomion, and me in Dor Malvegil) and with the dwarves of Darendor, and perhaps with the elves of Lindonaire. Each through our own Seer Stone, courtesy of the black elf king himself."

"Duergar, the League, assassins, Seer Stones, and svarts," said the Duke shaking his head. "Midgaard has turned upside down. Reality crumbles around us while myth and legend take hold. My head spins with this news."

"If I didn't see much of it myself, I would not believe it," said Malvegil. "Yet it's all true."

"Truth is sometimes in the eye of the beholder," said the Duke. "Especially in Lomion. Here nothing is ever as it seems. I want to see the stone in action, but we have a meeting to go to, you and I. One that may make your head spin."

"A meeting with whom?"

"The Freedom Council," said Harringgold with a smile.

Malvegil looked elated. "You've done it? You've organized it? For real?"

"They await me even now. You've made me late. Let's go before we miss anything."

"What of the Seer Stone?"

"Bring it with us," said the Duke. "The others need to know of this new danger, and the stone will serve as support for your words."

"The stone must not fall into the hands of the League," said Malvegil. "I'd rather not move it again. Not now that it's here, safe."

"There will be guards enough at this meeting, don't you worry," said the Duke.

***

The Vizier, Rabrack Philistine, known as the Royal Wizard, and lately, as the Grandmaster of the Tower of the Arcane (the High Seat of Wizardom in all Midgaard), entered the back door of Fister Mansion in disguise. Two guards that stood outside recognized him as he made his way down the alley, or rather, they recognized the man he impersonated, one Par Trask, greeted him by name, and opened the door to permit him entry. The six guards stationed in the antechamber eyed him, but made no move to bar his entry. His disguise held, at least against the guards, but of that, he'd had no doubt. The real test was yet to come.

One of the guards said he'd escort him to the meeting room and led the way down the corridor. The hall was narrow and smelled of tobacco smoke; the plaster walls were scuffed and scratched; the paint chipped; the carpet frayed and worn. They turned one corner and then another; they went down a short flight of stairs where half a dozen guards were stationed, and then passed through some battered double doors. Beyond, it was as if they'd entered another building entirely. Here, the flooring was wood planks, polished and bright, the walls wainscoted in cherry wood, the paint above, white and fresh, the ceiling high and coffered. They walked past several doors until they reached the end of a broad corridor. Two guards stood by a grand door ten feet tall, carved with intricate geometric designs. His escort left him and as the Vizier approached the door, he saw that to the right, the corridor opened up to a large reception room, sparsely furnished with chairs and couches. There lounged some two dozen soldiers, bullyboys, and mercenaries of every type imaginable — the bodyguards of those who had arrived before the Vizier. How odd most of those ruffians looked in such a regal room; many sitting on the floor and making more chatter than was proper.

"Good evening, Par," said one of the door guards. The Vizier nodded and managed a half smile as he prayed that the man didn't ask for some secret code or password. He didn't have it, whatever it might be, and there was no hope of guessing it. Given all the muscle on hand, he'd be hard pressed to get clear of there, if it came to it.

The guard knocked on the door using a curious pattern of raps and taps: a code! The Vizier felt the hair on the back of his neck stand up. Notwithstanding the importance of the knowledge that he stood to gain, he regretted being there.

At that moment, as they unlocked the door, it was all he could do not to run. Not to flee for his life. It didn't matter that this was a unique opportunity to surveil his enemies — it was just too risky. Too dangerous. Foolhardy, even. Reckless. He turned his head, and searched for a clear path that he could run through, but he was committed; it was far too late to go back now.

The door opened to a good-sized meeting hall. It hosted a curious collection of villains. Men that the Vizier dreaded seeing. Men that he feared would see through his disguise in an instant.

He made it through the door, barely noticed; a nod of greeting here, a hello there. Most of the traitors didn't even look at him when he entered. They just kept on their plotting and gossiping, awaiting the official start to their traitorous festivities.

Nevertheless, as he walked to his seat, he was more afraid than he'd ever been in his life. More so than the day that the Harbinger of Doom held a sword to the back of his neck. He never heard him coming, that demon. At first, his magic failed him, for he sensed nothing until the cold edge of the Harbinger's blade rested against his neck. When it did, every fiber of his being that made him a wizard felt ablaze. He knew at once who accosted him. He sensed the waves of malice and evil that radiated down that blade from the demon's hand. He nearly peed himself.

He relived those moments a thousand times. They haunted him day and night — how close he'd come to not only losing his life, but also losing his immortal soul. He'd been but a hair's-breadth away from being damned for all eternity — from being pulled down into whatever hell the Harbinger had climbed out of. He hadn't had a peaceful night of rest since that fell day.

Yet walking into that den of traitors in the Fister was somehow worse. It was even worse than the fear he felt on the day that he led the coup against Pipkorn and the other Grandmasters of the Tower. On that day, he was in control; he had planned every move, every moment, and had contingencies set up for every conceivable countermove and happenstance. And, as importantly, powerful allies from within and without the tower supported him. Nonetheless, things went awry, as they always do in times of combat and strife. Too many missteps; too many of his enemies escaped. Yet, despite it all, victory was his; complete and total. He won the Tower of the Arcane — the High Seat of Wizardom —his dream for more years than he could recall.

But this time, he was alone. He didn't know what to expect. He hadn't even known who would be in attendance at the meeting. He had guessed many of the names: Harringgold, Sluug, Pipkorn, but not all of them. There were surprises; he anticipated that there would be. The problem was, there was nothing he could do to control the situation, and that greatly troubled him. It made him vulnerable. It put him at risk; great risk. If they found him out, he had almost no chance of escape. They'd kill him for certain, but first, there would be interrogation and that meant torture. And it might go on for a long time. Who knew what horrors, what indignities, those villains might inflict upon him. They were capable of anything, the heartless bastards. The very thought of it sent shivers through him and he had to force himself to concentrate on what was said around him. After all, that's what he was there for — all that he was there for. To hear what those men said. To hear it from their own lips; to know their plans and schemes.

All those feelings, those fears that he felt in the meeting room, were alien to the Vizier. He'd lived long — longer than any would guess by looking at him. Most would mark him in his fifties, perhaps early sixties, but in truth, he was 142 years old — his years and health preserved past their time by adept use of esoteric magics beyond the ken of normal folk, and nearly as far beyond his more pedestrian brethren of the Tower. He was confident in his powers — his prowess and knowledge — but that day, he ventured into a pit of vipers. They called themselves the Freedom Council, which of course was a laughable misnomer. In truth, they were a cadre of the most violent, self-centered, dangerous, and downright stupid members of the Tower of the Arcane, the High Council, the Council of Lords, and other groups and individuals, various and sundry, of generally questionable repute. In short, they were the opposition to the new order that he championed. They were the old guard of Lomion aristocracy, motivated by ignorance, avarice, racism, narcissism, and xenophobia. He hated them and all that they stood for — as did every righteous citizen with an awareness of such things. That was why he orchestrated Pipkorn's overthrow, for Old Pointy Hat was one of their leaders — acting in secret to achieve their nefarious ends. And in so doing, Pipkorn acted against the interests of the Tower, he betrayed the realm, and most importantly, be betrayed the trust of the citizens of Lomion. Pipkorn's loyalties, if he even had any concept of the word, lay not with the Arcane Order, but with the Freedom Council and their schemes to oppress the weak and line their own purses.

The Vizier had hoped that the coup would be the end of Pipkorn, either by his death, imprisonment, or banishment, but the old snake had slipped the many nooses, nets, and knives that the Vizier set against him. How he'd managed it, the Vizier still didn't know. Nonetheless, he wasn't surprised, for evildoers have a grand talent for escape; somehow, it's in their very bones. It would have been so much better for the realm if the old bastard had died that day as the Vizier had planned.

And it would have been much better for Par Trask.

Poor old Par Trask never saw it coming; in part, because he didn't have any enemies, but mostly because The Black Hand was very good at such matters. It was probably a knife in the back, or else a garrote. The Vizier didn't know. He didn't ask; he didn't want to know. In the end, it didn't really matter, did it? Dead was dead after all; best not to think about it, especially since it wasn't personal.

Trask was an affable fellow who suffered from various infirmities despite a modest age, but the older he grew, the more his views tipped toward Pipkorn's side. How a decent man like Trask grew so uncaring about his fellows over time, the Vizier didn't understand. Corrupted somehow, he must have been. Must have had some hidden vice that they exploited and used to coerce him over to their side, but what it was, would likely remain forever unknown. Perhaps that was for the best.

If it was up to Pipkorn and his ilk, everyone would be left entirely on their own — to fend for themselves. If they didn't have enough food, they'd go hungry. If they weren't able to work, they'd spend their days as paupers or beggars. The Pipkorns of the world just didn't care about anyone except themselves. And in the end, come to think of it, neither did Par Trask, the old fool. Whatever sense of fairness and justice that he once had was long gone. And so, the Vizier supposed, he got what was coming to him. He should be grateful it was quick.

The Vizier didn't like to use The Black Hand, but considered them an invaluable tool for trying times. Used sparingly, his conscience permitted dealings with them, though he avoided the details of the deaths — it made it easier that way. Cleaner.

No one could deny that there were many bad people in the world — some, like Pipkorn, truly evil, truly vile. Sometimes, you just had to get rid of that sort — for the common good. The Hand allowed one to do that, and yet keep one's own hands clean.

The Vizier's quest to rid Lomion of evil made him one of The Hand's most valued customers.

In Trask's case, it had to be done — evil or not. The Vizier had to know what went on in the Freedom Council meeting. The future of Lomion might depend on it. The very existence of the League of Light might depend on it. He had to use whatever means at his disposal to stop the Freedom Council, the traitors. To do that, he had to know precisely what they were up to. That meant attending their meeting himself and hearing every word that they spoke. He wouldn't trust that task to any of his agents. They might miss some subtlety, some nuance that might affect his strategy.

His attendance was impossible, of course, but for his thaumaturgical skills. He had powers other wizards only dreamed of. Skills his colleagues thought lived nowhere but in song and story. He could take the place of one of the Freedom Council members; he could assume their identity; become their doppelganger. He had the power, but strangely, not while they yet lived.

His target needed to be dead. Why? Even the Vizier didn't know; one of the many mysteries of the magical weave. Wizards harnessed and controlled only a tiny fraction of the weave's near limitless power, and that power played by its own rules, rarely revealing its intent to those who tapped it.

So he had to take the place of someone. Who

better to impersonate than Par Trask? The man hardly spoke, thank Azathoth. Though his magery could make him look like Trask, exactly like Trask, the magic alone would not aid him at all in copying the sound of Trask's voice, his speech patterns, or his mannerisms. The Vizier had to rely on his own memory, mimicry skills, and acting ability to accomplish that. He had those skills too, in some abundance, but was much less certain of them than his magic. That was part of what had him scared. Would he make some false move? Would he do something uncharacteristic of Par Trask that got him noticed, that raised suspicions? His best chance to avoid suspicion was to be as quiet as possible and not engage the others. But quiet or not, it may be that one or more of the great wizards in the room would see through his illusions. For amongst the Freedom Council sat several wizards of the Tower of the Arcane. Some of them, masters of the mystic arts, and at least three (Pipkorn, Mardack, and Spugnoir) were grandmasters. Some of them had powers even the Vizier did not grasp. Not to say that they wielded greater power than he — just different power, for the magical weave was as varied as the tribes of men that tapped it. He'd rarely relied on illusions to fool such men and never in such close quarters for an extended time. If one of them did see through his illusions, he'd be done for. He wouldn't even know it until it was too late; until he was already found out. The very thought was maddening and sent his stomach into flips.

To limit his risk of getting trapped, he wanted a seat by the door. If they unmasked him, close to the door there'd be at least some chance of escape. But by the door was where most of the action would be — for there stood the head of the table and at it, sat Pipkorn. The Vizier's instincts told him to find the farthest chair in the back corner so as to draw the least attention. That would give him the least chance of being found out. Of course, if he was, there would be no escape, no chance of it at all. Not from back there.

Instead, he wound up in a seat at roughly the middle of the table, too close to the main players for comfort, and too far from the door for any escape — the worst of all possibilities.

The meeting room was large, with seating for thirty around the table, and for dozens more about the room's perimeter. Within ten minutes of the Vizier's arrival, nearly every table seat was taken by wizards from each of the major spires of the Tower of the Arcane (some that the Vizier had thought killed in the coup), including the three Grandmasters; nobles and lords (or their representatives) from most of the major Lomerian cities and several Dors; local nobles and guildmasters from Lomion City; and one member of the High Council — Lady Aramere of Dyvers. Her presence surprised the Vizier. He knew of course that she often sided with the opposition in council meetings, but not always, so he didn't think that she was one of them. Quite disappointing for he didn't dislike her much. Where Duke Harringgold was, or tat snake, Jhensezil, the Vizier had no idea.

Not until he saw all those prominent Lomerians assembled together did the Vizier fully appreciate the depth and extent of the League of Light's opposition. Collectively, the Freedom Council wielded immense power, commanded armies of guardsmen, knights, and mercenaries, and hoarded vast wealth that they could bring to bear against their enemies — against the League. It would be a long and bloody battle to bring those people down. But down they must go, for the good of the people and the good of the realm.

Just as Pipkorn was about to call the meeting to order, Harringgold arrived with Torbin Malvegil in tow. The Vizier only partly held back a gasp of surprise at seeing Malvegil alive, but happily, his reaction wasn't noticed in the general din of greetings that erupted from about the room. Malvegil was even more popular amongst the traitors than the Vizier had thought. All the more reason to eliminate him quickly, before the real struggle began. He would have words with The Hand over their failure. They should never have permitted Malvegil to enter the city alive.

Once everyone had retaken their seats, Grandmaster Mardack, that pompous blowhard, stood and raised his hands to draw the attention of the other conspirators. Even he had trouble settling them down. A raucous bunch, scattered and confused — evidence of the rabble that they were.

Just then, there was a loud knock on the meeting room door. The guards had shut and barred it when the last of the cabal had arrived. That's the only way that they would meet — in secret. Like a den of thieves.

The councilors looked to each other in

bewilderment and fear — as if they'd been caught red-handed.

"Everyone that we expected is here," whispered Samwise Sluug from Harringgold's right, though nearly everyone in the room heard what he said — the man seemed physically incapable of speaking quietly. "And the guards know not to disturb us."

"Well, see who it is," said Pipkorn.

"What if it's the chancellor's men come to arrest us?" said Lady Aramere.

"Then it won't go well for them," said Malvegil.

Harringgold nodded at Sluug.

Sluug (long, lean, and grim) moved to the door. Lord Mirtise of Dor Linden joined him. Both held swords at the ready.

"Drydan," said Sluug to the guard captain stationed on the other side of the door. "What is it?"

"Open in the name of the king," said a deep voice, strangely familiar.

"It is the king, my lord," said Drydan. "The king, himself."

A gasp erupted about the room. The Vizier was as surprised as the rest. Wizards readied spells. Some few put their hands on their faces in anxiety or disbelief.

Several decks of cards appeared around the table, as did dice, and Spottle paraphernalia. One man dumped a case of Mages and Monsters figures onto the center of the table. They were ready for someone to show up uninvited and were prepared with a cover story. Truly devious were those men.

Sluug looked to Harringgold.

"Open it," said the Duke. He did.

And there stood his majesty, King Selrach Rothtonn Tenzivel, tall and regal, his expression inscrutable. He held a large ale mug in his hand. Behind him stood Baron Morfin and his son, Gallick. The Vizier cringed at the sight of them. Gasps and mumbles of "Morfin, it's Morfin" came from around the room. Tenzivel scanned the hall, pausing at each face, taking note of each and every man and woman in the room.

"Your majesty, welcome," said Mardack. "I had no idea that you were aware of our little social club. Will you join us? Can we refill your mug? Some mead or wine? And you too, Morfin. Welcome back from the dead."

Morfin nodded.

"Close the door," said Tenzivel sternly after he, the Morfins, and Captain Korvalan of the Dramadeens (the king's bodyguards) stepped inside. "There are more of you than I expected," he said, his voice ever so slightly slurred from drink.

The Vizier wasn't surprised. He hadn't seen the king fully sober in many years. Such a disgrace.

"And some faces, I haven't seen in years," said Tenzivel. "Some of you have traveled far to be here. No common game of cards is this."

"It's merely a bit of harmless fun," said Mardack gesturing toward the gaming materials on the table. "A bit of gambling, drinking, and gaming to pass the time amongst old friends."

Even Tenzivel wasn't fool enough to believe that hokum.

"Such camaraderie," said Tenzivel. He scanned the haphazard placement of the gaming pieces and the cards. Par Triman held several cards the wrong way, facing them outward for all to see.

"So long as there are people willing to stand up to injustice, we may yet prevail," said Tenzivel.

What's this? worried the Vizier. Will he join with them? That would complicate things.

The councilors looked to the king expectantly.

"You are not the only ones that can shield your true intentions with a facade, though some are more skilled at it than you."

The Vizier cringed. Could Tenzivel somehow see through his disguise? The old fool had no magic that the Vizier knew of, but Tenzivel had always been full of surprises.

The king made his way around the table, reached out, plucked the cards from Par Triman, and turned them the correct way.

"The time for hiding draws to a close," said the king. "I'm resuming my rightful position, and together, we will take our republic back from the traitors that seek to destroy our way of life."

Not likely, and it's you who are the traitors, you lying bastard.

Mardack squirmed. "So you know—"

"Your purpose?" said Tenzivel. "Of course I know your purpose. And you have my support. That's why I'm here."

"Your majesty, if I may," said Mardack, "How did you know that we were meeting here?"

"I am the king; I have my ways. Now," he said looking around, "have I missed anything?"

"We were just getting started," said Mardack.

"Then proceed," said Tenzivel.

Pipkorn gave up his seat at the table's head to the king and found another on the side of the room, the Morfins beside him.

Mardack stood. "Thank you all for gathering here for the first formal meeting of the Freedom Council," he said, though he appeared a bit flustered, uncharacteristic for him, and he glanced repeatedly at the king. "As his majesty noted, many of you traveled far to be here; some, weeks from home. Some came via roads far less safe than they used to be. Others of us, traveled not far at all, but risk our very lives to be seen in public — in our own capital; in our own home. How far things have gone," said Mardack shaking his head. "How far Lomion has fallen."

"Too far," said Tenzivel.

"Indeed," said Mardack. "This council's purpose, make no mistake, is to decide on and then take such actions as are necessary to preserve the Republic, to preserve the freedoms that Lomion has embodied and that we all hold dear."

"To restore the Republic, not preserve it," said Malvegil. "That's what we need to do. What's gone rotten isn't worth preserving, and Barusa and his cronies have rotted us to the core. Forget about preserving; it's too late for that."

"The Articles of the Republic still stand," said Mardack. "They're the core of our system. So long as they remain the law of the land, the Republic yet lives. We need only take such measures and reforms that insure that the Articles cannot be thrown down."

"Reforms?" said Malvegil. "Half measures and political correctness are what's got us to where we are today. We've had too much compromise, too much acquiescence. We need no more of that."

"We must move within the system, with prudence and caution and due respect to the opposition," said Harringgold. "They are Lomerians too."

"To Nifleheim with the opposition," said Malvegil as he rose to his feet. "They're traitors every one. They want to tear down the Articles piece by piece. The edict taxing Dors at fifty percent. That is theft. The—"

"That was overthrown," said Mardack. "It was voted down by the Council of Lords. We need concern ourselves with that measure no longer."

"The expansion of the Tribunal?" said Malvegil. "The granting of citizenship to those who openly profess to hate us?"

"The upcoming common session of the two Councils," said Tenzivel. "That is where they will vote down the Articles."

"Then we must insure that they don't have the votes," said Mardack.

"You may be making too much of these things," said Par Gatwind in a soft voice with a slight accent characteristic of those originally from the Southron Isles. Sitting, one could tell that Gatwind was a large man, but not until he stood could his immense girth be truly appreciated.

"Am I?" said Malvegil. "Have you people thought about why they took these steps? Why they are trying to change or throw down the Articles? Have you? Have you thought about it?

Anyone?"

"I think we've all thought about it, and at great length," said Par Gatwind, his thick black beard crusted with crumbs from the table's offerings. Owing to his often drowsy appearance, girth, and soft-spoken manner, few would guess that in years past he had been an accomplished soldier and vaunted leader of fighting men. "The League's overriding philosophy of equality for all compels them to give lavishly to the poor by taking from most everyone else."

"Stealing from everyone else," said Malvegil.

"As you say, though they don't see it that way," said Par Gatwind. "Nearly half the Council of Lords has always espoused a version of that philosophy. The League's methods are all that differentiates them from many others. Those of us gathered here find common ground in the recognition that the League's approach is doomed to fail, however lofty and altruistic may be their intent. When the wealthy have had all their assets redistributed to the poor, the system will collapse. It is inevitable. The League and their supporters are too shortsighted to see this. What they think is fairness and kindness will only lead to our ruin. If we don't stop them, the Republic may collapse, and at a minimum, it will leave us in a weakened state that will make us vulnerable to our enemies for years to come. This is what we must prevent. That is why I am here."

Many about the room nodded in agreement.

"Par Gatwind," said Malvegil, "you too are short sighted. You're taking the League's stated goals at face value. You believe that they want to help the poor and the downtrodden. They don't. They are merely using that as a means to garner popular support. In truth, they don't care about the poor at all. They have one goal and one goal only — to seize power; to take control of Lomion and rule it as they will. That means suspending the Articles of the Republic, confiscating wealth, confiscating private property, and confiscating arms, so that we cannot defend ourselves against them. It means taking sole control of all military units, and disbanding or destroying those units that they can't control. It means eliminating all local governance — putting every town, city, and Dor under the direct control of the capital. And hear these words clearly — they plan to kill all those who have the power to oppose them. We're heading quickly toward a purge. A purge that will see most of us in this room, maybe all of us, dead — unless we take sufficient measures to stop it."

"This inflammatory language gets us nowhere," said Par Gatwind. "This is nothing more than wild conjecture, hyperbole, speculation, and alarmism. It's insulting to every loyal Lomerian. Some — no, most, that support the League are good people. They're not interested in killing anyone. What you're saying makes no sense and frankly makes you sound unhinged, sir."

"The High Council would never allow these things that you claim," said Lord Smirdoon of Lockely Bay to Malvegil. "It violates all that the Republic stands for. It would never be allowed."

Before Malvegil responded, old Grandmaster Spugnoir pounded his fist to the table, an action so uncharacteristic that everyone went quiet and turned their attention to him. Spugnoir was a caricature of a wizard come to life — ancient and pale with bushy whited hair and beard to match, multi-pocketed robes, and even a pointy hat. "The Tower has already been purged," he said. He looked around the room, scanning face after face. "Do you hear me, you fools? The tower has already been purged, or are you so addle-pated that you've forgotten that? Rabrack Philistine and his cohorts attacked the Tower from within and murdered more than a hundred wizards. More than one hundred! Some of them were your friends, Gatwind. Every wizard here tonight has been in hiding since that purge for fear of our lives."

"You're equating two things that have nothing to do with one another," said Gatwind. "The coup was the Vizier's doing. Why assume that it was part of some conspiracy by the League?"

King Tenzivel stood up and pointed his finger at Gatwind. "Do you think that the Vizier orchestrated the coup just because he couldn't stand to wait his turn to become a Grandmaster?" said Tenzivel. "No. No. And no. He did it to remove opposition to the government takeover that he's backing. Who wields more power to stop him, to stop the League, than do the Tower Wizards? No one. That's why he took over the Tower. That's why he killed your brethren."

"You think that the Leaguers are good people?" said Grandmaster Spugnoir as he looked around at his colleagues. "That they just want to help the poor? They didn't need to sack the Tower of the Arcane to accomplish that, did they? We

163

had nothing to do with poor or rich — we're scholars and historians."

"The Council has been attacked as well," said Duke Harringgold. "Malvegil took a dagger in the back the last time he visited the city. And they made another attempt just today."

Gasps of surprise came from around the room.

"And as you well know, I've been holed up in my palace these past three years," said Tenzivel. "I did that to stay alive and to keep my House alive, and for no other reason. And where do you think Morfin has been these past months? A prisoner! Held in a cell below Tammanian Hall on the Vizier's orders. He escaped only today. Do you think all this happened by chance? Do you think that the League did these things because they want more robust gifting of food and monies to the poor? We are in the midst of an overthrow of our Republic, of the destruction of our way of life. And as Malvegil said, even if you're willing to sit back and let it happen, more than likely, they'll kill you anyway, for nearly all of you have been marked as opponents to the League's measures. The purge isn't coming, my friends; it's here."

"We are the only ones that stand a chance, any chance at all of stopping this," said Malvegil. "You must all open your eyes and see the truth before it is too late."

"I can't accept that," said Gatwind. "I won't accept it. Conspiracies wound within conspiracies. It's too devious. Too unbelievable."

"I agree," said Lady Aramere. "You see your own fears, not reality.

"Here, here," said Par Triman and Lord

Smirdoon.

Many others nodded their heads.

"There is little evidence to back up the claims that I've heard here tonight," said Lord Smirdoon. "It seems mostly supposition. I believe that the Vizier acted alone. His own lust for power drove him to do what he did. I've seen no evidence to dispute that thought."

"This is how great nations die," said Spugnoir in a strong, slow voice. "When good men are blinded by fear and naiveté. When they fail to act. When they become apologists for the evildoers. I have lived longer than anyone here has, by many, many years. I have seen this all before and I have studied it in the histories. This is how it ends. This is how freedom dies unless those of good heart take up arms and fight. We're born with our freedom. It's our natural right, but it can and will be taken away if we don't defend it."

"Let us put it to a vote," said Mardack. "As Gatwind said, we've all given this much thought in recent weeks and months. The debate tonight, eloquent and spirited words notwithstanding, is unlikely to have changed many minds. And so I put it to you: do we work within the system to preserve the Republic or do we take aggressive action?"

"What precisely do you mean by aggressive action?" said Gatwind.

"He means, kill them before they kill us," said Tenzivel.

"I've no objection to such a vote," said Gatwind, "so long as it is binding on us all. Meaning, we must not split as a council after this.

We can't have some of us working within the system, while others go on the attack. We must all work together in common cause."

"Then if the vote is to fight, you will pledge to do so?" said Harringgold. "On your oath?"

"If that is the will of this council," said Gatwind. "I will support it. On my oath."

"Does everyone agree?" said Mardack.

Heads nodded all around, including Par Trask.

"Any opposed?" said Mardack.

There were none. At least none who spoke up.

"Shall it be a secret ballot?" said Mardack.

"No," said Tenzivel. "There are far too many tricksters in this room. Every man must speak his mind in front of us all. If you don't have the guts, you don't belong at this table."

"Very well," said Mardack. "Every councilor will write their vote on a piece of parchment. When all are ready, we will go around the room and each councilor will reveal their vote and speak it aloud for all to hear. That way, the vote is not only transparent, but later votes cannot be influenced by earlier ones, for your spoken vote must match what you wrote down. Does that satisfy everyone?"

It did. The vote was taken. Twenty favored working within the system. Fifteen voted to fight, including Tenzivel, Pipkorn, Spugnoir, Harringgold, and Malvegil. Mardack voted against them.

"The die is cast, and our fates are sealed," said Malvegil.

"We will hold you to your oaths," said Gatwind. "There must be no violence."

"The Malvegils always keep our word. We will not fight, unless we are attacked. I can only hope that they kill you before me, so at least I'll have the chance to piss on your grave, you stinking idiot."

Gatwind's jaw tightened and his fists clenched, but he said no more.

***

The meeting soon ended. Tenzivel asked several of the councilors to remain to speak further with him. The rest left. With the door again locked and guarded, Tenzivel faced Harringgold, Pipkorn, Spugnoir, Malvegil, and Mardack. Captain Korvalan loomed over Tenzivel's shoulder.

Mardack couldn't wait for Tenzivel to say his piece. "That was well played by all," said Mardack as he looked from Pipkorn to Spugnoir. "Until Pipkorn sat down and gave me the floor, I hadn't even noticed anything."

"His disguise was impressive," said Pipkorn. "I didn't see it at first myself. Master Spugnoir flashed me a signal."

"I studied transformational magic at great length many years ago," said Spugnoir. "Compared to a true master of that art, Philistine is an amateur."

"What are you talking about?" said Tenzivel.

"Par Trask was the Vizier in disguise," said Mardack.

"What?" said Tenzivel, Malvegil, and Harringgold in near unison.

"We had that snake in our grasp and you let him go free?" said Malvegil. "And after hearing our plans, no less? Why? What were you thinking?"

"They staged it," said Tenzivel. "You put on a performance for him, didn't you?"

"We did," said Pipkorn smiling.

"Explain what you mean?" said Malvegil.

"Gatwind is our man," said Spugnoir.

"What?" said Harringgold. "So his position—"

"He only pretended to oppose us," said Spugnoir.

"The vote was rigged," said Pipkorn. "The speeches, the opinions — all rigged. Every wizard in the room was in on it. Except for the Vizier."

"We knew the League might try to infiltrate us," said Mardack. "We had this contingency plan set up in advance, just in case. Gatwind played his part masterfully."

"So Trask is dead?" said Harringgold.

"Almost certainly," said Spugnoir. "The nature of the magic."

"By my count, the vote would have been twenty-four in favor of attack, but for our little performance," said Mardack.

"So we won the vote?" said Harringgold. "That means—"

"That we go to war," said Malvegil, a broad smile on his face.

"Well done," said Tenzivel, his characteristic slur in his voice. "Well done. Like the old saying goes, nothing in Lomion is as it appears." Tenzivel held out his mug toward Mardack. "Take it."

Mardack eyed the mug suspiciously and then took it.

"Drink," said Tenzivel.

"Thank you, your majesty, but I prefer not to imbibe at this time."

"Shut up and drink it," said Tenzivel. "Now."

Mardack looked to the others but they all seemed as confused as he did by the king's demand. He looked into the mug, sniffed it, and no doubt wondered if that was what Tenzivel had been drinking all along, or something else.

"It's not poison," said the king. "Take a sip."

Mardack relented and sipped from the cup. "It's not mead," said Mardack. He took another sip. "It's honey water." He looked to the others. "Honey water. There is no alcohol in it."

"And there never has been," said Tenzivel, his voice clear and strong.

"You gave up the drink?" said Malvegil.

"I never took it up in the first place. It's always been honey water or some such. All these years."

"You had us all fooled," said Pipkorn. "You're a better actor than Gatwind."

"Had I not convinced everyone that I was a hot-headed addle-pated drunk, the League would have found a way to do away with me long ago. I had to bide my time until you men were ready to act. Now it seems that time is here."

"Well played, my Lord," said Harringgold.

"As you said, nothing in Lomion is as it appears," said Pipkorn.

"It has always been that way," said Tenzivel, "and I suspect it always will. Harringgold — you're our tactician. I want you to develop plans for how we can outmaneuver the League. If that does mean violence, so be it. One way or another we have to put a stop to the League and that may mean putting an end to all its leaders. I have my own plans for that already. Plans I've spent much time preparing. We'll gather again in three days' time —— just we few that are here. No one else is to know about any of this. We'll compare our plans. Finalize them. And then begin this. If Odin smiles upon us, this is the beginning of the end for the League. We will take our country back."

"Or else get dead trying," said Malvegil as he placed the box that contained the Seer Stone on the table. He opened it and told the tale of the duergar to the others.

***

The Vizier, still disguised as Par Trask, looked furtively about as he slowly made his way north on Stone Street, a block up from Fister Mansion. A figure lurked in the shadows between two buildings and spoke when the Vizier drew near. "A masterful disguise," said the man. "I hardly recognized you, even though I knew what to look for."

"A mere trifling," whispered the Vizier, careful that no one else was about that could overhear them. "Your performance, unaided by the art, was all the greater. You couldn't have done better: you fooled them completely. We now know all that we need to know to finally finish them. To finally rid Lomion of those traitors."

"Yes, my master," said Par Gatwind as he stepped from the shadows, an evil smile on his face. "Now we have them, and soon we will crush them all."

15

ALDERS FOR DINNER

Rom Alder sat in the command tent, staring at the tabletop. Dirk of Alder, blue armored, young, and rangy, paced back and forth on the other side of the tent. "They killed Uncle Brock." He glanced at Rom after each pronouncement, though Rom did not look his way. "Who do those people think they are? Do they think there will be no repercussions? No reprisals? I will see them dead. Every Eotrus will hang from their Dor's walls before I'm done with them."

"You talk tough for a little man," said Bald Boddrick from his seat opposite Rom, a large ale mug in his hand. In truth, Dirk was nearly six feet tall and approached two hundred pounds. To Boddrick, however, that was small.

"Let the boy blow off some steam," said Bithel the Piper from the seat next to Boddrick. Captain Kralan of the Myrdonians, hawk faced and black haired, nodded at Bithel's pronouncement, as did Captain Martrin of the Lomerian Guard.

Rom looked up for a moment. "He's an Alder," he said to Boddrick before he resumed staring at the table.

"You can't just wipe out an entire noble family in anger," said Boddrick to Dirk. "You want to talk about repercussions; you'll have them if you do that."

"They drew first blood, unprovoked, no less,"

said Black Grint, whose nickname spoke to his disposition, not his complexion, which was ghostly white, just like his hair. "We'd be in our rights to kill them dead. All of them."

"Not the women," said Sentry of Allendale, tall and lean, with a thick mustache. "Not the children. We're not animals. And some might say that the writ provoked them a bit, don't you think?"

"Do they even have any women?" said Boddrick. "I ask you, have any of you seen an Eotrus woman? Even once, ever?"

"Not I," said Bithel.

"That's because they keep them hidden away, their ugly and their stench so strong as to turn a man to stone even as he's puking out his guts," said Boddrick.

"You're wrong," said Black Grint. "They don't hide their women. They keep them on display for all to see —— in pens in the barnyard."

There was laughter all around, except for Rom who still stared down, deep in thought.

"They breed with pigs, they do," said Grint. "Sometimes, when they get truly desperate, they get all cozy with gnomes, I hear. Alas, we'll have no fun with any Eotrus women. Except for Boddrick, for he likes pigs. Oh, and Sentry, for he has a fondness for gnomes."

More laughter.

"She wasn't a gnome," said Sentry. "She was just short."

"I saw a beard," said Grint.

Sentry shook his head as they all laughed again.

Rom looked up, his expression grim. When he spoke, the others shut up. "Eleanor Eotrus was one of the great beauties of her day. A noble woman, from a proud lineage."

There was a pause for several moments during which no one said anything, tension in the air.

"She was a Malvegil by birth, was she not?" said Sentry.

"Aye," said Rom.

"The Malvegils are almost as bad as the stinking northerners," said Boddrick. "Swamp dwellers, they are, surrounded by flies, fleas, and muck for every moment of their lives. Your Eotrus woman was probably half swamp viper and half stink bug."

Rom's cold gaze shifted to Boddrick. "Remind me why I suffer your presence?"

"Because I've killed forty-seven men in the wars, and fifty-two men in the service of House Alder. I've never been defeated in battle. In fact, no man can stand against me and live. That's earned me the right to say whatever I want, whenever I want, to whomever I want. If any don't like it—"

"When you were still pooping your pants, I'd already killed more men than that," said Rom, his eyes and voice icy cold. "So control your wagging tongue before I cut it out."

On the face of it, Rom's statement appeared no more than a boast, for he looked only fifteen years Boddrick's senior, twenty at the most.

Boddrick stared back at him. "I answer to Mother Alder, not you, old man, so I'll wag my tongue all I like. If you—"

The table upended. In a flash, Rom was at Boddrick, lifted him up (all four hundred pounds of him) and slammed him on his back to the tent's dirt floor. Boddrick lay stunned, the wind knocked out of him. All the others gaped in surprise. Their hands instinctively moved to their weapons, though no one drew them; they all seemed uncertain of what to do. It was plain to see, Rom could have put his dagger through the big man's chest or throat, just as easily as he had bodyslammed him.

"Have you anything else to say?" said Rom to Boddrick.

Unable to catch his breath, Boddrick shook his head.

Rom looked around. "Who do you answer to?" he said, eyeing the men, each one in turn.

"To you, my Lord," said Sentry, bowing.

"To you," said Bithel.

"To you, uncle," said Dirk.

"On this mission, you, my lord," said Captain Kralan.

"Aye, you," said Captain Martrin.

Black Grint stared back at Rom, matching his steely gaze, and not looking the least bit concerned. After a few moments, he nodded his head. That was all the response he'd offer, and Rom accepted it.

"Get out of here, all of you, and go get some sleep," said Rom. "I'm sending for reinforcements from the city. We're going to be here a while."

"You mean to siege them?" said Sentry.

"I mean to see them all dead," said Rom.

Rom awoke with a start. There was a commotion in the camp. Men yelled. Screamed. The Eotrus! he thought. They've sallied forth to attack. Rom scrambled to his feet. He hadn't expected them to leave the safety of their walls. But he had slept in his armor, just in case. Prudence and caution, as much as strength and skill — it's what keeps a soldier alive. He grabbed his sword and made for the tent flap, listening for horses as he moved. If they had charged into camp on heavy horse, he'd need his spear, but he heard no pounding hooves, so it was sword and shield, his weapons of choice for close combat. He didn't understand the screaming. Just as he reached for the tent flap, he heard the growls of some beast. Something he couldn't identify.

Rom stepped out of the command tent, which, along with the other officers' tents, formed a tight ring around a fire pit. Captain Kralan was there, sword in hand. So was Captain Martrin, and the troop bugler, and several others. Beast-like growls came from all sides and dark shapes leaped amongst the tents and bedrolls throughout the camp. Men screamed and wailed and cried out for help. Not the Eotrus. A pride of mountain lions? A wolf pack? The sounds weren't right. The shapes weren't right. What the hell are they?

An overwhelming animal stench assailed Rom's nostrils. It was so bad that it almost made him gag. Then a troll crashed into Martrin, crushing him face down to the ground, claws flailing. Rom didn't know what the troll was — he had never before seen its like. He hesitated a moment as he processed what he was looking at.

But only a moment. Then he stepped forward and with one powerful swipe of his sword cut the top half of the troll's head off. He didn't need to know what it was to kill it. It collapsed on Martrin, who was dead, a huge chunk of flesh torn from the back of his neck.

"Bugler, call for a wedge," said Rom as he turned around. But the bugler was down, a troll tearing into his face with its claws and teeth. The bugler's sword protruded out the troll's back — he had caught the thing coming in, but in its fury, the mortal blow hadn't stopped it.

Rom dashed over. The troll lifted its head and growled. Rom thrust the tip of his sword deep into the thing's upper chest. Despite the blow, it rose up, still some life left in it. Rom kicked it in the gut as he wrenched his blade free. The thing still stood, blood spurting from its chest. It should have fallen from either of the two mortal wounds it had suffered. But it didn't. If anything, it looked as if it was gathering its strength for another attack. Rom stepped in and bashed it in the face with his shield. He heard the sounds of its bones cracking from the powerful impact. The troll fell back as a cut tree. It howled in agony as the bugler's sword, which still stuck through its torso, did more damage during the fall.

Rom spun around for fear of other trolls that might be behind him.

Men fought with trolls throughout the camp. There were dozens of the beasts, maybe scores. The camp had been caught by surprise and many men were dying for it. How that happened, Rom didn't understand. They'd posted a strong guard around the entire encampment. Then Rom heard a low growl behind him and spun back to see the troll he'd just dropped rising to its feet. Its face and chest wounds didn't appear to be bleeding — at least not the way such wounds were wont to do. The troll came at him fast, despite its injuries.

Rom was quicker. He slashed the creature in an arc from its right shoulder down across its body to its left thigh. It kept coming. Rom took a few quick steps backward and repeated his slash, this time going from the left shoulder down across to the right thigh. Still it came, and the wounds didn't bleed the way they should. He couldn't believe that it still came on. Nothing could take such punishment. Rom sidestepped, backpedaled, and swung his sword high in a powerful arc. The troll put up its forearm to block the blow and simultaneously ducked. Rom's sword severed its arm and lodged two-thirds of the way through its head. The creature dropped, wrenching Rom's sword from his grasp.

Rom turned, his shield held protectively, but no more opponents were close. He brought the shield's edge crashing down on the fallen troll's head, crushing it to pulp and freeing his sword, even as its one remaining arm clawed at him and attempted to pull him down.

Rom turned to see Captain Kralan turn his back on a troll he had just stabbed in the chest, in order to face another troll that leaped toward him. Rom yelled a warning, but it was too late; the first troll raked its claws across Kralan's back and brought the knight to his knees. Unfortunately, Kralan had not had the foresight to keep his armor on during the night. Both trolls pounced on the fallen man and tore him to pieces. There was nothing that Rom could do, so he turned aside.

"Get into formation!" shouted Rom. "To me! To me!" he said, turning around and around to make certain that no troll could pounce on him from behind. Two Myrdonians appeared a moment later, one limping from a gash in his leg, and took their places, back to back with Rom. Then Black Grint showed up, his sword and main gauche both dripping with troll blood. More men came and they expanded their circle, soon two rows deep. Within another ten seconds, Rom had a core of fifteen men around him. The trolls avoided them, instead picking off men that stood alone or in smaller groups. Twenty seconds later, he had forty men with him. Most had a weapon or two, but no armor or other gear.

Dozens of trolls rampaged through the camp to the south of Rom's position. What men still lived in the northern part of the camp stood about Rom in a tight circle two to three rows deep.

"The fighting is thick back by the wagons," said Black Grint.

"We can't get to them," said Rom.

"What are they?" asked a Myrdonian.

"Mountain trolls," said Black Grint. "Down from the north. Bash their heads in or cut their heads off, else they'll just get up again. That and fire is the only way to stop them."

Two trolls charged from one side. Two more came at them from another direction.

"Stay in formation!" shouted Rom. "Aim for their heads."

The trolls fought like demons and wouldn't stay down. In the space of two minutes, Rom lost a half dozen of his men, and only managed to kill two of the trolls. Two more moved away, presumably too hurt to continue, or else in search of easier targets.

Then from the east came eight trolls carrying swords and hammers and shields — some of strange design; others that they had looted from the fallen soldiers. The men nearly panicked when they saw that the trolls were armed, but Rom's powerful commands held them together. The trolls charged Rom's contingent in a single line, shoulder to shoulder. They barreled through, scattering the men. And worst of all, they used their weapons to deadly effect. Their style, crude compared to that of Lomerian knights, but effective all the same. The fighting was close and bloody and more chaotic than almost any battle Rom had seen, and he'd seen many. The trolls' strength and agility was so far beyond a man's, that it was almost impossible to stand against them, even with numbers. They tore apart Rom's line, scooping men up and tossing them, tearing off arms and legs, howling and slavering all the while. The soldiers slashed them, stabbed them, and pounded them with hammers, but they withstood terrible punishment and kept fighting, getting up again and again until some blow finally staved in their skulls. When it was done, ten men only still stood alongside Rom and Black Grint. All the rest were dead or dying along with the trolls.

The fighting was still thick by the wagons. Through the scattered firelight, there seemed to be several dozen trolls between Rom's position and the rest of his troop who were making their stand by the wagons.

"We run for the Dor?" said Black Grint.

"Aye," said Rom. "It's our only chance."

***

"Dead gods," said Sarbek as he and Ector ran toward where Indigo stood along the parapet atop the Outer Dor's main gate. "What's going on out there?"

Indigo lowered a spyglass from his eye and passed it to Sarbek.

"As best as I can tell," said Indigo, "the trolls are having the Alders for dinner."

"They attacked a full brigade?" said Ector.

Indigo nodded. "By the time I got up here, the fighting had spread throughout the camp. The trolls must have come at them from at least two sides, probably three at once. And they must have come in quiet, because it looks as if they took the Alders unawares, most still in their bedrolls and tents."

"How many trolls do you think?" said Sarbek. "I can barely see anything. It's too dark out there."

"I couldn't tell," said Indigo, "but to scatter a full brigade like that — there must be at least fifty. Probably a hundred or more. It looks like at least several squadrons, maybe a full company fled to

181

the south. I didn't see any large mass of trolls going after them, so they may have gotten clear. The main fighting is in the southeast corner of the camp by the wagon train. Another major battle was at the northern edge of the camp, where they have their command tent — that battle looks to be over, but I can't tell who won."

"They're still going at it by the wagons," said Sarbek. A see a thick ring of men and the trolls keep charging them, pounding away. What's this? A squad is headed this way, running for their lives."

"How many?" said Ector.

"My guess is thirty, maybe thirty-five," said Sarbek, "but there are trolls after them, picking off the stragglers."

"Are we letting them in?" said Indigo.

"We can't stand here and watch them get eaten while pounding on our gate, now can we?" said Sarbek.

"Why not?" said Indigo.

"Son, sometimes, you scare me," said Sarbek.

"The feeling is mutual," said Indigo.

"Now," shouted Sarbek. The gatemen pulled open the Outer Dor's main gate. The ragged contingent of soldiers ran in, several trolls on their heels. One troll leaped forward and pounced on the legs of the man farthest back, taking him down less than ten feet outside the gate.

The moment the soldiers were in, Eotrus crossbowmen fired from atop the wall and from the barbican area. Dozens of bolts skewered the trolls as they reached the gates. Two went down at the threshold, one staggered in. Within seconds, swordsmen cut it down, and staved in its head.

The troll that had taken the straggler bounded forward through the gate, howling, then stopped, for a huge mass of soldiers faced it. Before it got its bearings, Indigo charged toward it, pike in hand, and caught it in the upper abdomen. His momentum carried him forward and he slammed the troll against the wooden scaffolding beside the gates. The pike's blade cut through the troll's body and embedded in the wood beyond, pinning the troll to the wall, its feet dangling just above the ground.

"Do we finish it?" said Indigo to Sarbek as more pikemen pressed their blades close to the troll.

Sarbek paused to consider that for a moment. "Sverdes may have some use for it. Bind it with ropes, lots of ropes. Put a muzzle on it before you pull it down. Then hog-tie it. Keep ten men on it and throw it in a cell under constant guard. Ten men on guard — no fewer. Keep it tied up even within the cell. We've seen what these things can do; I'll take no chances with it."

One of the trolls felled by the crossbowmen was dead, for two shafts had penetrated its skull. The other stirred despite a dozen bolts sticking from it. As it tried to sit up, Rom Alder stepped forward and lopped its head off with his sword. Rom looked toward his encampment. No other men ran toward the Dor, but here and there along the path that they had run, trolls hunched over bodies, feasting on men, tearing them apart.

"Close the gate," said Rom.

"Stand down," said Sarbek approaching him, a dozen crossbowmen supporting the castellan. Most of Rom's men collapsed to the ground as soon as they knew they had escaped the trolls. The Eotrus quickly disarmed them. Black Grint and two Myrdonian Knights stood back to back, weapons ready, as Eotrus crossbowmen and swordsmen surrounded them. "I'll not tell you again," said Sarbek. "Drop your weapons now, or we will kill you where you stand. You've seen me do that before, so you know it's no idle threat."

Rom's eyes narrowed and his jaw clenched. He let the sword fall from his grasp.

"Who are you?" said Sarbek.

"I am Rom of House Alder."

"The witch mother's brother?" said Sarbek. "Well, well, quite a prize indeed." Sarbek shouted to his men. "Bind their hands and put them in the dungeon." After they'd bound Rom's hands before him, Sarbek said, "You will join us on the wall."

Atop the wall gathered Sarbek, Ector, several Eotrus knights, and Rom Alder. They studied the battle through spyglasses, one of the knights holding one up to Rom's eye.

"There's still a wedge of men fighting by the wagons," said Ector who had the best vision of the group. "Eighty or ninety of them in a ring. They're holding the trolls at bay."

"They've got torches, and several of the wagons are ablaze," said Sarbek.

"There are too many trolls," said Rom. "They'll all die out there."

"That they will," said Sarbek.

184

"You have cavalry," said Rom. "Use them."

"I do, but I'll not lose half our horse for a chance, and it's only a chance, to save a handful of your men," said Sarbek. "Their fates are in Odin's hands now."

Ector eyed Sarbek but did not contradict him.

"My grandnephew is out there," said Rom. "Save him and you will be rewarded. You have my word on that."

"I will not sacrifice Eotrus men to save an Alder," said Sarbek. "I don't expect if you were in my position, you'd do any different."

Rom didn't respond.

They watched through the spyglasses for several minutes as the trolls made charge after charge against the Alders, trying to scatter the men, but they held together in a tight core.

"That cadre of knights fight like devils," said Sarbek. "Is that Boddrick amongst them?"

"Aye," said Rom. "No one else is that big. And Bithel the Piper will be beside him, if he still lives. The man in the blue armor is Dirk, my nephew."

"I see several men in Myrdonian green amongst them," said Ector.

"An entire brigade," said Rom. "Not since the wars have we had such losses."

"That's because the south is soft; life is easy there," said Sarbek. "It's we here on the borderlands that do all the fighting. It's we that suffer all the losses to keep you people safe in your beds, in your fine houses and fancy clothes, and parties aplenty. You see that out there," he said pointing toward the battle, "that's just one little piece of the wild that we've been holding

185

back for hundreds of years. Them and a hundred threats like them. Maybe after today, you'll have a bit of appreciation for that."

"You knew they were out there?" said Rom. "The trolls?"

Sarbek didn't immediately answer.

"Did you set them on us?" said Rom. "Are they your allies?"

"Don't be a fool," said Sarbek.

"Even so," said Rom, "You should have warned us."

"You'd never have believed us," said Sarbek.

"I'd have taken precautions," said Rom. "For one, my nephew would have been at my side — not out there. He's going to die because of your treachery. You'll pay for that. Every one of you will."

Sarbek turned and faced him. "You stinking Alders are all the same. You came here to arrest or to kill the entire Eotrus family on fabricated charges, and to take all their holdings for your own, and you accuse us of treachery?" Sarbek's hand lashed out. He punched Rom squarely in the jaw. Rom's head turned and he reeled back; but just as quickly, he turned back to Sarbek, his eyes focused, a scowl on his face. Sarbek punched him again. He threw all his strength into the blow. Rom responded just as he had before, though this time his scowl was stronger and blood trickled from his mouth.

"You're a weak, little man," said Rom. "In House Alder, we'd have you scrubbing the water closets."

"Get this bastard from my sight," said Sarbek.

"Throw him in the deepest darkest cell you can find. Then throw away the key."

The knights took Rom away just as Indigo joined the others on the wall.

"How do they fare?" said Sarbek to Ector. Ector raised his spyglass back to his eye and studied the battleground. "It's over," he said.

"Darned tough men they were," said Sarbek. "I wish that we could have saved them."

"What we do now?" said Ector

"We hope that them trolls got their fill of fighting and head back whence they came," said Sarbek. "Failing that, we hope them that we saw out there tonight was all of them. If there are a lot more coming, we're headed for the deep stuff, right quick."

"Sir Gabriel always said, hope is not a strategy," said Ector.

"It ain't, but sometimes, it's all you got."

16

UNTIL DEATH DO US PART

"**D**o you truly believe that this duergar threat is real?" said King Tenzivel to Lord Malvegil as they walked through the Fister Mansion's halls, guards in front, Duke Harringgold, Grim Fischer, and more guards behind them.

"The dwarves of Darendor believe them," said Malvegil. "And they're no friends of the svart. Bornyth Trollsbane told me himself that he'd seen them."

"But do you believe them?"

Malvegil chose his words carefully. He didn't want to speak of the incident that happened twenty-five years prior, but he had to. He couldn't take the chance that Tenzivel would disbelieve the svarts and not support preparations to deal with the duergar. "Many years ago, I encountered creatures in the Dead Fens that walked when they should have been dead. They were just as the svarts describe. We had no name for them at the time, but duergar is as good as any. So yes, I believe them. The threat is real." Stoub turned and eyed him. He'd served as Malvegil's chief bodyguard for many years, but hadn't heard that story. Few had.

"Unfortunate timing, then," said Tenzivel as they approached the rear door of the Fister.

"Fighting on more than one front will make things much more complicated. I want to hear everything about your previous encounter with these things."

Guards were massed at the Fister's exit; many more than when they had come in. Whoever set up the security wasn't taking any chances.

Captain Korvalan shouted in alarm and drew his sword. "Assassins!"

Malvegil saw a flurry of motion as the door guards reacted. Many crossbows fired. In front of him. And behind.

Bolts pincushioned several of the guards that walked in front of Malvegil and the king. At such close range, their armor was useless. They went down.

Malvegil reached for his sword.

A bolt slammed into Tenzivel's chest. Then a second. The king's eyes were wide; his mouth open in shock as he slumped down, his chest spurting blood. "Dead gods, save the Republic," he said as he fell, grasping at Malvegil's arm.

Stoub turned and shoved Malvegil to the side. Two bolts hit Stoub in the back, then a third; he went down clinging to Malvegil, half atop him. Malvegil looked into his eyes for the briefest of moments as life left them. Two more bolts struck Stoub's back as Malvegil pulled himself free.

Swords clanked behind Malvegil. More attackers from the rear. He heard Fischer cursing them.

The exit guards moved to the side, lowering the crossbows they had fired on the group. They were Black Hand — they had to be. In through the doorway charged a band of howling mercenaries, sword, axe, and spear — foreigners by their look —— men of the Southron Isles, reavers and cutthroats, paid killers. A score of them at the least. They dashed past The Hand assassins and made directly for Malvegil and those few that still stood with him.

Korvalan and Malvegil and a couple of other guards braced to meet their charge. Two bolts were already embedded in the Dramadeen commander's torso, though he paid them little heed. Malvegil raised his sword, but then his back exploded in pain. He felt the bolt sink in and hit his spine. They shot him from behind, the cowards. As he fell, he didn't feel anything. In her chambers in Dor Malvegil, Lady Landolyn screamed.

The guards behind Harringgold grunted as crossbow bolts struck them in their backs.

"The Hand!" shouted Fischer from Harringgold's side. The Duke drew his sword as he spun around. A bolt slammed into his left shoulder. Fischer barreled into him and knocked him to the ground as more bolts flew over them. The Duke banged his head when he hit the floor. He felt Fischer grab him by the arm and drag him into a side passage. How the gnome had the strength to move him, he didn't understand. Harringgold shook the cobwebs from his head and pulled himself to a sitting position. Three men turned into the passage, crossbows in their hands. Grim flung a dagger at one man and while it was still in flight, he threw another at the second man.

The first dagger hit its victim's throat. He immediately fell, gurgling and sputtering blood. The second dagger hit its target in the belly. That man staggered back and dropped his crossbow. One of Harringgold's guardsmen cut him down from behind.

The third assassin fired his crossbow, but his shot went wide. He drew a sword and charged. Grim met his charge head on, though the man was almost three feet taller than he and probably half again his weight.

The Hand swordsman was skilled. Very skilled. His sword danced like death. The man dodged and parried and spun. He threw elbows and kicks as often as he swung his sword.

Grim Fischer was better. Ten seconds of dueling and the assassin was done, sliced and stabbed in half a dozen places. Grim finished him with a stab through the chest.

"Get up," yelled Grim to Harringgold. The sound of fighting still thick in main passage. "We've got to get you out of here."

"The king?" said Harringgold. "The king!"

"We can't help him. There are too many of them."

Several more assassins poured into the corridor. A lone House Harringgold guardsman tried to hold them back.

"We're moving," said Grim as he dragged Harringgold to his feet. Blood soaked the Duke's shirt and ran down his arm and torso. Even his pants were wet with blood.

When they rounded the next corner, Grim pulled a sconce on the wall, then pressed the wall at a certain spot. A small hidden door swung open. They squeezed through and closed the door behind them, Grim checking that no blood trail stopped at the hidden door. With the hidden door closed, no light entered the space. Wherever they were was pitch black.

A light appeared in Grim's hand and softly illuminated the area directly around them. It wasn't much, but it was enough to see a bit. They were in a narrow corridor of masonry walls, cobwebs, and stone floor. The stone looked newer than the rest of the construction; added no doubt, over old, creaky wooden floors to permit silent passage.

"Where are we going?" said Harringgold as they raced down the corridor as fast as the Duke could move.

"We can get back to the meeting room from here," said Fischer. "If the wizards are still there, they can help."

Several turns and one staircase, all within the hidden corridor, brought them to a small door, much like the one through which they entered. Fischer carefully popped open the panel and peeked out. It put them in the anteroom outside the meeting hall. Several guards still lounged about the place. Harringgold didn't recognize them, but Fischer did.

The guards were alarmed when the panel opened but relaxed when they saw that it was Fischer and the Duke.

The sounds of the battle hadn't reached that deeply into the large building, so the guards had no idea about what happened.

"They still in there?" said Fischer.

"Aye," said the door guard as he wrapped on the meeting room door.

"Get a tourniquet around the Duke's shoulder and fast," said Grim.

Two other guardsmen rushed over to aid Harringgold.

Pipkorn opened the door, an annoyed look on his face, Mardack and Spugnoir behind him.

"The Hand hit us by the exit," said Grim. "A score of them, maybe more, and a squadron of mercs."

The wizards looked shocked.

"The King?" said Pipkorn.

"I don't know," said Grim. "It was a wild melee. I lost track of him from the start."

Pipkorn stared over toward Harringgold.

"He'll live if we can get the bleeding stopped," said Fischer.

"Master Spugnoir, see the good Duke home, will you?" said Pipkorn. "Now let's find the king."

Two corridors down, four men turned into their corridor, running toward them.

"That's them," shouted Fischer as the assassins aimed their crossbows.

Pipkorn extended his arms toward them. Twelve-inch diameter spheres of translucent yellow erupted from the wizard's palms and shot toward the assassins. The first two assassins dodged to the side, but the spheres changed course and struck them both in the head. The third man dived to the floor, but the sphere hit him as well. The fourth dodged back around the corner, but the fourth sphere followed him. When

193

the spheres hit, they enveloped the men's heads and stayed there. They sat on their heads like transparent helmets. The men clawed at the spheres in a panic, trying to pull them off, but their hands passed through them as if they weren't even there. In moments, it was clear that the assassins couldn't breathe. They were suffocating under those tiny domes.

"Impressive," said Mardack.

The assassins thrashed about to no good end. One ran at Pipkorn, but Fischer threw a dagger that dropped him in his tracks.

"You men," said Pipkorn as he pointed to four of the guards that had accompanied them from the meeting hall. "Restrain those two. Fast. I need to drop this spell before it kills them or we won't be able to question them. You go on ahead," he said to Mardack, Fischer, and the remaining guards. "I'll be just behind you."

By the time that Fischer and Mardack arrived near the Fister's rear exit, the battle was over. Bodies filled the corridor. Here and there a man groaned or called for help, some life still left in them. They found Tenzivel slumped against the wall; two crossbow bolts in his chest. Fischer checked him. He was dead. The king was dead.

Torbin Malvegil's body was face down near the king; a bolt sticking out of the middle of his back. A few feet away, Captain Korvalan was on his knees, facing the exit, leaning on his sword. His eyes were closed. Half a dozen bolts were stuck in him and he had many other wounds, his armor torn and battered. Blood pooled around him. He too was dead. The corpses of a dozen mercenaries and several brethren of The Black Hand were heaped about him. A dozen more mercenaries lay dead about the foyer, along with several Dramadeen and House Harringgold guardsmen.

"He held them back," said a voice. One of the Dramadeen officers, Korvalan's second in command — a hulking brute called Mavron, stepped from the shadows, a bolt sticking from his shoulder, multiple cuts and bruises about his body, his sword drenched in blood. "He kept them off the king, though it did no good," he said pointing to the king's body. "They wanted the king's body, the devils. But he wouldn't let them take him. He wouldn't die until he killed them all. Not until he killed them all. He was my captain."

"It seems you did you part as well," said Mardack.

"Not like him," said Mavron. "He was my captain. He was a hero."

Mardack searched around, looking for something. "Do you see the box — the box that Malvegil carried?"

"No," said Grim. "One of his guardsmen had it. This one," he said pointing to a dead soldier. "He carried it." They looked all about, but it was nowhere to be found.

Pipkorn dashed down the corridor breathing heavily.

"The King is dead," said Mardack to Pipkorn. "And The Hand has the Seer Stone."

17

THE MONKS OF IVALD

The people of Jutenheim spilled out of their homes and businesses to watch the expedition pass by. Most did so stoically, but some waved and cheered, and a few offered catcalls and taunts. Not once in the lifetime of any of the locals, save for perhaps the crone, did Jutenheim witness a large expedition set off over the great cliffs. It was an event, and one that caught them by surprise.

Children followed them through the streets, skipping along and laughing, wonder and excitement in their eyes. No fewer than a score of local men offered up their swords, wanting to join the expedition and share in the adventure, and no doubt, in the presumed spoils. Ginalli was inclined to take them on, to make up for the losses in manpower that they'd suffered, but Ezerhauten argued against it.

"They're undisciplined, untested, and have no loyalty to our cause," said Ezerhauten. "They will be far more trouble than they are worth, and may well hinder your noble purpose." Fear of the last clinched it, and Ginalli turned them away.

The Jutens were accustomed to strange folk visiting their port, but they'd never seen anyone as large as Mason, the man of stone. Although he wore a hooded cloak and gloves that covered his stony features, there was no way to hide his great height or bulk. The people pointed and stared as he passed. Some named him an 'ogre', others a 'jotun' (their word for "giant"), while still others called him an 'ettin'.

The Pointmen were at the expedition's van; a few officers on horse, but most traveled on foot. Behind them came four more squadrons of sithians — all that remained of Ezerhauten's stalwart company. Behind them, pulled by ten horses and driven by Teek the lugron, came Glus Thorn's coach. Park Keld sat beside Teek in what Keld called the 'place of honor.' Before and behind the coach rode most of the expedition's surviving wizards: Father Ginalli, Par Brackta, Par Rhund, Par Weldon, and Stev Keevis. Mason walked just behind the wagon. Behind him came a troop of lugron, some three dozen strong. Curiously, Korrgonn, Mort Zag, and Glus Thorn were nowhere to be seen. Presumably, they either rode within the coach, or else waited in Thorn's tower, across the great magical divide. The Rose was left only with its remaining crewmen and those others too injured (e.g., old Par Oris, who clung voraciously to life) or too ill to make the journey over the cliffs.

A steep, windy, and rather treacherous road carved into the rock brought the expedition halfway up the cliffside within a couple of hours. A gang of children followed them nearly half that far. The road ended at a flat area of about one acre in size that was notched into the cliffside. There sat the monastery. The building was stone and built directly into the cliffs. Its gates were of stone, steel, and wood. They stood closed. No one was about.

Rothmar and Frem rode at the expedition's vanguard. "You'll have to go on foot from here," said the blacksmith. "There's a steep path that continues up. It goes behind and over the monastery. It's mostly walkable, with some difficulty. At some parts, you'll need to do a bit of climbing, and I expect that you'll need to use the ropes to haul up your baggage. Kordan will show you the easiest path; he's been up to the top hundreds of times — a good lad."

"You've been a great help," said Frem. "It would have taken a couple of days to organize this caravan without your help. Thank you."

"You're most welcome, but it does not begin to pay the debt that I owe you."

Ginalli walked over, Ezerhauten beside him. "What do you know of this temple?" said Ginalli to Rothmar.

Rothmar took his time in replying, eyeing Ginalli. Frem had warned the Juten about the priest. "It's a monastery, not a temple, as far as I know, though I've never been inside." He turned and looked at Frem as he spoke more. "The monks are a mysterious lot though they cause us no trouble. They rarely come to town for supplies and always keep to themselves. They've always been that way. It was the same when my grandfather was a boy."

"I've heard they've been to the valley floor," said Ginalli. "That they can guide us, for a price."

"I know nothing of that," said Rothmar,

"though it wouldn't surprise me if it were true."

"Tell the monks that I would speak with them," said Ginalli.

"Tell them yourself," said Rothmar. "For they know me not. Young Kordan will take you up to the top, if the monks don't. I go no farther."

Ginalli's eyes narrowed. "Then your service to us is done, Juten. What do I owe you for the use of the horses and for bringing us this far?"

"You owe me nothing," said Rothmar. "Frem Sorlons has already paid me."

Ginalli eyed Frem suspiciously and then walked toward the great door of the monastery. No doubt, Ginalli meant to get to the bottom of that remark when he had time. He didn't like his lackeys making deals on their own with anybody, even when things worked out well. The trouble was, Ginalli's mind always wandered to the crises of the moment, whether they were real, imagined, or inflated, and he forgot about the minor things of the past. That was his way. More likely than not, Frem would never have to explain himself, and that suited Frem just fine.

The monks would not open the monastery's great doors. After a time, they agreed to permit entry of four visitors through a small steel door that stood to the side of the main ones. Ginalli selected Keld, Ezerhauten, and Frem to accompany him. Up until recent days, Frem wasn't certain that Ginalli even knew who he was, but lately, he always picked Frem for some duty or other. That was good, mostly, for it put him in the know, but in general, Frem preferred a lower profile.

The door ushered them into a dark, narrow corridor that sharply turned this way and that before ending at the grand entry hall just behind the building's main doors. There was no reason for those turns, save as a security measure, to box in anyone that broke into the place — a feature more common to a fortress than a monastery; not that Frem had much knowledge of monasteries. Several armored guards stood behind the main entry doors and eyed the group as the side corridor spilled them out into the entry hall.

That hall was huge. The ceiling, sixty or eighty feet high; the hall's depth, at least twice its height. Great carvings dozens of feet high adorned the walls; great tapestries too. It was cool inside, and the air was fresh, not damp and musty as Frem expected. A breeze from somewhere carried through the place. The hall had few windows, and hence, was rather dark, rather mysterious. Frem did expect that.

A silent, nondescript monk in robes of dull brown led them to a hall off the main and seated them at a large wooden table. The room's floor was of stone tile. The ceiling, high. Oil-burning sconces along the walls; paintings of varied skill between them — pastoral scenes of woodland and jungle. The tabletop was thick, carved from some huge, ancient tree — a tree far larger than any Frem had seen in Jutenheim. So they felled it in the interior, beyond the cliffs, Frem figured. That likely meant they had a hoist system. Perhaps they wouldn't have to climb down to the valley floor after all; that thought gave Frem much comfort. He had no love of heights and no fondness or skill at climbing. Still, it was better than skulking in caverns.

"They deny us at the front door, then usher us through the servants' entrance," said Keld, bitterness in his voice. "Then they don't even offer us a refreshment? Nothing? As if we were dogs." He shook his head; his jaw set; his clenched fists resting on the tabletop. Frem couldn't stand him; nobody in the company could. The wizards didn't like him either. Except for Ginalli who valued him above almost anyone else. Why? No one could fathom.

Several monks marched into the room; several well-armed guardsmen with them.

"I am Brother Abraxon," said one monk dressed in armor, a variant of a monk's robe (but open at the front) atop it. He wore a sword at his hip.

"You are in charge here?" said Ginalli.

"I am," said Abraxon. "We do not often host visitors in Ivald Monastery, especially not foreigners, but I'm told that you plan to journey to the interior. Is that so?"

"It is," said Ginalli. "I do not recognize your sigil. What god or gods do you follow?"

"We are adherents of the most holy Vanir — may their wisdom and insights into our future guide our every endeavor."

"And may we follow our true path," muttered the other monks and guards while placing a fist over their hearts.

"My apologies, but I profess ignorance of this Vanir," said Ginalli.

"No apology is needed. Vanir is the name of a

pantheon of gods whom we follow. Not a single deity. Alas, the Vanir are little known in the far northlands. Even our neighbors in Jutenheim follow the Aesir (rivals to our gods), so we choose to keep separate from them, and thus avoid clashes of faith, fortune, or philosophy."

"Ah, that explains much," said Ginalli. "I have great respect for the religious beliefs of others. I hope you do as well."

"We do," said Abraxon.

"I am glad to hear that, for my journey here," said Ginalli in his smoothest, calmest, most lucid voice, "is one of profound religious significance. As you can no doubt tell from my accouterments, I am a priest of Azathoth, the one true...err, I—"

"You were going to say, 'the one true god,'" said Abraxon. "We know the saying. We are schooled in the beliefs of many religions here. It's part of our training. The remark would not have offended us."

"Then you spoke true when you said you respected the beliefs of others," said Ginalli. "Of this, I am grateful. I have heard that an ancient temple lies somewhere deep within Jutenheim. I believe this temple has religious significance to my order. My journey here is thus a pilgrimage to that temple, to learn the truth of things. To see it for myself. To know whatever there is to know about it. When I heard that there was a monastery or temple on these cliffs, I journeyed here at once, on the chance that this may be the temple that I'm searching for."

"Alas, it is not. Members of our order constructed Ivald more than eight hundred years ago as a monastery dedicated to the Vanir. Ivald has remained a monastery, populated by the monks of our order, throughout all the intervening years. There is no temple here and nothing of Azathoth."

"I thought as much upon our entrance. But do you know of this temple that I seek?"

"I recall stories of it," said Abraxon nodding his head. "Though no one in my time has visited it, if even it still exists. For certain, it is long abandoned."

"Might there be some writings about it in your records? Or some monk amongst you that has knowledge of it?"

"We must check," said Abraxon. He called for their curator of records. A bespeckled man, olden and stooped, soon appeared, a large book under his arm. Neither his memory (which seemed razor sharp despite his years) nor his journal held any record of the temple, though, like Abraxon, he specifically recalled hearing about it, and spoke freely of what he knew. He explained that part of the history of Jutenheim was carried down by the monks in an oral tradition. Some portions of that tradition had never been written down. The legend of the temple, it seems, fell into that oral tradition. The old monk recalled several points about the look of the place, but none that told of where it was or what purpose it served. He promised to poll his brethren to see if any remembered more.

"Can you provide a guide?" said Ginalli. "To bring us safely to the valley floor and as far beyond as your people know? I would be most appreciative and I would provide a generous donation to your order."

"We are familiar with the valley. Mayhaps we can arrange something. I must tell you that the interior of Jutenheim is a dangerous place even for well-armed men."

"So I've been told several times," said Ginalli. "We are well equipped to handle dangers."

"I don't doubt it, as you've brought a veritable army to my doorstep. Odd for a religious pilgrimage."

"Not so odd when the journey is overlong and fraught with dangers," said Ginalli. "We've lost all too many of our company since we set out from Lomion City."

"And finding this temple is so important that you'd risk losing more? Maybe even your own life in this pursuit?"

"Once started, a pilgrimage must be completed," said Ginalli. "It's one of the prime tenants of my humble order," he lied. "I could not divert from this path now, even if I wanted to."

"Then we must help you," said Abraxon. "If for no other reason than to foster the spirit of respect and friendship between our respective faiths. I shall speak with my brethren and we will discuss the best approach to speed you to where you're going. We know a fair portion of the interior and we can provide copies of what maps we have. At a minimum, we should be able to tell you where not to look, thus narrowing your search. And you'll need equipment: ropes, climbing gear, and more. Beyond anything you may have acquired in Jutenheim. Their boasts, notwithstanding, the

Jutens know little or nothing of the interior. We've been there. We know what it takes to survive there. It will take some time to prepare the minimum of gear and supplies required, and longer for thorough preparations."

"We must leave as soon as possible," said Ginalli. "Tomorrow morning at the latest."

Abraxon seemed surprised. "Much of what you'll need can't be prepared that quickly."

"We are well equipped already," said Ginalli. "But if you can supplement our supplies, we'd be most grateful. We'll make do with what we have and whatever you can provide in this limited time."

"Very well," said Abraxon. "We'll do what we can. My people will work all night if need be. We can make accommodations available for you and your men tonight as well. As to your donation?"

"Three thousand pieces of silver," said Ginalli.

Abraxon smiled. "Plus expenses for equipment and supplies?"

"Yes," said Ginalli.

"And have your men map the interior as best you can, adding to the maps that we provide you. As detailed as you can make them. Copies to us on your return."

"Agreed," said Ginalli.

"Done," said Abraxon. "We have a deal."

Hours later, they gathered again in the same meeting hall. This time, Glus Thorn joined them, as did several other monks. The monks laid a number of maps on the table.

A middle-aged monk called Brother Bertold

was in charge of the maps and was the monastery's resident authority on Jutenheim's interior. "Getting up the cliffs will be a challenge," said Bertold. "At a minimum, it will take a full day, but it may take two if there are any delays or mishaps. We can show you the fastest and safest route and lend you the use of ropes, pulleys, and small hoists that we've set up to ease the journey to the summit. The good news is that getting down the other side will be easy. We've a few small buildings up there and a robust hoist system. In a matter of a few hours, we should be able to get your entire party down safe and sound, baggage included, with no risk at all. We use the hoists all the time to bring up crops and game."

"Crops?" said Ginalli.

"We prefer to be as independent from Jutenheim as we can be," said Brother Abraxon, "for the religious reasons I previously explained, so we grow most of our food in fields near the base of the cliff's landward face. We also do a bit of hunting and fishing down there. The land is fertile and protected from the more dangerous parts of the interior by a wide lake and a large bog."

"So we'll find no immediate dangers on the other side of the cliff?" said Ginalli.

"None," said Abraxon. "To be fair, we do see the occasional bear and mountain lion, but such will of course be no threat to a large party."

"The bog, however, will be difficult," said Brother Bertold. "Mosquitoes as big as your thumb. Alligators, poisonous spiders, snakes big enough to squeeze a man to death, some big enough to swallow you whole, poisonous plants, fever, quicksand. It's a death trap. How bad it will be for you, I can't say. It all depends on how much trouble you run into, and that is more luck than anything else. Without our help, it could be that you get lucky and your whole party makes it across the bog alive, or it could be that the bog takes you, one and all. But with this," he said pointing to one of the maps, "your chances of success increase a hundredfold. This map marks three paths that we know to be reliable and safe. Several others are also shown that are unreliable — because they become submerged at times when the bog water runs deep."

"How long to cross it?" said Ginalli.

"If good fortune is with you," said Bertold, "seven to ten days. If you build rafts to cross the lake, you could cut that time down to five to seven days, but of course, it will take time to build the rafts. We've only a couple of canoes. Given the size of the lake, using them won't save you much time. Figure ten days to get across either way."

"Is there any chance that the temple could reside within the bog?" said Thorn. "Or be submerged within the lake?"

"We've never seen any structure within the bog, no ruins, nothing," said Brother Bertold. "If it had been there, we'd have a record of it, for the place is well mapped as you see. As for the lake, our oldest maps show it just as it is today. It's probably been there thousands of years, so no, the temple cannot be there."

"Can we go around the bog?" said Thorn.

"If you go east and hug the base of the cliffs,

you can skirt it," said Bertold. "You'll be in the bog half the time, on rocks or solid ground the rest. It's definitely a safer way to go, but it will add two or three days to your journey, assuming that you ultimately want to head south, which I believe you do. If your temple is out there, it must be to the south."

"What is to the east?" said Thorn.

"Seven or eight days of hugging the cliffs will bring you to wide open fields where you can see for miles," said Bertold, pointing again to the map. "Beautiful country, if you don't mind the lions. We've been through that area a number of times over the years and saw no buildings. If you went that way, once you pass the eastern edge of the bog, you'd turn south. Another five days marching south, skirting the edge of the bog the whole way, would put you as far south as if you headed straight across the bog, albeit, you'd be many miles east. All told, that path adds two to four days to the journey."

"But it's safer?" said Ginalli.

"Safer in that you avoid most of the bog and its evils," said Bertold. "But you have to spend several nights in the eastern fields. That means fending off lions during the night and mayhaps alligators from the bog as well.

"Unacceptable," said Thorn. "We need a faster way."

Bertold looked to Abraxon.

Frem caught that glance, as did Ginalli. "Is there a path that can bring us south faster?" said Ginalli.

"There is," said Abraxon, "but it is dangerous

as well."

"Explain," said Thorn.

"Beneath our underhalls are tunnels that lead down through the mountain. At the base of the cliffs, the tunnels turn south and east. They continue under the lake and the bog. There is a path that brings you out a day or two south of the bog."

"And what is the danger?" said Ginalli.

"Besides the normal dangers of any deep cave or tunnel," said Bertold, "of which there are many, the place is infested with black elves."

"Ha! Black elves," said Keld. "You jest; they are but figments."

"Is that legend or truth?" said Ginalli.

"Truth," said Abraxon. "They've made incursions into our underhalls more than once. No doubt, you've noticed that we run this place more like a fortress than a monastery. The black elves are the reason why."

"The elves will kill you as soon as look at you," said Bertold. "Once they—"

"Let's say we get past the elves," said Thorn. "How much time would this route save us?"

"It would cut your journey in half, at least," said Abraxon. "Assuming that you don't get lost, or pinned down by the elves."

"I'm not interested in skulking through any more caves," said Ezerhauten. He looked to Ginalli. "I trust that you haven't forgotten what happened in the tunnels below Tragoss Mor?"

"None that were there will ever forget that experience," said Ginalli. "But these are different tunnels. And time is of the essence."

"Why, if I may ask?" said Abraxon. "What do a few days matter, one way or another?"

Ginalli leaned back in his seat and paused, as if considering how to answer that question, or whether to answer at all. "Like all religions, ours has its rivals," said Ginalli. "A group of men follow us on a ship called The Black Falcon. They seek to thwart our pilgrimage. They don't believe that our mission is a spiritual one. They think that we're on a treasure hunt. They're trying to get to the temple before we do, to steal its riches. The trouble is, they won't find any riches, for we believe that there are none to find. But they may find old scrolls, carvings, and religious relics that are priceless to us, but of no commercial value to anyone else. In their zeal and general stupidity, they'll probably destroy it all. That would be a terrible loss to our faith. One that we cannot abide. Thus, we've been moving with all possible speed, to make it to the temple before these others can desecrate it. Every day counts. We must keep well ahead of them to avoid more conflict, more bloodshed."

"Bloodshed?" said Brother Abraxon, a concerned look on his face.

"Yes, I'm afraid so," said Ginalli. "Our journey has been long and the criminals I mentioned have dogged our heels the entire way. They've caught up to us once already. We tried to talk to them, to explain that ours is purely a religious pilgrimage. But they wouldn't hear it. Thugs and thieves every one of them; their minds fixed only on loot and slaughter. They attacked us. Tried to kill us — to murder us. Regretfully, much blood was spilled —

which I will tell you is contrary to every belief that we hold dear. Only in self-defense may we fight. And that is what it was. If we hadn't had the forethought to hire Lord Ezerhauten's company for protection, we would have all been murdered. In the battle, we captured two of their number and are holding them still, humanly of course. We're taking them with us to the temple in hopes that if our enemies do show up, their fear of us harming the hostages (not that we ever truly would) may keep them at bay. We've no interest in another pitched battle. But as you've noticed, we're prepared for it, if it comes."

Abraxon nodded. "You've had a hard road on this pilgrimage of yours. I do not envy what you've been through. If good fortune is with you, the tunnels may prove an easier path. They should save you five days at least. And we can make certain that if those criminals show up, that they take the longer path. If they seek our council, we'll lay out the same overland options to them as we just presented to you, save that we will remain silent about the path through the tunnels. We'll tell them that we helped you, as they'll no doubt be able to find out from others, but we'll say that you went down the cliffs and across the bog, but which route you took, you shared not with us. Acceptable?"

Ginalli nodded.

"Perfect," said Thorn.

18

WIZARDS' FIRE

More than a thousand leagues away from the Isle of Evermere, Grandmaster Pipkorn witnessed the battle on the schooner through Tanch's eyes as he gazed into his magical font in which floated one of the twenty fabled Rings of Talidousen. Sweat dripped down the grandmaster's furrowed brow; his breathing, heavy. He'd already aided Par Tanch, enhancing his spells beyond Tanch's ken, beyond what even the Talidousen Ring was capable of. The strain was difficult for Pipkorn to bear, for hurling a spell over such a distance was far more taxing than throwing it in person. But it had to be done. Their mission had to succeed. If Theta failed, it would be the end of everything.

But for all Pipkorn's efforts, their deaths were at hand. Even Theta could not survive the horde that charged at them. And remotely, Pipkorn could not save him, or any of them. Not against an entire army of bloodthirsty fiends — creatures beyond even Pipkorn's experience. But he could help do some damage, terrible damage, and then rely on luck and providence to see them through.

***

Tanch knew what he had to do. The trouble was forcing himself to do it. The group's only chance was for him to unleash the full power of his Scorched Earth spell against the Evermerians. There were so many of them, and spread out over such a span, he didn't know whether he could stop enough of them to cause the rest to flee. But it didn't matter. He had to try. He had to do his part. He had to do everything he could to survive. Who could fault him for that? And so he pushed his fears aside, pushed his conscience aside, and focused on his will to survive, his burning need to live. Though what it was that he lived for, even he could not say.

Tanch waved his arms and made strange gestures with his fingers; he murmured certain words that he had only spoken once before — words that tapped the mysterious wellspring of energy that comprised the grand weave of magic. And as he did, he felt some portion of himself reach through the ether, across the dimensions, and into the weave itself. The eldritch energy surged into him, and spread throughout his body, covering every surface, inside and out, making him one with it — with the magic. He welcomed that power as an old friend, though he feared it more than a bit, and never fully trusted it. He brought all his energies to bear to contain it, to control it, even if only for the briefest of times. The magic grew in power as the moments ticked by, growing heavier, weighing him down. He called on more of it, and more still, as much power as he could master, and then some; far more than he had ever wielded before. It filled him up until he thought he'd explode. Almost so much that he wanted to explode just to be free of it.

Then he felt the power surging and pulsing within the Ring of Talidousen that he wore on his right hand. He felt the ring's reserves of strength and power and marveled at them, for they dwarfed his own. How an inanimate object could hold such power was beyond Tanch's comprehension. He felt the power stream from the ring into him, adding to what he commanded himself. It was so heavy, that power. He didn't understand why it didn't crush him; flatten him to nothing. But somehow, it didn't. He still stood. He was still in control.

Just before he was about to let loose the magic, he felt even more power surge into his spell, strengthening it. Much more power. He could no longer contain it all. The overflow of that sorcery took shape outside his body, hovering invisibly about his person, unseen by any but Tanch himself. Tanch couldn't believe it; he'd heard of such clouds of magic, but only in story and legend — only in tales of the great archmages of the ages. How could such a thing happen to him? The cloud of eldritch energy grew brighter, stronger, more powerful, and weightier. But from where the new power came, Tanch had no idea, though he welcomed it. The raw energies that spun about him were more than he could gauge, more than he could understand. It was all Tanch could do to hold the spell back, to restrain it long enough for it to build to its full potential. Yet he dared hold it no longer, for the Evermerians thundered down the pier toward him. They'd be at his and his companions' throats in moments.

And then death erupted from Tanch's hands. A geyser of flame shot from his fingers even as spheres of coruscating energy, gold and orange and red, launched from his palms. The fire blasted toward the onrushing Evermerians, far too fast for them to react. In the blink of an eye, the magic incinerated those closest to him. It left nothing but ash. Those farther away burned slower but with equal finality. Simultaneously, the spheres of energy flew amongst the Evermerians, humming as they went, turning and weaving with intelligence — homing in on their victims. One after another, the spheres exploded and tore apart anything and everything within ten yards of the center of each blast. Though far more destructive, the explosions were reminiscent of the sparkling fireworks thrown by hedge wizards on midsummer's night. Fleeting visions of those fireworks dominated Tanch's last thoughts as he collapsed to the deck, smoke rising from his body.

***

Ob, Tug, Dolan, and the men in the longboat with them had been rowing toward the schooner as fast as they dared, trying to maintain silence, and thus secrecy, for the night was dark, and the Evermerians hadn't yet spotted them. But they had been too far out, too far west. They didn't make it to the schooner in time, not nearly.

They threw themselves down as the roaring flames shot from Tanch's fingers. Even behind him, still a goodly ways from the schooner, the heat was oppressive; the air, difficult to breathe. They flattened themselves to the bottom of the longboat while the fireballs exploded along the strand, not knowing whether they would live through it or be taken by the flames. Waves of heat battered them, tongues of flames licked over their heads, and the superheated water of the bay roiled, steamed, and rocked the boat, threatening to capsize it. They covered every part of their flesh that they could to protect it from the steam and the condensing droplets of hot water that rained around them, wincing each time a droplet burned their flesh. Then they heard the screams from shore. There's nothing quite like the sound a person makes as their body is eaten by flames. It's something that sticks with you, even though you'd like to forget it; a truly horrific sound and one that Ob had heard all too many times in his life. Never had he heard such screams from so many voices at once. This time it was hundreds of them. Hundreds. And in addition, crowded as they had been only moments earlier, the blast must have killed many hundreds more outright, maybe even thousands.

Ob sat up in the boat and saw the docks aflame. Half the stretch of the boardwalk was fully engulfed, including many of the buildings closest to the water. Several of the long piers were on fire. Many Evermerians ran screaming from the boardwalk area, but for others it was too late. Many, fully enshrouded in flame, ran wildly about the burning boardwalk, screaming, careening into things, and one by one falling to the ground, writing for a time, until finally, they moved no more. The smell of burned meat was heavy in the air. Those things were inhuman monsters, cannibals, and worse; yet still, such suffering was a difficult thing to watch, even for an old soldier like Ob.

Then Ob realized that the schooner was afire.

"Put your backs to it, boys," he said as he looked for any sign of life aboard the schooner, though he saw none. "We've got to get to them before they get all toasty."

Graybeard cursed and muttered as he watched the flames spread across his ship.

"Was it the wizard that did that?" said Tug as he scanned the destruction. "Does he have that kind of power?"

"I expect so," said Ob, "since he did something similar in Tragoss Mor."

"That was a lot smaller thing than this," said Tug.

"Here the need was greater," said Ob. "I guess we all underestimated Mr. Scaredy Cat. He really has something to him after all. A lot to him, I suppose. Had me fooled but good. Thought he was nothing but a hedge, and a useless one at that. That sure ain't the truth, and I'm not afraid to admit it. That's the gnome way, you know. Then again, old Mister Fancy Pants may be behind it. I don't put nothing past him, that stinking foreigner."

"Are you saying that one of yours did that?" said Captain Graybeard as he pointed to the inferno.

"That's right," said Ob. "We got powers, we do;

all sorts of powers. Those aren't even our best men over there."

Graybeard was speechless.

A minute or so later, they had the longboat pulled up to the east side of the schooner. The smoke was thick and at first, they didn't see any movement. Then something moved on deck, but Ob couldn't tell what.

"Ahoy, Theta, you stinking bastard," yelled Ob. "Artol! Magic boy! You alive?"

"Captain," shouted Tug.

Dolan stood up and was about to leap from the longboat over to the schooner when Ob restrained him. "You're in no shape for acrobatics, boy. I'll go. Me and Tug."

And they did. Tug threw a grappling hook with a rope ladder attached to it up over the schooner's gunwale. He climbed it with shocking ease considering his massive bulk. Ob scurried up no easier. Captain Graybeard and two of his men came along to help.

They crouched low to avoid as much of the smoke as they could and moved toward the back of the boat.

"We were about to go over the side," said Artol as he stepped toward them through the thick smoke, Glimador a step behind him. "Would have been a cold swim."

"Everyone okay?" said Ob as he tried to look past Artol. He spotted Theta and Slaayde kneeling beside Tanch and Bertha. Bertha wasn't moving. Tanch was flat on his back and seemed to be having a seizure. His face was bright red. His clothes were scorched. "Oh, shit."

"What about the others?" said Ob to Artol. "Slaayde's men; the lugron and that other fellow?"

"Dead," said the big soldier.

Just then, a rogue wave hit the schooner and nearly swamped the longboat, spray flying onto the piers and the boardwalk, dousing some of the flames, though the water didn't carry far enough to put out most of the fires.

Within a minute, they had everyone piled into the longboat and started rowing out into the bay. Graybeard and his men were none too happy to leave their ship behind, but they had no choice, for the schooner would never sail again; not with the damage that it had taken.

They were a hundred yards from shore when Ob said, "Oh, boy, we're still in the deep stuff," as he pointed toward shore. "That's her, ain't it? She's still alive, the bitch."

They all looked toward the shore. On the west side of the docks, there gathered the surviving Evermerians. A hundred at least were engaged in fighting the fires with buckets of water drawn from the bay. The rest lined up along the strand, the Duchess at their center.

"It's her," said Dolan.

"Dead gods," said Ob. "It looks like there's more of them now then there was before. How can that be?"

"Before, it was only the men," said Dolan. "Now their women are out there too. Lots of them. And from what I can see, they've got bigger teeth than the men."

Ob sat down next to one of the schooner men

and helped with an oar. "We've got to move quick. Everyone get on an oar. If they take to the water, or pull out some longbows or bigger stuff, this will get ugly fast."

Tanch convulsed where he lay, shaking, and foaming at the mouth.

"Is there anything we can do for him?" said Artol to Theta as they both pulled their oars.

"Not until we get back to the ship," said Theta. "Even then, whether he lives or dies is out of our hands. It's all up to what strength he yet has within him."

"He saved our butts," said Artol.

"That he did," said Theta.

"You'd have gotten out anyway," said Artol. "Wouldn't you have?"

Theta tilted his head to the side in a semblance of a shrug. "It would have been a long, cold swim."

"Aye," said Artol.

19

MAPS, SPEECHES, AND STOWRON

Brother Bertold led the way down the stairwell to the monastery's underhalls. Frem and the Pointmen followed closely behind him. Their job, to secure the entrance to the tunnels while the rest of the expedition prepared their gear and hauled down the supplies. Wall sconces lit their way, supplemented by lanterns carried by Bertold and several of the Pointmen. The stairs were wide and solid, though uneven from age and wear. The steps and the walls were stone, bluish gray in color, and here and there streaked with white or black. The stone had a dull, natural finish, easy on the eyes, though the dark color made the place all the gloomier.

Unless the black elves decided to raid the underhalls while they waited, the Pointmen had landed the easy duty for once, and that was fine with Frem and his men. They'd had it hard for the whole mission and deserved a breather.

It was a full thirty feet down from the monastery's main level to the first underhall. The next underhall was twenty-five feet farther down than the first. Each deeper level had a lower ceiling, so the stair runs got shorter. Even so, it was a long way down to the seventh underhall, the bottommost level of the monastery.

As he trudged down the steps, Frem's mind drifted to that stair far beneath the city of Tragoss Mor — the one that led down toward the Keeper's abode. They'd lost men on that stair (a treacherous, narrow, slick thing), and a lot more at the bottom. Gargoyles, or some such, made of stone, came out of the walls and decimated their troop. Frem lost several friends that day. In truth, the monastery stair was nothing like that other one, but going down all that way, in the dark —— try as he might, Frem couldn't keep those terrible memories at bay.

"Nothing much down here except the crypts, a bit of cold storage, and the entrance to Svartleheim," said Bertold as they reached the bottom of the stairs. "That's what we call the tunnels. It means, land of the black elves. Oh, and this is Brother Rennis," he said as he pointed to a lanky young monk that sat at a table adjacent to the base of the stair, a cudgel that looked too big for him to wield leaned against the wall beside him. A bell hung from the ceiling; its pull chord next to the monk's head. Rennis had a reading lamp, a pile of books, a barrel of water, a mug, and not much else. A watch station of sorts.

"Watch your heads," said Bertold. "There are some low clearances down here. Rennis, anything to report?"

"All quiet, brother," said Rennis. "Have the tunnel guards been checking in on schedule?"

"Yes, brother."

"That's a good lad," said Bertold. "Keep your

ears open, but keep up with your studies."

A couple of turns and a trek of about two hundred feet from Rennis's post put them in a large bare hall with an ironbound wooden door at its back. Two monks in armor, sword, and shield, stood the watch, another big bell at their watch station.

"Beyond that door, my friends," said Bertold, "lies Svartleheim and the shortcut of which we spoke." Bertold unfolded a map and laid it on the guards' table. Frem leaned over the table and closely examined the map as Bertold spoke. The monk went over the route in detail, pointing out various landmarks and places to avoid. Frem and his officers paid close attention and asked numerous questions. The rest of the Pointmen lounged about, happy for a bit of rest. They didn't pay attention to the discussion, trusting to their officers to handle such things.

"Much of what I've told you comes down via the oral tradition," said Bertold. "Besides these maps, we've little in writing about the tunnels. I've only been in there twice myself, and never past the Eye of Gladden."

"What's that?" said Putnam.

"Stone carvings; can't miss them. Once past the eye, keep to the main passage for three days and that should put you here," he said pointing to a side tunnel on the map. "Follow the map, do not stray from the path I've shown you, and if Wotan smiles upon you, five days from now, you'll see the light of day on the other side."

"How many elves are in there?" said Putnam. "Tell us true. What can we expect?"

"No idea," said Bertold. "You may not encounter any. The first time I went in to scout the place, I wandered about the tunnels for hours, exploring and verifying the maps, even adding a bit to them. That entire time, I saw and heard nothing of the elves. No sign or trace. But I was in the upper tunnels, going no farther than about two hundred feet down from this spot."

"The second time we went in, we headed straight down the main passage. Five hundred feet below where we stand and a couple of miles in, we reached the Eye of Gladden. It was there that we found bones and artifacts. Before we could examine them, we thought we heard the elves coming, so we hightailed it out. Might have been nothing, might have been them; I don't know. We played it safe and we got out. I haven't been back there since. I'm darned curious, but I don't want to get dead. Then again, the brothers of old that made these maps went the whole way through the tunnels and back again, so we know it's not impassable."

"Have some others not made it?" said Putnam.

"I'm afraid so," said Bertold. "The most recent was twelve years ago, three years before my first trip in. A dozen men down from one of the big port cities wanted to go on safari to hunt big game, but they had no time or interest in braving the bog. Old Brother Hordin, he was the keeper of maps before me, thought it a good opportunity for exploring the tunnels, so he agreed to guide them through. Five other brothers went with him. None of the foreigners and only one brother came back, and he has since passed. He told how the elves jumped them two days in. Seems the foreigners made a racket and insisted on building a fire. It attracted more attention than they could handle. You'll have to watch yourselves in there. Especially when you're in deep."

"What of the incursions that Brother Abraxon mentioned?" said Frem.

"The elves got past our door a few times in recent years and caused some mischief. That's why I haven't ventured back in. I know they're in there, lurking, and I don't want to chance running into them. It seems as time goes on, they've been getting bolder. What they're hoping to find up here, we've no idea. Maybe they're just exploring. Or maybe looking for food — there can't be much down there. Who knows? Anyway, that's why we set these guard posts."

"You man them day and night?" said Frem.

"Have to," said Bertold. "We can never tell when the elves will come calling."

"Is there any other way into the tunnels?" said Frem. "Besides this door?"

Bertold hesitated a moment before responding and looked down as he spoke. "We know there is. There has to be, because we've seen the elves outside in the night on several occasions and the people of Jutenheim have seen them too, going back generations. Try as I might, I've never been able to find their secret exit, and Wotan knows, I've tried. They must keep it well hidden. If you've no more questions, I need to find your commander. I have a twin of this map to give him, so you'll have two in case one gets lost or damaged. Good luck to you," he said, still looking down; he made no offer of a handshake.

As Bertold made his exit, Frem looked down at the thick layer of dust his fingers picked up from the tabletop.

Frem and Putnam sat on the far side of the hall facing the door to Svartleheim. As big as it was, the room was beginning to get crowded with packs, gear, and men. Half the company must have been there by that time. The other men chatted, but Frem was silent, lost in thought.

"Are you starting to brood now too?" said Putnam to Frem. "Bad enough that Sevare hasn't been himself since last night. I don't need you going all funny too."

"Sevare hasn't been himself for a long time. And last night, he almost got dead, so cut him some slack. That black elf spell hit him square in the chest."

"Bah, nothing could kill that bugger," said Putnam. "But he's not in proper form, I'll admit, and that's no good, especially since he's the only first-rate wizard the company has left. Ezer will have to staff up good after this mission is done."

"A bit of optimism from you after all, sergeant?" said Frem.

"What do you mean?"

"Ezer can only staff up if he and some of us are still alive."

"You think we won't be?" said Putnam. "You think it's going to be that bad?"

"Not sure," he said, shaking his head. "It has been pretty bad so far, this trip has, but I don't know." Frem took a drink from one of his canteens and then refastened it to his belt. "I was just thinking that I'll miss Little Storrl on this one. His cheerfulness always makes the dark times a bit easier, and it's going to be awful dark in there."

"At least the lad is alive," said Putnam. "I'll miss Maldin more. He's a bruiser that one; a good man to have at your side in a tight scrape, but he'll not see action for quite a time, if he recovers at all."

"I didn't think he was going to make it back to the ship," said Frem. "A tough man."

"We're all tough men," said Putnam. "This life makes us that way, or else we wouldn't last long in this business. Don't look now — here comes the toughest of the bunch."

Ezerhauten arrived with the latest load of supplies. Frem got his attention and they moved to a private spot to speak.

"I'm thinking that we should tell the wizards about our run-in with the black elves," said Frem.

"I already did," said Ezerhauten. "Before the meeting with the monks."

Frem looked surprised. "The elves will make a connection between us invading their territory and the loss of their men. They'll assume we took out their boys and come at us hard."

"That's exactly what I told the wizards," said Ezerhauten.

"What did they say?" said Putnam.

"Ginalli nearly shit himself. In fact, I think he did," said Ezerhauten, scrunching up his nose "Thorn said svarts were of no concern to him. He said that he had ways to deal with them. And that was that; end of discussion."

227

"What about Korrgonn?" said Frem. "Had he no opinion?"

"I haven't seen him in days," said Ezerhauten. "He's gone hermit. Why, I've no idea."

"So we're going in," said Frem. "Like it or not?"

"We are," said Ezerhauten. "Believe me, I don't like it any more than you do; I've always hated caves and tunnels, long before Tragoss Mor. But we're stuck with it, so we'll go in and we'll do our jobs, just as we always do."

"Fine," said Frem. "But do you smell anything fishy?"

"You mean besides whatever Thorn has up his sleeve about dealing with the elves?"

"That stink is ripe," said Frem. "I'm talking about the monks."

Ezerhauten took his time answering, his wheels spinning. "They seem decent enough to me. Ginalli paid them good, and they're doing their part." But then, Ezerhauten narrowed his eyes and looked all around, the way he did when he got suspicious of things. "That isn't much of a barrier," said Ezerhauten of the door to the tunnels. "You'd think they'd seal it up proper, or at least barricade it or brace it with timbers or iron. I don't see any of that down here. It's just a stout door with a crossbar. Yeah, that strikes me odd, and it's starting to smell. That what you were getting at?"

"Aye," said Frem. "And there's more. The monk told me that they man this room day and night; have been for a goodly time, maybe years, but the guards' table is covered in dust — a thick layer of it. They'd eat on that table, don't you think?

They'd game on it. They'd nap with their heads on it. It might be dirty, stained, and such, but it would never have a thick layer of dust. And the room is too bare, like it's not really used."

Ezerhauten nodded. "I noticed that the guard post at the base of the stairs was bare too; not lived in like you'd expect."

"They do have the essentials that they'd need," said Putnam. "Even the bells for warning. And they have their story down straight, smooth as syrup."

"That they do," said Ezerhauten. "But that may just mean they're smart, and that enables the worst kind of stink. Frem, you figure that they set up these guard stations just for us? Just for show?"

"I'd bet on," said Frem. "I bet that door stands wide open most of the time."

"The black elves happening by for tea and crumpets whenever they like?" said Ezerhauten. "I'm having trouble getting my arms around that one, but maybe it's so. Maybe they've got some alliance with the little buggers, or some common cause. There's more to this than we can see."

"We could be walking into a trap," said Frem.

"Or maybe their table broke," said Putnam, "And they just pulled this one out of storage today or yesterday. Maybe it's been sitting in some storage closet for years and that's why it's all full of dust."

Ezerhauten bobbed his head from side to side. "Well, that could to true too. Sometimes the simple answer is the true one. Sometimes it's not." He looked at his men for some moments.

"Either way, and no matter what Thorn has up his sleeve, this one is going to be difficult. I can feel it in my bones. Maybe the worst yet. Stick close together in there and watch your backs."

"We always do, Commander," said Putnam. "And we'll watch yours too."

"I'm counting on it," said Ezerhauten.

A short while later, when preparations were nearly complete, Ezerhauten recalled Frem and the other squadron captains topside. Putnam went along out of curiosity, even though he didn't enjoy the stairs.

They had Thorn's coach pulled up in front of the monastery's main doors. Par Keld was cursing every monk in sight, demanding that they open the doors and stand aside. He wanted to drive the coach into the main hall. Teek sat stoically beside him munching on a cigar, the horses' reigns in his hands. It didn't look like the monks were going to comply. Things were close to getting ugly when Brother Abraxon showed up and directed that the doors be opened.

Keld parked the coach inside the hall, then jumped down and raced to the side of the coach to open the door. It seemed he wanted to make certain no one had that honor but him. The Leaguers were there: the wizards and the lugron: Par Brackta, Par Rhund, Par Weldin, and Stev Keevis. Mason was there too. Out of the coach stepped Ginalli, then Thorn and his gnome apprentice, and then Gallis Korrgonn himself. Frem hadn't seen the Nifleheim lord since the meeting where Thorn killed Captain Rascelon. The wizards all bowed as Korrgonn greeted them. Then Mort Zag began to squeeze his bulk through the coach door. The monks gasped in surprise at his appearance and drew back from the coach.

"Be not alarmed," said Ginalli to the monks. "Our dear friend, Mort Zag, is one of the red giants of the far northern mountains. A peaceful and thoughtful people, despite their brutish appearance. You have nothing to fear from him."

It took the giant, or demon, or whatever he truly was, a full minute to squeeze himself through the door. No one dared laugh. But Frem really wanted to.

Ginalli never missed an opportunity to make a speech, so Frem wasn't the least bit surprised when he stepped forward to do so. "Beloved faithful of Azathoth," he said, arms extended, palms outward, "let us thank our newfound friends, the honorable monks of Ivald, for their generous aid and support in our holy quest. The faithful of Azathoth will be forever in their debt. Let the hand of friendship always be warmly felt and freely given between us and all adherents of our respective faiths." He smiled, turned, and warmly embraced Brother Abraxon, who seemed surprised by the gesture, but embraced him back, smiling, the requisite three manly pats on the back. The other wizards turned, and shook hands with and thanked those monks nearest to them. The lugron seemed confused by the speech. When Ginalli spoke fast, as he often did, his accent confounded them. Some stood there doing nothing. Most shook hands with each other. A few understood the intent and shook hands with the monks near them.

"We set off now on the final leg of our quest," said Ginalli. "Once we pass into the tunnels below this sacred place, there will be no going back. There will be little rest, no place of comfort or ease. And no help. We will be fully committed. And there will be hardships, perhaps even more than we have already faced, and those have been all too many, as you all well know. We must ready ourselves for those trials, mentally, physically, and spiritually. We must keep in mind that every step of the way, our lord is with us, looking down at us from the heavens, supporting our quest with his love and his blessings. And we must rejoice that he has sent us his own son to face these trials by our side. Together, through strength and faith, we will persevere and we will succeed in our quest. After all we've been through, all that we've lost, all that we've sacrificed, we cannot fail. We must not fail. And we will not, so long as we keep our faith and never, ever give up, no matter the hardships. I believe in you, and I'm counting on you. On each and every one of you, to hold strong to your beliefs, to your faith, and to see us through these trials on behalf of our lord."

"Let us bow our heads in prayer," said Ginalli with a respectful nod toward Korrgonn.

Korrgonn made the sign of Azathoth across his breast and then spoke a prayer in some olden tongue unknown to Frem. The words he spoke echoed strangely in the air. Frem felt a pressure, an unseen force, an eldritch energy about him as those lost words vibrated through the air. There was magic to them. Olden magic of Azathoth from the days of yore. Magic of a bygone age perhaps best forgotten. Of its nature or purpose, Frem could only guess. A blessing for their journey? A binding to hold them to their course? Or something else? Something darker? Something sinister? Frem did not know. He didn't understand Korrgonn. He didn't bother to try. But Ginalli was a different story. He wondered if anyone else saw Ginalli for what he was. Or were they all too dense, as Frem pretended to be. Did they recognize that every word that Ginalli spoke was carefully chosen and designed for one purpose only — to achieve his ends, to further his cause, the truth be damned? In the end, it didn't matter. Frem knew what his duty was and he would do it, even if it meant he'd never return home. Even if it meant that he'd never see Coriana again. Frem was a good soldier. No one could deny that.

Ginalli stepped forward, still not done. "By now, we've all heard about the black elves that lurk in the tunnels. With Lord Ezerhauten's company at our side, we're well equipped to handle such threats, but Master Thorn has brought us additional allies that will further safeguard the faithful during the remainder of our quest.

"What's this?" muttered Ezerhauten from Frem's side.

"These friends are called the stowron," said Ginalli. "They are among Azathoth's faithful. You may trust them as you trust each other."

As if on cue, Par Keld opened the coach door again, and out stepped some odd looking characters. They were short and stooped and wore black robes with cowls that completely covered their faces. Each carried a wooden staff capped with bone, their hands deathly pale. They stood straight up, but walked a bit hunched over in an odd side-to-side gait, vaguely reminiscent of that of an ape. Six stepped out. The last two each led a blindfolded man that had his hands bound before him. One was Jude Eotrus. Frem didn't recognize the second man, but he was older, and was missing one of his arms below the elbow. The monks didn't react to the prisoners since Ginalli had already spun his tale about captured criminals.

"Are we ready to set out?" set Ginalli.

"Aye," said the gathered group.

"Nord," said Thorn to one of the stowron, "bring forth your brethren and waste no time about it. We need to get moving."

"Brethren?" muttered Frem.

Nord climbed back onto the coach, which stood empty. He closed the door and then immediately opened it again. More stowron now crowded within the coach, having appeared out of nowhere. Two, four, ten of them, and they kept coming. They lined up in the hall in a column of twos.

"Oh boy," said Ezerhauten. "I didn't expect this."

"We go," said Thorn after about twenty stowron had disembarked from the coach. More were still coming out. The wizard turned and headed for the underhalls, everyone else following.

Ezerhauten scrambled to catch up to Ginalli,

Frem on his heels. He wanted to hear what they said firsthand. "Who are these men?" said Ezerhauten.

"The stowron, as I said — allies of Master Thorn's. Quite reliable. They live in caverns; did you know that? They have for generations. They're probably as comfortable there as are the elves."

"Can they fight?" said Ezerhauten.

"Quite competently," said Ginalli.

"Why was I not informed about this?" said Ezerhauten. "I'm in charge of the military aspects of this mission. It's essential that I know what our assets are, and what their capabilities are. Otherwise, I can't—"

"You're in charge of your company, Commander, nothing more. Master Thorn is in charge of the stowron. You're a hired hand here, Commander. A valued one, but still just a hired hand. Don't forget that. You do as we tell you. Understood?"

Ezerhauten's teeth clamped together. A few breaths later he said, "Understood."

20

THERE BE TROLLS

Sarbek burst into Ector's chambers just after dawn. "Ector! Get up! Up, boy, up," he shouted as he marched through the antechamber and the sitting room toward Ector's bedchamber.

Ector met him at the bedchamber door, still half-asleep, his robe disheveled, his face flushed and with an odd expression.

Sarbek was immediately suspicious. "Have you looked out the window, boy?"

"You just now woke me up."

Sarbek pushed past him.

"Wait," said Ector as he unsuccessfully tried to bar the knight's path. The young woman in Ector's bed looked mortified and frightened, covers pulled up to her chin. Sarbek glanced at her, just long enough to note who she was, said nothing, and made his way to the window. He threw the shutters open. He turned and gestured Ector to the window to stand beside him. The window faced to the north, and thus looked out on the opposite side of the Dor from where the previous night's battle took place.

"Can't see much from here — but look there," he said pointing at the tree line in the distance beyond Dor Eotrus's outermost wall.

"What is it? More Alders?"

"More trolls. Can you see them? Your eyes are better than mine."

"Not without the spyglass," said Ector. "It's too far."

"There is a mess of them out there," said Sarbek. "I saw them from the roof. A lot more than we thought. Worse, now they're organized. Some got uniforms on them and weapons too. Some are marching in as units and standing up like men — but they otherwise look like the trolls we've been fighting, except maybe taller. That's a stinking army assembling out there, all coming down from the north. And they've also got the ones on our south side what fought the Alders. From the look of this, they're planning to encircle us."

"A siege?"

"Maybe," said Sarbek. "Don't know if they've got the smarts for that, for a proper siege takes some doing. But maybe. Hell, the way them things climb and bounce about, they might not need any ladders. They might be able to come on over the wall on their lonesomes."

"If they can climb the walls, we don't have a chance," said Ector.

"True, if we try to hold the whole Dor and the Outer Dor too," said Sarbek.

"So let's not," said Ector. "Let's withdraw to the citadel and barricade ourselves in. Fight them in the corridors if we have to, so that they can only come at us a few at a time."

"I won't give up the main walls," said Sarbek. "Besides, if they can scale the main walls, then once they're inside the Dor, they'd just scale the walls of the buildings and the citadel. Then they'd come in through the windows and swarm us. We can't fight on that many fronts. We've got to think, to come up with some strategy."

"What if they continue moving south?" said Ector. "We've got to warn Lomion City."

"I've sent ravens already," said Sarbek. "I've also sent more ravens to our bannermen."

"A few days ago I didn't even believe in trolls," said Ector. "They were just monsters from children's stories. Now we're under siege by them."

"That's the north, boy," said Sarbek. "It's wild. And it spews its worst at us, time and again. It's what makes us Northmen strong. Or else, kills us dead."

***

Hours later, Sarbek, Ector, Malcolm, Indigo, and the beardless dwarf, Pellan, stood on the main roof of the citadel.

"How soon until the Outer Dor is fully evacuated into the keep?" said Ector as he looked over the parapet. A steady stream of people, wagons, and livestock filtered through the Dor's gates, soldiers aiding them and guiding their way.

"Within the hour," said Indigo, "except for a few holdouts that won't leave their homes or shops. What do you want us to do about them?"

"Nothing," said Ector. Sarbek turned and studied his face.

"Every civilian is free to do as they like," said

Ector, "so long as we fully inform them of the danger. Make certain the holdouts understand that if the trolls come for them, we will not sally forth to help them; not even if we can. I'll not allow my men to die rescuing someone who chose to be reckless and needlessly remain in harm's way. They can choose to risk themselves, but not others."

"Some of the holdouts are families," said Indigo. "What of the children?"

"Tell the parents that we won't allow their children to die because they are stubborn fools. Tell them that I ordered their children to be taken into the keep so that we can protect them. Tell them that if they don't let us take them, we'll arrest them all, the whole family. I'd rather take away someone's freedom for a short time, than rip their children from their grasps."

"What if they put up a fight?" said Indigo.

"Try not to harm anyone, but do whatever you have to, to bring those children to safety."

Sarbek looked surprised and a slight grin formed on his face. "You've got more of your father in you than I ever thought." He turned toward Pellan. "How about the supplies?"

"Two or three more hours and all the food, water, and essentials will be inside the keep and secure," said Pellan. "We're using every spare man we have, including a couple of hundred civilians."

"That may not be quick enough," said Sarbek. "Not nearly. They could come at us at any time. Get another hundred civilians to help; more, if you need them. Within the hour, I want it done. And get all the women and old men what can't fight and all the children into the citadel's underhalls. Put all the supplies down there too. All of them. And don't place them anywhere near the entrance. Get everything essential to the most secure areas."

"That will take longer," said Pellan. "There's a lot of footage down there."

"Do the move in two stages," said Sarbek. "Drop the stuff near the entrance to the underhalls, and have other folks carry it from there to secure locations deep inside. Don't put everything in one spot; spread it around in several of the most secure areas. Conscript anyone and everyone you can for the work."

"Like you conscripted me?" said Pellan with more than a hint of bitterness in her voice.

"Yes, just like that," said Sarbek. "We do appreciate your service, captain; you've been a big help."

"It's my sword that you'll need, not my quartermaster skills, before this adventure is done," said Pellan.

"I expect that all our swords will be bloodied afore we're done with the trolls," said Sarbek.

"You think to abandon the keep itself?" said Pellan. "Is that why you want everything down in the underhalls?"

"Depends whether they can scale the walls," said Sarbek. "If they can, we won't be able to keep them out. We can't stand toe to toe with them in the open, or we'll end up just like the Alders. If they come over the main walls, we'll retreat to the underhalls. We'll fight them room to room in the narrows. That will work to our favor. We'll bleed them for every step inside they take. And if we bleed them enough, maybe they'll decide we're not worth the trouble and move on. Maybe. Anyway, if they get over the walls or through the gates, the underhalls are our only chance.

"But if they can't easily scale the walls," said Ector, "then we can hold the keep. We must."

Sarbek nodded. "As I said earlier, I'll not cede the whole Dor to those things without a fight."

"Retreating to the underhalls is no path to victory," said Pellan. "All it does is buy us time for relief to come, unless they're smart enough to smoke or burn us out. Then it will be a deathtrap."

"That's a risk that we'll have to take, if it comes to it," said Sarbek. "Now go get those supplies positioned. We need it done before they come at us. I don't want to have men hauling supplies during a battle and I don't want to leave anything useful behind."

"Aye," said Pellan, and she dashed off down the stairs.

"Indigo — I want you to station one-fifth of our archers in the citadel's windows," said Sarbek. "In position to fire at anything in the courtyard. I need them to hold their positions no matter what. They are not to withdraw even if the trolls overrun the grounds. They are not to abandon their posts, even if the rest of us retreat to the underhalls. They make their stand here in the tower."

"Aye, Castellan," said Indigo.

"Put the rest of the archers on the main walls, holding one squadron in reserve in the courtyard to hold back any breach in the gates or walls. If we fall back to the redoubt — one out of every three archers are to go below to help hold the stair and the underhalls. The rest are to go up into the towers to join their fellows. There they will remain, making their stand, and holding back the trolls' efforts to get to the underhalls."

"We'd be sacrificing them," said Ector. "I don't—"

"In war, such things are necessary," said Sarbek. "Your father would agree. The lads will do their duty; they're good soldiers. Indigo, preselect who is to go where. Draw lots if you have to, but waste no time about it. I want everyone to know what they are supposed to do, and where they are supposed to go ahead of time, to minimize the confusion."

"We should give a weapon to every man who can hold one," said Ector, "and get them on the walls. Any woman willing, give her one too. Shields and clubs would be best or thin blades. Battle swords are no good if you don't know how to use them."

"Forget the thin blades," said Indigo. "It won't stop trolls."

"You're right," said Ector. "I keep forgetting that we're not dealing with normal foes. Clubs, maces, bludgeoning weapons. Give them those."

"I will see that it is done," said Indigo.

Sarbek, Ector, and Malcolm remained on the roof surveying the work below and watching for any movements of the trolls.

"How many of them do you think there are out there?" said Ector.

"I don't know," said Sarbek. "From what we've seen, at least five hundred, but there could be more, maybe a lot more back in the woods or still on their way down from the mountains."

"What do they want with us?" said Malcolm.

"To kill us," said Ector. "That's all they wanted up at Mindletown. Pellan said they wiped the place out; the whole town."

"This may be the start of an invasion," said Sarbek. "Just the sort of thing we're based here to stop. Just the sort of thing we've always stopped before."

"Like when the lugron came down from the highlands?" said Malcolm. "And the time that they came from West Rock? Or when the Spantzileers came over the eastern hills?"

"Aye," said Sarbek. "We stopped them bastards but good those times and many others. But by the gods, why did the trolls have to show up when we're at our weakest? If they'd come just six months ago, we'd have your father, and Sir Gabriel, Talbon and his wizards, Stern, Ob, Brother Donnelin, Jude, Claradon, Marzdan, Balfin, Kelbor, and all the rest with us. In all my years here we've never been anywhere near this weak."

"Could they know that somehow?" said Malcolm. "Is it possible?"

"Who knows?" said Sarbek. "Maybe they've been watching us from the woods for years, biding their time, waiting for the best time to strike. Or else, maybe it's just our bad luck. Either way, we've got to deal with them. We've got to stop them here and safeguard the realm, even if the bloody southerners don't deserve it."

"We've never had to stop trolls before?" said

243

Ector.

"Not an army of them anyways," said Sarbek, "And none at all in my time."

"If we hold up here," said Malcolm, "we're giving up our cavalry — one of our best weapons. Are you certain that that is the right thing to do?"

"The way they took out that brigade," said Sarbek, "tells me that we can't hope to defeat them in the field —— not with the limited number of heavy horse that we have in the garrison. If all the banners come in and assemble at Rikers and Roosa, as we've directed, and if we still hold the walls, we can sally forth our horse and join with them. With a couple of brigades of cavalry, we'll break their lines and send them running back to their caves. But it will cost us. It will cost us dearly."

"How long until all our bannermen are assembled?" said Malcolm.

"In three to four days they might be at twenty to thirty percent strength," said Sarbek. "To get to seventy or eighty percent will take a week at least. Two weeks will bring all that will come."

"We can't hold that long," said Ector. "Not even close."

"We can and we will, if they can't scale the walls," said Sarbek.

"What are they waiting for?" said Malcolm as he looked through his spyglass. "They're just standing about out there at the tree line. Wait — — I see smoke, over there," he said pointing to the west.

Sarbek and Ector focused their spyglasses on the same area and then panned around. "There is smoke coming from the east, and from the north too," said Ector.

"They're setting fire to the outlying farms," said Sarbek. "No chance that they'll pass us by now. They're cutting us off. Only question is, when will they come at us?"

"There are a lot of good folks out there," said Ector. "On those farms."

"Many of them came in yesterday," said Sarbek. "We sent riders to every farm and homestead within a few miles. Most of the folks are fine. No doubt, some are dead. We'll make them trolls pay. We will track them to their lairs and wipe them from the face of Midgaard."

Horns blared in the distance, from the south.

"What's that now?" said Sarbek as they all turned their spyglasses to the south.

"Reinforcements from Lomion?" said Malcolm. "Maybe the Alder's brigade was only the vanguard of a larger force."

"If that is the case, the Alders meant to siege us," said Ector. "There may be a whole corps coming. I don't know what's worse —— that or the trolls."

"Maybe they'll kill each other off, like last night," said Malcolm.

The horn blared again.

"The sound of that horn isn't right," said Sarbek. "It's not made of metal. That's a true horn — ram, most likely," he said. "Our military don't use that."

"Then who?" said Ector. "Rangers?"

"Could it be elves, up from Doriath?" said Malcolm.

"It's the trolls," said Sarbek.

"Pfft," went Malcolm. "They're animals. They don't use horns."

Then sounded a horn blast from the east, and then another from the west.

"Apparently they do," said Ector. I see movement through the trees to the north."

"They're getting ready to come at us," said Sarbek.

Then began a repetitive blaring of horns from all sides.

Trolls began marching out of the southern woods in lock step. They wore metallic armor — a mishmash of plate and chain and ringmail, worn over hides. Some of it was scavenged from the remains of the Alder brigade — weapons too. Most of those trolls carried weapons, and more than a few of them walked upright like men. Here and there were pockets of the wild trolls that had chased Sarbek and Ector down from the north. The wild ones capered about, dragging their knuckles on the ground, howling. Between both groups, there were several hundred trolls in all.

A few minutes later, more trolls marched out of the woods from the east and from the west, and an even larger group from the north. Those trolls were different from the others. Every one of them walked upright. Every one was fully clothed and equipped with heavy armor and weapons of strange design. These trolls were huge — nearly all were seven feet or more in height. They were hairless and muscled, their skin leathery, their eyes a piercing, otherworldly green. They marched forward, row after row, company after company, from the east, the west, and the north.

"Dead gods, how many of them are there?" said Ector.

More came through the trees, all in formation. They came by the hundreds. Then they came by the thousands. A sea of trolls spat up from some subterranean depth only imagined in man's darkest nightmares.

"Dead gods," said Ector.

Sarbek's face went deathly pale. He shook his head and looked from one side of the parapet to the other. "We've no chance. No chance at all," he said quietly.

"Sir Sarbek, what do we do?" said Malcolm.

"I'm sorry, boy, but there are too many. There's just too many. We've no chance at all. I've failed you. Failed your father. There's just too many."

21

MOURN THE FALCON

Sir Seran Harringgold sat at the dining table in the Captain's Den of The Black Falcon, nursing a goblet of sweet Cavindish wine as he listened to Sirs Kelbor and Trelman debate their next move. For that night's game of Mages and Monsters, Seran was teamed with Ganton the Bull, undeniably the toughest man of the bunch in a real fight, but a bumbler at gaming strategy. Brute force is all he knew on the battlefield or the gaming table. At least he was comfortable following Seran's lead. They'd played enough games over the last several weeks for him to gain the Bull's respect and to develop quite the rivalry with their opponents. Seran had grown up playing M&M and was an expert. The problem was, Kelbor and Trelman were experts too, and for all intents and purposes, it was two against one. That challenge made it all the more fun, especially playing with Ob's gaming pieces, which were old, rare, and exceptionally finely crafted. They just had to make certain to put them back exactly as they found them, or else Ob would have their heads.

The game that night was intense; they'd battled for hours, interrupted only when Tug returned from one of his supply runs. Each time that he did, Seran inspected the haul — not that it was his job to do that, he just felt that he should. On the last trip, he didn't assign any troopers to the detail, instead allowing Tug to take only his own men. They planned to spend the night in Evermere and were anxious to get over there. Not that the soldiers wouldn't have liked to do the same, but he wanted to keep them out of trouble.

The game dragged on until midnight and beyond. Seran was tired but he forced himself to give the game his full attention. He made himself think of it as a real battle and made his moves accordingly. Hunger, fatigue, illness, or whatever else that got in the way, had to be put aside, just as in a real battle, or else you'd end up dead. Treating the game that way made it more real, more intense, and made him a much more deadly opponent.

Seran heard yelling on deck. He and the others halted the game and listened for a moment; the uproar continued. As one, the knights made for the door. Then they heard the explosions, one after another. The docks were engulfed in flames by the time that Seran made it to a spot where he had a clear view of Evermere.

"Guess it wasn't a friendly port after all," said Kelbor. "Very disappointing. Would have been nice to have a day or two of rest and relaxation."

"Plenty of time to rest after you're dead," said Bull.

"Ten silver stars say that Tanch is behind that," said Trelman as he pointed at the flames.

"Taken," said Bull. "Scaredy Cat doesn't have

the juice, not by a long ways. I say it was Theta."

"He's no wizard," said Trelman.

"That fellow's got powers," said Bull. "And a bag of tricks as deep as Old Pointy Hat's. He even scares me, and I'm not scared of anybody."

"What do we do now?" said Trelman. "Take the ship through the reefs or go in with longboats?"

"Or do we wait?" said Kelbor.

"Even Slaayde wouldn't pilot the ship through that," said Seran. "I'll not trust the mate to do it. Actually, I wouldn't trust the mate for much of anything."

"Agreed," said Kelbor. "That man's a snake. Longboats it is then."

"We'll leave half a squadron of troopers on board and a skeleton crew to man the ship," said Seran. "The rest of us are going in."

"You want these reavers with us?" said Bull.

"They're good in a fight," said Seran. "But mostly I don't want them on the ship without us. What if they got the notion to sail away into the sunset?"

"Aye, then we'd be in deep for certain," said Bull.

"Maybe we should clear this with Claradon?" said Trelman.

"We should," said Kelbor, "but we don't have time, and he's still half out of it. We've got to move, or our people may end up dead."

As the knights gave the orders to proceed as they'd agreed, sailors readied the sails and the ship turned and started moving toward the mouth of the bay — against Seran's orders.

Seran ran to the bridge deck. "What are you

250

doing?" he yelled to N'Paag, the First Mate.

"Rescuing the captain," said N'Paag. "Look at that inferno over there," he said pointing. "I'll not leave my captain to burn alive. We're going in to get him and your people too."

"You can't pilot the ship through the reefs, especially not in the dark," said Seran. "Slaayde wouldn't even chance it."

"I'm a better pilot than him. I can do it."

"We can't take that chance. If the ship runs aground or is damaged we may never get off this island. Our mission is too important."

"My captain is too important to leave there to die. We're going in."

"Turn the ship away from the bay," said Seran sternly.

"No. Shove off, Tin Can. While the captain is away, I command The Falcon."

Seran stood glaring at him. Two seamen hovered behind N'Paag looking as if they were expecting a fight. Another stood a couple of steps directly behind Seran.

"Best you shove off, like the mate says," said the man behind Seran.

"Or else things might get unfriendly," said one of the men behind N'Paag.

Seran looked toward the main deck. He was alone in this. The other knights and soldiers were helping to prepare the longboats. No one else had even noticed his dispute with N'Paag. Not being seamen, they hadn't realized that N'Paag's maneuvering made no sense if they were going to launch the longboats. They must have thought he was just bringing the ship into better position to deploy them.

"I'm not letting you take the ship into that bay," said Seran. "Stand down, or you — all of you — will spend the rest of this voyage locked in the brig."

The seamen laughed.

"You stand down, Mister Tin Can, or you'll get a thrashing like you've never had before."

"And if you get us riled enough," said one of the seamen, "you'll get dead."

Seran pulled his sword, but before he brought it to bear the man behind him tackled him, taking him from his feet with some clever tripping maneuver at the same time that he pushed him forward. Before Seran could do anything, three blades pricked his throat.

Then, out of nowhere, the whole ship rose in the water.

Yells of surprise came from all across the deck. The ship rose up and listed to the side just as if it were hit by a huge swell in a storm, yet the sky and the sea were calm.

The men holding Seran scrambled off him, and tried to figure out what was happening. Seran pulled himself to his feet.

He saw a dark shape rise from the water in front of them, at the very mouth of the bay. The night was too dark for him to see much, but whatever it was out there, was huge. Bigger even than the largest whale. Much larger than The Falcon herself. N'Paag spun the wheel hard to port. As luck would have it, or perhaps providence (if you believe in such things), a strong wind came up that aided The Falcon's turning and got them headed away from the bay.

The breeze carried with it the thing's scent — an overwhelming fishy smell like you'd get on the deck of a big fishing vessel. What the thing was, still wasn't clear, for it was too dark. It seemed huge, and rather round and featureless.

"Take the ship around that point," said Seran to N'Paag. "If we're lucky, that thing won't follow us."

"That's what I'm doing, Mister Tin Can. And I don't need no advice from you. You run along now so that we don't have no more troubles. Man the catapult," shouted N'Paag. "Man the ballistae."

Crewmen uncovered the ship's weaponry and prepared them to fire.

"What is that thing?" said Trelman.

"A sea monster, you numbskull," said Bull. "Some people don't got much going on betwixt their ears," he said to no one in particular. "You got to think a little bit, like I do."

"Claradon is coming," said Kelbor. The men turned to see Claradon Eotrus step through the door from below decks. He hobbled on crutches and looked pale and unsteady as he shuffled toward them, Kayla, Sergeant Vid, and several troopers in tow.

"What's happening?" said Claradon.

"A sea monster is all," said Bull to Claradon. "We've got things well under control, as usual."

"The port is on fire," said Kelbor, "and that thing, whatever it is, is blocking the mouth of the bay. We're maneuvering around the point, hoping that it won't follow."

"I can't see it — just a dark shadow," said Claradon. "What is it?"

"We can't tell other than it looks a lot bigger than the ship," said Kelbor.

"We can't leave our people stranded over there," said Claradon. "They're obviously in trouble. It looks like the whole waterfront is on fire. That didn't happen by accident."

"I doubt we can stop that thing with the ship's weapons," said Kelbor. "If we don't and it comes at us, we're dead. It'll swamp us and crack the hull."

"I agree," said Trelman. "Fighting anything that big is suicide. But could we try sneaking by it in the longboats?"

"Or wait it out," said Bull. "It came out of nowhere; maybe it will go back there."

"I've an idea," said Claradon. "But if it doesn't work, we're going to have to fight that thing head on. Get to the weapons. Make certain they're ready. Get the archers in place. And see if they have any harpoons aboard. If they do, pass them out — all of them — to any man that knows how to use one, and get them to the gunwales, ready to throw."

An earsplitting honking sound, non unlike an elephant's trumpeting, came from the thing in the water and went on and on for several seconds, followed by a loud, clacking sound, akin to huge jaws snapping.

"It's turning toward us," said Bull.

"Oh, boy," said Claradon.

***

A deep, loud, bellowing call of some large creature sounded from far out in the bay.

The men in the longboat all went quiet and stayed their oars.

"What the heck was that?" said Ob.

"It sounded like it came from out by The Falcon," said Artol. "But I've never heard anything like it before."

"Nor have I," said Ob.

"I heard a sound like that once," said Captain Graybeard. "Out in the Southron Isles, by Hargone Bay. The locals said it was a monster from the deep. Something not seen much anymore. But every time that it did show up, fishing vessels went missing, their crews never found."

"A sea monster," said Ob. "Now that's just wonderful. Another thing straight of out the fairy tales. Maybe another old enemy of yours, Mister Fancy Pants? Or an old pet that you set loose when he got too big?"

Theta made no response. He kept his eyes fixed on the mouth of the bay.

"Back on the oars, men," said Ob. "We need to get to the ship and quick, sea monsters be damned."

The throng of Evermerians began to chant something from the eastern end of the docks — a rhythmic sound that may have been words, but no one in the longboat could make out what they said.

Far out in the bay, a large ball of yellow and orange fire flew through the air.

"What the heck?" said Ob as all the men

255

turned and gaped in surprise at the crackling fireball. The flaming projectile arced down and smashed into something atop the water, far out at the mouth of the bay. The fireball exploded and spread flaming pitch across the object and the surrounding water over a wide swath. Then came the roar — the same trumpeting sound as before, but even louder, angrier. A great shape rose up out of the water: a giant creature, but of what nature, they could not yet see, though the bay was growing lighter by the moment. The clouds high above were clearing; the moonlight beginning to shine through.

"What in Thor's name is going on out there?" said Captain Graybeard.

"N'Paag is using my catapult," said Slaayde. "That was one of my pitch bombs. Ravel cooked up the recipe years ago, after we saw something like it in action way down south."

"They must have been coming in to get us and that thing blocked the way," said Ob, "so they're trying to clear it out."

"But what is it?" said Artol. "It looks huge. It looked like the whole mouth of the bay moved and rose."

"Fire," said Seran and the catapult crew launched a second sphere of flaming pitch and metal shot at the sea monster.

"Got it," shouted Bull as the pitch exploded on impact.

The flaming bits and the growing light gave them a better look at the creature. It was enormous, even larger than they had thought. It had a hard, round back, unlike any fish or whale.

The thing turned in the water and dived down, extinguishing some of the fire that raged along its back, only to resurface again almost immediately, covering a third of the distance between it and The Falcon in a matter of moments. Now they saw its gigantic head, its webbed legs, and scorch marks across its thick shell where the projectiles had hit it. It looked like an enormous sea turtle, no less than a hundred and fifty yards across. It was angry and it was coming at them.

"Ballistae, fire!" said Claradon from the bridge deck. "Archers, fire," he shouted. Bolts from the two large ballistae mounted on deck fired. One shot bounced off the creature's shell, but the second caught it between its foreleg and neck, sinking deep. The archers and crossbowmen fired, scoring several hits, but the arrows and bolts bounced off it, unable to pierce its thick hide. Another catapult shot flew toward it, but the turtle ducked its head and neck into the water and the shot blasted into its shell, spreading flaming pitch across much of its back. The thing's head popped out of the water, and screamed a monstrous, otherworldly wail that was so loud that it vibrated the bodies of the men in the longboat, still so far away. As it closed on the ship, honking and pounding the water with its forelegs, the men threw their harpoons. Those that hit bounced harmlessly off its shell or its hide. As the thing barreled toward The Falcon, some of the seamen jumped over the side to escape the inevitable collision. But the knights of Dor Eotrus did not flee. It was not their nature. They held their ground. Claradon stood on the bridge deck, sword drawn, ready for action despite the grievous wounds that still plagued him. Kayla, Sergeant Vid, and a squad of soldiers stood around him. Kelbor, Trelman, Bull, Seran, and a full squadron of troopers stood, weapons ready (including many pole arms and harpoons), at the bow. They all braced themselves as best they could.

Just before the turtle would have collided with The Falcon, it submerged, diving down at a steep angle, its maneuverability impressive for a creature a fraction of its size. The ship was not hit except by the beast's wake. The turtle was gone, beneath the waves. The men looked to all sides, searching for any sign of it, but found none. As quickly as it came, it now seemed to be gone.

Some moments later, there was a huge jolt. Then the sound of cracking timbers. The ship rose up out of the water, higher and higher, knocking the men on deck from their feet.

"By Odin," yelled Ob, rising to his feet, even as the sea turtle lifted The Falcon out of the water. "Shit! Claradon! Shit!"

"My ship," shouted Slaayde as he struggled to his feet to try to get a better look. "My ship!"

The turtle had launched itself to the surface, head first, under The Falcon. As it came up, it lifted the ship with its head, the ship rising thirty, forty, perhaps even fifty feet out of the water, before it and the turtle crashed down to the water's surface. The turtle slipped back down below the surface. The Falcon, however, came down hard on its side, great timbers cracked and snapped. The vessel's hull was shattered, a ruin.

Timbers, deck boards, and men flew in all directions, tossed into the icy water. Much of what was left began to sink.

"Put your backs into it," shouted Ob. "We've got pick up the survivors before they freeze to death."

"This is your fault," shouted Slaayde as he pointed at Theta, his face twisted in rage. "There's a curse on you and anyone with you. You've been the death of many a friend and good sailor since this darned voyage began, and now I've lost my ship. My ship! My whole darned crew! I'll see you dead for this! I'll see you dead!"

"Back down, Slaayde," said Artol. "You don't know who you're talking to."

"Screw you, you big bastard," said Slaayde. "I'll see you all dead before I'm done."

The giant turtle burst from the water again. It rose up high, and then crashed down directly atop The Falcon's wreckage.

"No," shouted Ob. "Claradon, my boy, oh no."

The turtle's jaws snapped at figures bobbing in the water. It grabbed one between its jaws, the silvery glint of a knight's armor shown in the moonlight as the man was snapped in half. Then a second knight followed him to the afterlife. The turtle's webbed forelegs thrashed and pounded the water all around the wreckage. Its intent was clear: to kill any and all survivors from The Falcon.

"We've got to move," said Ob. "We've got to get out there." He turned toward Tanch, anguish on his face, his eyes, wet. "We've lost him, dammit. We've lost him," he said to Tanch, though

259

the wizard was still unconscious.

"You folks don't have other ships hanging about out there somewhere, do you?" said Graybeard.

"Just the one," said Dolan.

"And now all we've got is this stinking longboat," said Ob.

"They're coming," said Dolan.

They all looked toward shore. The Evermerians were putting longboats, dinghies, and canoes into the water. Dozens of them. Enough to hold a few hundred people. They piled into the boats and started rowing toward the longboat, still chanting and yelling.

"Oh, shit!" said Ob.

"That's it then," said Slaayde. "We're all dead. There's no way out of this. No way out. You stinking bastard," he said, still glaring at Theta.

The turtle roared behind them as it smashed and ate anyone that it found alive in the water.

Then the vast throng of Evermerians still ashore, those who couldn't fit into the boats, ran into the surf, and began to swim out into the bay, toward the longboat, howling and screaming. There were thousands of them. Thousands.

22

WELCOME TO SVARTLEHEIM

"**W**ho the heck are these guys, Commander?" said Par Sevare as the stowron marched down the hallway leading to the door to Svartleheim.

"Reinforcements," said Ezerhauten. "The good news is that Thorn is putting them on point. So your necks won't be stuck out as far as usual. He made me turn over the map to one of them. He wants the company in the center, protecting the wizards."

"He's putting the lugron in back?" said Putnam. "They'll bolt at the first sign of trouble."

"He's placing two squadron of stowron in the rear," said Ezerhauten. "The lugron will be just behind us. You still have that other map?"

"Yup," said Frem.

"Keep it close and don't let it get damaged," said Ezerhauten. "I've a feeling that we'll be needing it."

The soldiers moved aside as the stowron marched through the hall and passed through the door to Svartleheim. A full squadron passed. Then another. Then another.

"How many are they?" said Putnam.

"A full company," said Ezerhauten. "About two

hundred strong."

"This changes things," said Putnam. "Changes everything."

"That it does," said Ezerhauten. "Our odds of getting through this mission alive just changed dramatically."

Ezerhauten positioned 2nd and 3rd Squadrons directly behind the stowron vanguard. Then came the Pointmen and the wizards, all mixed together. Mason got the duty to carry the big metal case in which the wizards stowed the Orb of Wisdom that they obtained from Mason's old master, the Keeper, in his lair beneath Tragoss Mor. It was with that orb, whatever it was, that Korrgonn hoped to open another gateway to Nifleheim and bring forth Azathoth. Korrgonn and Mort Zag stuck close to that case. Korrgonn never let it out of his sight. And Mort Zag never let Korrgonn out of his sight. Not bad having a giant (or a demon, Frem thought) for a bodyguard. Not that Korrgonn needed one. No mortal could stand against him and live, little less, defeat him.

Par Keld and Teek got babysitting duty, watching over the prisoners. They took off their blindfolds, but kept their hands tied, which made movement in the tunnels all the slower and more difficult.

Behind the Pointmen and the wizards were 4th and 6th Squadrons. Ezerhauten figured that if the elves were smart, and if they really wanted everybody dead, they'd come at the expedition from behind, so he wanted fully half the company lined up behind the Pointmen. Frem thought that was smart, especially since they passed more side tunnels along the way than Frem could count. The elves could come at them out of any or all of those. Some of the side passages were nearly as large as the main, but most were only wide enough for one man to pass through stooped. Some were tiny, too small for a man to fit, but maybe not too small for the elves.

The main tunnel was wide enough in most spots for two large men to walk comfortably side by side. Some of that tunnel (and the side ones) were natural, probably lava tubes left over from when Midgaard birthed Jutenheim. But the main tunnel was bolstered, shored, and braced at regular intervals with stone pilasters carved right into the walls. Someone had made the tunnel. But who, why, and when, Frem had no idea.

The main tunnel's ceiling was no less than seven feet high, stretching to ten or more in many places. But the path wasn't clear. Rocks and boulders were strewn randomly about, such that you'd have to walk around them or climb over. And the floor wasn't level; it was sloped downward throughout, sometimes at a shallow slope, sometimes steep, and sometimes it dropped off and you had to climb. Those things made it difficult and dangerous to move with any speed. Especially since it was so dark in there — dark as the grave.

Without their lanterns, they'd have been lost. To conserve fuel, they had a lantern lit for every tenth row of men, which left things dark indeed for those farthest from the lanterns, though the stowron didn't seem to need the light. Frem and all the Pointmen had steel and flint that they could use to start a fire if need be. Most of the other men of the company had the same. Not that there was a lot on hand to burn. They made certain that they had a bunch of torches prepared and stowed in their packs, just in case. The sithian company was always prepared; that was a large part of the training that Ezerhauten instilled in them.

The air in the tunnels was very cool, but not freezing. And it was dry. Bone dry. But it was not nearly as stale as it could have been. More than likely, that spoke to there being numerous exits from the place, despite Brother Bertold's inability to find them. The rock surfaces were dusty. Putnam or Moag could've read tracks from them, if there were any, but since more than two hundred men marched ahead of them, any elf tracks were long gone.

There was no distinct smell to the tunnels. All Frem noticed was the scent of lantern oil and that of the dust kicked up by those ahead of him. No animal smell. No bats. Nothing. And that wasn't a bad thing.

A hundred yards in, the path turned downward and to the east. Soon they were climbing more than walking. That was a challenge considering the large packs that they carried over their shoulders or strapped to their backs, especially for the men that had lantern duty. They could see better, but it was hard to climb with a hand encumbered.

After some two hours, Frem figured the lead men were close to the Eye of Gladden. That's where the elves hit them. Frem heard a series of explosions, then yells, and a chorus of hissing sounds (which turned out to be the stowron). The tunnel was jammed up with men, so there was nothing much Frem and the Pointmen or the wizards could do. There was no open area to form up and maneuver. No line of sight to the battle. No lines of communication either, save by repeating a message over and over down the line. That was never reliable. Ezerhauten shouted at the wizards and the lugron to shut their traps so that he could hear what was going on, but they paid him little heed.

Then Thorn ordered them to quiet down. He must have had some sense of tactics, but the others surely didn't. They didn't even listen to him. Then Thorn threatened them. That didn't work either. Then he conjured some unseen force and used it to pick up one of the lugron and smash his head against the tunnel wall. Thorn pounded him into the wall over and over, until there was nothing left of him but pulp, and his body fell apart. That shut them up.

"We could push our way to the front," said Putnam.

"That we could," said Ezerhauten. "And then we'd see what was what. Of course, if we're losing, we'd get trapped up there, and we'd get dead."

More explosions sounded at the front. The stowron started backing up.

"Ginalli, they've got Diresvarts up there hitting your stowron," said Ezerhauten. "If you want to knock them back, you'll need to send a couple of your wizards through the line. Otherwise, we may get pinned down here, or worse, the stowron may rout, and then we're screwed."

"Stev Keevis, Par Rhund," said Ginalli. "Make your way to the front and blast whatever elf wizards you can find. Only the wizards. Then get back here. Let the stowron deal with the grunts."

"Commander, I want a squad of your men to go with them," said Ginalli to Ezerhauten.

"Markus," shouted Ezerhauten to 2nd Squadron's captain, "send six men forward with the wizards. Stick to them like glue."

Ezerhauten marched up to Ginalli. "The frontal assault may be a diversion. I want to send a squad of my Pointmen to the rear in case they come at us from that way."

"Do it," said Ginalli. "But I want you here."

"Take your squad to the rear," said Ezerhauten to Frem. Then he lowered his voice so that only Frem could hear him. "If things get ugly, get out. That's an order."

Ezerhauten expected the main attack, if any attack came at all, to come from the rear, when they were deep into the tunnels. With their chance of escape back into the monastery cut off, and assuming that the elves had sufficient numbers, they could bleed the expedition to death in the dark. But when they got hit so early on, and so hard from the front, elf wizards and all, Ezerhauten thought he had been wrong. He figured that the elves lacked discipline or patience and came straight at them as soon as they learned of their incursion into Svartleheim. That surely meant that the frontal assault was it. The elves wouldn't have had time to set up a rear attack so quickly. They couldn't have gotten behind the expedition so fast. So when he sent Frem to the rear, he thought he was sending his best men out of harm's way, to insure that they'd live to fight another day regardless of how the battle played out.

What Ezerhauten didn't count on, was that the elves had been lying in wait for them just as Frem had feared. And that therefore, the main attack was going to come from the rear. He had sent Frem and his men into a meat grinder.

Frem, Sevare, Putnam, and their men moved toward the rear. Frem went a bit paranoid along the way and conscripted a full squad of troopers from 4th Squadron (nearly all of them Sithian Knights), and pulled them along to the rear with him for support. They arrived at the back of the column just in time to see all hell break loose.

The elves smashed into the expedition all along the middle to rear section of the line, pouring out of the side tunnels — all of the side tunnels, all at once. There were hundreds and hundreds of the little buggers. And they had at least a few of their wizard-priests, the Diresvarts, amongst them, tossing spells of death and destruction. Luckily, the very rear of the column, where the last thirty or forty men were (Frem and his men amongst them), was at a spot where there were no side tunnels. In moments, they were cut off from the rest of the expedition when elves ran howling out of the side tunnels and cleaved through the line of men ahead of them.

No elves were behind them. For a moment, Ezerhauten's words rang in Frem's ears. Maybe he ought to turn his men and make a run for the monastery while the getting was good. But he couldn't. The monks couldn't offer any real help; though they had weapons and some guardsmen, they were not a fighting force. The only reason to flee would be save himself and his men. Frem was a soldier, not a coward. So long as there was any chance at all, he wouldn't turn tail; he wouldn't abandon his company or his commander; he couldn't. He had to fight his way back to 4th and 6th Squadron and to Ezer and the rest of the Pointmen. He'd make his last stand with them, if it came to it.

Frem had his men form up shoulder to shoulder, shield to shield. Putnam was the rear-guard, watching for any sign of elves from behind. Frem's men plowed forward. The knights from the 4th Squadron slammed into the elves, sword, hammer, and mace, their heavy battle armor impervious to most of the elves' attacks. They crushed any black elf in their path. But they could not advance far. Once they reached the point where the side tunnels met the main, they couldn't go by them without letting the elves get behind them, for there were elves packed into every tunnel. If they blew by the side tunnels, they'd entrap themselves —— elves to their front and to their rear. As much as he wanted to rejoin the rest of his company, Frem was not reckless. He knew good tactics from bad. He'd not entrap himself and the men in his charge. That would be a fool's mistake, or a rookie's. Frem was neither.

So all that Frem's men could do was relieve the beleaguered stowron nearest to them. They saved a few lives, but not many. Frem was surprised to see that the stowron made a darned good account of themselves. When they got going, they fought like demons. They were as agile as acrobats, and vicious with their staffs. When they lost their weapons, they punched, kicked, and clawed with the best of them. They were warriors. They gave the elves what for. But the black elves had earned their reputation honestly. They were terrible opponents, despite their diminutive size. Fierce and fearless. Wounded, or outnumbered, they didn't retreat. They plowed forward, always aiming their attacks for the vitals or the neck or the eyes. And they knew what they were doing. They were no raw recruits; they'd seen battle before.

Then Frem heard Putnam's whistle. Four pips, which meant a major attack from the rear.

Frem's heart raced, but he kept his wits. He kept ten men facing forward and ordered them to hold. He turned the rest. He barreled down the line, pushing by the others, and pulling Sevare along with him. When he got to the rear, he saw a dozen dead elves lying in the tunnel. Putnam, Clard, Sir Carroll, and Sir Royce stood amongst them, weapons bloodied. Men were passing pikes up to them. Frem moved up to Putnam.

"We're in the deep stuff now, Captain," said Putnam. "Real deep stuff."

"What is it? What did you see?" said Frem.

"The monks," said Putnam as a battle cry rang out before them. From around the bend, just entering the edge of the lantern light, charged every monk and guardsman from the monastery. All in full battle garb. Howling for blood. Several black elves charged along with them, thick as thieves. Brother Abraxon at the van.

"Oh, shit," said Frem.

23

THE GOD OF LIGHTNING

"By Odin," said Artol, defeat in his voice as he gazed at the throng of Evermerians that chased them. "There's no way we can stand against that many."

"Dolan, try to rouse the wizard," said Theta. "We need him."

Dolan repeatedly shook Tanch, but to no avail. He lightly slapped his cheek. He doused him with cold water. Tanch did not stir. He was out for the duration. "He's barely breathing," said Dolan.

"That's it, we're finished," said Slaayde. "We're dead men thanks to you, you stinking bastard."

"What of the monster?" said Graybeard.

"We'll get by it," said Theta. "But there is no hope against that horde. So shut up and row."

They pulled the oars with every ounce of strength they possessed, but the Evermerians continued to gain ground. The longboat was simply not as fast as some of the canoes and small boats piloted by the Evermerians.

"Two more minutes and they'll be on us," said Artol.

"Keep rowing," said Theta.

"I'd rather fight them with some strength left," said Artol as he heaved at the oars.

"Keep rowing," said Theta.

The lead canoe drew close to the longboat. Two of the Evermerians put down their oars and prepared to jump over.

"Dolan," said Theta. "Give the man in the back of the boat an arrow in the eye."

Dolan lifted his bow, nocked an arrow, turned, pulled, and shot, all within three seconds. The arrow struck exactly as Theta had directed. The canoe rocked. One of the other Evermerians lost his balance and fell into the water. But one of them leaped toward the longboat.

A normal man wouldn't have made it halfway to the longboat from that distance, but the Evermerians were no normal men. Captain Graybeard stood and swung his oar at the man, striking him full in the face, slowing his momentum. He landed atop the gunwale, but before he could steady himself, Slaayde put the point of his dirk through his ear. The Evermerian went limp and slipped in the sea. Short several rowers, the canoe fell behind, now too slow to hope to catch the longboat. Two other canoes took its place.

"Again," said Theta.

Dolan turned and shot a rower in the nearest canoe, and then one in the canoe behind. Both Evermerians fell dead, one shot through the eye, the other through the forehead. Both canoes continued to gain on the longboat, albeit more slowly.

"One more in each," said Theta.

And Dolan shot again. Each arrow hit, though it took three shots to get the second man to drop his oars and pitch over the side.

This pattern continued on and on as the minutes wore on. Dolan singlehandedly took five more boats out of action before he ran out of arrows.

Theta ordered that they all produce whatever knives they carried. Amongst them, they found a dozen blades that could be thrown. Three more boats fell victim to Dolan's knife throwing skill, which was nearly was impressive as his bowmanship.

"Everyone, keep rowing," said Theta. "Dolan, remember the time that we met the Vhen in the Trachen Marches?"

"Aye," said Dolan as he started scrounging around in his belt pouch, searching for something.

Theta pulled out a piece of hard leather from a pack he had stashed in the longboat. He unfolded it. It was stitched together into a conical shape and had some sort of metallic lining. He affixed something to the side of his battle hammer's head and lit a piece of tinder in no time flat.

Dolan found what he needed, held it in his hand, and then also expertly lit a piece of tinder. "Ready," said Dolan.

Theta stood up, his hammer in one hand, the leather cone held in the other. He put the narrow end of the leather cone, a rudimentary bullhorn, to his mouth and spoke.

A half dozen of the Evermerian boats were now within ten yards of them, many of their warriors readying to leap across to the longboat.

"I am the lord Angle Theta," he shouted, his voice amplified tenfold by the bullhorn. "I am the

273

god of storms and death! I am the god of lighting! Taste my wrath and burn!" He held his hammer high and sparks flew from it. A tiny explosion went off and arcs of electricity ignited around the hammer. Sparks flew in long streaks. They seemed to come down from the heavens, crackling and popping, called by some magic unknown. "Come forth and meet your doom!" Theta boomed so loudly that most of the men in the longboat momentarily dropped their oars to cover their ears. Dolan swung his arm to and fro, throwing across the water some objects he held in his hands. Even as streaks of lighting erupted from Theta's hammer, more crackling, fiery streaks skimmed across the surface of the water toward the Evermerian vessels, tendrils of crackling flame that began at the longboat and searched for victims.

The Evermerians that were nearby ducked and pulled back on their oars, shouting in panic.

The sparks from the hammer began to sputter out and Theta lowered the weapon and pointed it at the nearest boats as he mouthed words in some long forgotten tongue, whispering them to the hammer. A moment later, a streak of crackling blue energy shot from the tip of the hammer in a continuous stream. Theta aimed it at the nearest boat. The stream struck one of the Evermerians despite her attempts to dodge. Sparks flew as it touched the woman. The Evermerian caught fire and screamed as the stream of energy passed through her. It cut her in two. Cleanly. Searing her flesh as it passed through, such that there was little blood. Her body collapsed, the top part falling into the sea.

Theta turned the stream and cut the head off a man on the other side of the same boat. Two more fell victim on the next boat over before the stream dissipated. "Come forth and meet your doom!" Theta boomed once again as more sparks erupted from the head of his hammer.

The Evermerians were in a panic. Many dived into the water to escape. Some lay flat in their boats, hiding. Others turned their boats, rowing back toward shore.

Above it all, the men heard the Duchess's voice. "Keep after them, you cowards," she shrieked. "Kill them. They're running away; what god does that? It's just the wizard's tricks. Kill them!"

Theta sat down and leaned forward, his hands rubbing his temples, his eyes closed, obviously in a great deal of pain. Dealings with magic, it seemed, even affected him.

Two-thirds of the Evermerian fleet was routed or had fallen back. The rest came on, led by the Duchess herself in a large canoe equipped with outriggers on either side. The huge mass of swimming Evermerians still came on though they lagged behind the boats.

Slaayde shook his head and eyed Theta. "Charlatan or wizard?" he murmured.

Ob heard him. "A bit of both it would seem."

"The turtle is gone," said Artol. "It sank beneath the waves."

"Keep rowing," said Theta, though he didn't lift his head from his hands. "We've got to clear the bay before it returns."

"What's left of them bloodsuckers is gaining on us again," said Ob. "Heck, even their swimmers are gaining. Never seen nobody swim that fast in my life, and the cold doesn't bother them. They'll catch us unless you've more in your bag of tricks."

"It's empty," said Theta.

"Dolan?" said Ob.

Dolan held up one last arrow that he had stashed somewhere. "For the Duchess," he said.

"That's smart, boy," said Ob. "Right smart. Kill her dead and the rest may turn tail. But if it don't work, it's knife work for us. A bloody lot of it."

"If it doesn't work, we're dead," said Slaayde. "There are still a thousand of them out there. Maybe more. We've no chance. My ship! How did it come to this? Oh, Bertha, how did it come to this?"

A few minutes later, they reached the mouth of the bay where The Falcon had gone down. The lead Evermerian boats were again within ten yards and closing fast. Swimmers a few dozen yards behind them.

"Do you see any survivors?" said Slaayde as he looked around, desperation on his face. "Any of my men?"

"Nothing," said Artol. "Not even any debris. Not a single board remains."

Theta perked up. He turned and looked around, scanning the water all around them and peering into the distance. "Turn to port, now!" he shouted.

From the east, out of a patch of mist, came four Evermerian boats headed straight at them, only yards away. Despite a quick turn of the longboat, within moments they were surrounded and cut off from the open water.

"Bring me the wizard and their lightning god," shouted the Duchess from her boat, which was now well back from the lead boats. "Kill all the rest," she said, a patch affixed over her lost eye.

Dolan leveled his bow and shot.

Instead of trying to dodge the arrow, the Duchess put her hand up to block it. She didn't do that out of fear, or because she froze or didn't have time to move. She did it intentionally — because she was confident that she could pluck the arrow from the air in midflight, having done that many times before. She knew how intimidating such a feat was. What fear it would instill in the bulls. Not that they weren't afraid already, running for their lives, and with no hope of escape — not after the great turtle took their ship. There was nowhere for them to go.

Even with one eye, and one hand, she knew that she could catch that arrow. Her subjects would be in awe. Any doubts that they had in her, any loss of respect over her injuries, would be washed away. They would worship her. Her rule would remain unchallenged.

She reached out with her hand to catch the arrow, but she feared damaging her face any further. Who knew how long it would take her eye to heal? Years maybe, if ever. Her beauty marred. She'd make them pay.

Her hand was in just the right spot, at just the right moment. Few could hope to make such a catch, but she had the speed. She had the skill.

One eye notwithstanding. The problem was that Dolan carried no normal bow. His was stiffer. Arrows shot from it carried farther, faster, truer. It raced through the air directly at the Duchess's forehead. As her fingers closed about it, the shaft slipped through them, and only the feathers brushed her fingers. The arrowhead impacted her cheek, and stopped only when it smashed into her jawbone. She fell back screaming in agony and fury.

Moments later, she was on her feet again, cursing them. Blood streamed from her hand. Her face was a ruin. "Kill them," she sputtered, and spat blood. "Kill them, my lovelies. But bring me the wizard and the wannabee god. I will have my fun with them yet. Kill all the rest."

"That's it then, we're dead," said Slaayde. "The one shot that really counted, and Mister Dead Eye missed."

Theta stood up in the longboat, falchion in one hand, his shield in the other. Artol, Tug, and Dolan did the same. The others braced themselves on one knee, their weapons held at the ready.

"Come forth and meet your doom," shouted Theta.

From all directions at once, the Evermerians attacked, swarming them. Claws and swords, tooth and nail, hammer and dirk, the battle raged, and the bay ran red with blood and death.

END

BOOKS BY GLENN G. THATER

THE HARBINGER OF DOOM SAGA
GATEWAY TO NIFLEHEIM
THE FALLEN ANGLE
KNIGHT ETERNAL
DWELLERS OF THE DEEP
BLOOD, FIRE, AND THORN
GODS OF THE SWORD
THE SHAMBLING DEAD
MASTER OF THE DEAD
SHADOW OF DOOM
WIZARD'S TOLL
VOLUME 11+ (forthcoming)

HARBINGER OF DOOM
(Combines *Gateway to Nifleheim* and *The Fallen Angle* into a single volume)

THE HERO AND THE FIEND
(A novelette set in the Harbinger of Doom universe)

THE GATEWAY
(A novella length version of *Gateway to Nifleheim*)

THE DEMON KING OF BERGHER
(A short story set in the Harbinger of Doom universe)

Visit Glenn G. Thater's website at http://www.glenngthater.com for the most current list of my published books.

My Mailing List (for notifications of new book releases and special discounts)
http://eepurl.com/vwubH

GLOSSARY

PLACES

The Realms
Asgard: legendary home of the gods
—Bifrost: mystical bridge between Asgard and Midgaard
—Valhalla: a realm of the gods where great warriors go after death
Helheim: one of the nine worlds; the realm of the dead
Midgaard: the world of man
—Lomion: a great kingdom of Midgaard
Nether Realms: realms of demons and devils
Nine Worlds, The: the nine worlds of creation
Nifleheim: the realm of the Lords of Nifleheim / Chaos Lords
Vaeden: paradise, lost
Yggdrasill: sacred tree that supports and/or connects the Nine Worlds

Places Within The Kingdom Of Lomion
Dallassian Hills: large area of rocky hills; home to a large enclave of dwarves
Dor Caladrill:

Eotrus Demesne
Dor Eotrus: fortress and lands ruled by House Eotrus, north of Lomion City
— Citadel, The: a generic name for the main part of Dor Eotrus — the castle itself. It is also often used to specifically refer to the castle's central tower.
— Courtyard, The: open area between the main citadel walls and the central tower and other

buildings.

— Keep, The: synonymous with Citadel

— Odinhome, The: temple to Odin located in Dor Eotrus; also used as a generic terms for temple/church of Odin.

—Outer Dor, The: the town surrounding the fortress of Dor Eotrus. Also used generically as the name for any town surrounding a fortress.

— Underhalls, The: the extensive basement levels beneath the citadel.

Berrill's Bridge: a large bridge over the Ottowhile River, northeast of Dor Eotrus, on the West Road

Eastern Hills: in the northeast section of Eotrus demesne

Markett: a village east of Dor Eotrus, within Eotrus demesne

Mindletown: a town of 400 hundred folk, a few days northeast of Dor Eotrus, in Eotrus demesne. Recently wiped out by trolls.

Ottowhile River: a large river northeast of Dor Eotrus, passable only via bridges for much of the year.

Rhentford: small village on the road between Dor Eotrus and Mindletown. Recently sacked by trolls.

Riker's Crossroads: village at the southern border of Eotrus lands, at the crossroads that leads to Lomion City and Kern.

Roosa: a town

Stebin Pass: a pass through the foothills of the Kronar Mountains, northwest of Dor Eotrus.

Trikan Point Village: village east-northeast of Mindletown, in Eotrus demesne

Vermion Forest: foreboding wood west of Dor

Eotrus
Temple of Guymaog: where the gateway was opened in the Vermion Forest
West Rock: at the northwest edge of Eotrus demesne, at the foothills of the Kronar Mountains.
Wortsford: a northern town within Eotrus demesne

Dor Linden: fortress and lands ruled by House Mirtise, in the Linden Forest, southeast of Lomion City
Dor Lomion: fortress within Lomion City ruled by House Harringgold
Dor Malvegil: fortress and lands ruled by House Malvegil, southeast of Lomion City on the west bank of the Grand Hudsar River
Dor Valadon: fortress outside the City of Dover
Doriath Forest: woodland north of Lomion City
Dover, City of: large city situated at Lomion's southeastern border
Dyvers, City of: Lomerian city known for its quality metalworking
Grommel: a town known for southern gnomes
Kern, City of: Lomerian city to the northeast of Lomion City.
Kronar Mountains: a vast mountain range that marks the northern border of the Kingdom of Lomion
Lindenwood: a forest to the south of Lomion City, within which live the Lindonaire Elves

Lomion City (aka Lomion): capital city of the Kingdom of Lomion

—Dor Lomion: fortress within Lomion City ruled by House Harringgold

— Channel, The: moat around Lomion City, 150 ft. wide by 30 ft. deep; connected to Grand Hudsar Bay

—Fister Mansion: a fancy old hotel in Lomion City

—Grand Hudsar Bay: the portion of the Grand Hudsar River that meets Lomion City's south and east borders.

—Great Meadow, The: picturesque swath of grassland outside the city gates

—Tammanian Hall: high seat of government in Lomion; home of the High Council and the Council of Lords

—Tower of the Arcane: high seat of wizardom in all Midgaard; in Lomion City

—The Heights: seedy section of Lomion City

—Southeast: dangerous section of Lomion City

Portland Vale: a town known for southern gnomes that are particularly skilled bridge building masons

Tarrows Hold: known for dwarves

Parts Foreign

Azure Sea: vast ocean to the south of the Lomerian continent

Black Rock Tower: Glus Thorn's stronghold

Bourntown:

Darendor: dwarven realm of Clan Darendon

Dwarkendeep: a renowned dwarven stronghold

Dead Fens, The: mix of fen, bog, and swampland

on the east bank of the Hudsar River, south of Dor Malvegil

Evermere, The Isle of: an island in the Azure Sea, far to the south of the Lomerian continent.

— The Dancing Turtle: Evermere's finest inn

Grand Hudsar River: south of Lomion City, it marks the eastern border of the kingdom

Emerald River: large river that branches off from the Hudsar at Dover

Ferd: Far-off city known for its fine goods

Jutenheim: island far to the south of the Lomerian continent (see below for more details).

Karthune Gorge: site of a famed battle involving the Eotrus

Kirth: Par Keld is from there

Kronar Mountains: foreboding mountain range that marks the northern border of the Kingdom of Lomion.

Lent

Minoc-by-the-Sea: coastal city

R'lyeh: a bastion for evil creatures; Sir Gabriel and Theta fought a great battle there in times past.

Saridden, City of:

Shandelon: famed gnomish city

Southron Isles: islands in the Azure Sea

—Hargone Bay:

Thoonbarrow: capital city of the Svarts

Trachen Marches: Theta and Dolan fought the Vhen there.

Tragoss Krell: city ruled by Thothian Monks

Tragoss Mor: large city far to the south of Lomion, at the mouth of the Hudsar River where it meets the Azure Sea. Ruled by Thothian Monks.

Jutenheim

It's an island continent in the far south of Midgaard's southern hemisphere. It's also the name of the primary human settlement (a large town with a significant port) on the continent.

Eye of Gladden, The:

Grasping Grond, The: an inn

PEOPLE

Peoples of Midgaard

Emerald elves

Lindonaire elves (from Linden Forest)

Doriath elves (from Doriath Forest)

Dallassian dwarves (from the Dallassian Hills). Typically four feet tall, plus or minus one foot.

Gnomes (northern and southern), typically three feet tall, plus or minus one foot.

Humans/Men: generic term for people. (In usage, sometimes includes gnomes, dwarves, and elves)

Lugron: a barbaric people from the northern mountains, on average, shorter and stockier than volsungs, and with higher voices.

Picts: a barbarian people

Stowron: pale, stooped people of feeble vision who've dwell in lightless caverns beneath the Kronar Mountains

Svarts (black elves), gray skin, large eyes, spindly limbs, three feet tall or so.

Vanyar Elves: legendary elven people

Volsungs: a generic term for the primary people/tribes populating the Kingdom of Lomion

High Council of Lomion

Selrach Rothtonn Tenzivel III: His Royal Majesty: King of Lomion

Aldros, Lord: Councilor

Aramere, Lady: Councilor representing the City of Dyvers

Balfor, Field Marshal: Councilor representing the Lomerian armed forces; Commander of the Lomerian army

Barusa of Alder, Lord: Chancellor of Lomion; eldest son of Mother Alder

Cartagian Tenzivel, Prince: Selrach's son, insane; Councilor representing the Royal House.

Dahlia, Lady: Councilor representing the City of Kern

Glenfinnen, Lord: Councilor representing the City of Dover

Harper Harringgold, Lord: Councilor representing Lomion City; Arch-Duke of Lomion City

Jhensezil, Lord Garet: Councilor representing the Churchmen; Preceptor of the Odion Knights

Morfin, Baron: Councilor

Slyman, Guildmaster: Councilor representing the guilds; Master of Guilds

Tobin Carthigast, Bishop: Councilor representing the Churchmen

Vizier, The (Grandmaster Rabrack Philistine): The Royal Wizard; Grandmaster and Councilor representing the Tower of the Arcane

NOBLE HOUSES

House Alder (Pronounced All-der)
A leading, noble family of Lomion City. Their principal manor house is within the city's borders
Batholomew Alder: youngest son of Mother Alder
Bartol Alder: younger brother of Barusa, Myrdonian Knight
Barusa Alder, Lord: Chancellor of Lomion, eldest son of Mother Alder.
Blain Alder: younger brother of Barusa
Brock Alder: 6th son of Mother Alder
Dirk Alder: eldest son of Bartol Alder
Edith Alder: daughter of Blain; a child
Edwin Alder: son of Blain
Mother Alder: matriarch of the House; an Archseer of the Orchallian Order
Rom Alder: brother of Mother Alder

House Eotrus (pronounced Eee-oh-tro`-sss)
The Eotrus rule the fortress of Dor Eotrus, the Outer Dor (a town outside the fortress walls) and the surrounding lands for many leagues.
Aradon Eotrus, Lord: Patriarch of the House (presumed dead)
Adolphus: a servant
Claradon Eotrus, Brother: (Clara-don) eldest son of Aradon, Caradonian Knight; Patriarch of the House; Lord of Dor Eotrus
Donnelin, Brother: House Cleric for the Eotrus (presumed dead)
Ector Eotrus, Sir: Third son of Aradon
Eleanor Malvegil Eotrus: (deceased) Wife of Aradon Eotrus; sister of Torbin Malvegil.

Gabriel Garn, Sir: House Weapons Master (presumed dead, body possessed by Korrgonn)

Humphrey (Humph): Claradon's manservant

Jude Eotrus, Sir: Second son of Aradon (prisoner of the Shadow League)

Knights & Soldiers of the House:

— Sergeant Artol: 7 foot tall veteran warrior.

— Sir Paldor Cragsmere: a young knight; formerly, Sir Gabriel's squire

— Sir Glimador Malvegil: son of Lord Torbin Malvegil; can throw spells

— Sir Indigo Eldswroth: handsome, heavily muscled, and exceptionally tall knight

— Sir Kelbor

— Sir Ganton: called "the bull" or "bull"

— Sir Trelman

— Sir Marzdan (captain of the gate, deceased)

— Sir Sarbek du Martegran (acting Castellan of Dor Eotrus), a knight captain of the Odion Knights

— Sir Wyndham the Bold of Weeping Hollow: knight captain (deceased)

— Lieutenant, The: veteran cavalry officer (deceased)

— Sergeant Vid

— Sergeant Lant

— Sergeant Baret

— Trooper Graham

— Trooper Harsnip (deceased), Sergeant Balfin (deceased), Sir Miden (deceased), Sergeant Jerem (deceased), Sir Conrad (deceased), Sir Martin (deceased), Sir Bilson (deceased), Sir Glimron (deceased), Sir Talbot (deceased), Sir Dalken (deceased)

Malcolm Eotrus: Fourth son of Aradon

Ob A. Faz III: (Ahb A. Fahzz) Castellan and Master Scout of Dor Eotrus; a gnome

Sirear Eotrus, Lady: daughter of August Eotrus (deceased)

Stern of Doriath: Master Ranger for the Eotrus (presumed dead)

Talbon of Montrose, Par: Former House Wizard for the Eotrus (presumed dead), son of Grandmaster (Par) Mardack

Tanch Trinagal, Par: (Trin-ah-ghaal) of the Blue Tower; Son of Sinch; House Wizard for the Eotrus. Aliases: Par Sinch; Par Sinch Malaban.

Sverdes, Leren: House physician and alchemist

House Harringgold

Harper Harringgold, Lord: Archduke of Lomion City; Lord of Dor Lomion, Patriarch of the House. He has a brother in Kern.

Grim Fischer: agent of Harper, a gnome

Marissa Harringgold: daughter of Harper, former love interest of Claradon Eotrus.

Seran Harringgold, Sir: nephew of Harper

House Malvegil

Torbin Malvegil, Lord: Patriarch of the House; Lord of Dor Malvegil.

Landolyn, Lady: of House Adonael; Torbin's consort. Of part elven blood.

Eleanor Malvegil Eotrus: (deceased) Wife of Aradon Eotrus; sister of Torbin Malvegil.

Gedrun, Captain: a knight commander in service to Lord Malvegil

Glimador Malvegil, Sir: son of Torbin and Landolyn; working in the service of House Eotrus.

Gravemare, Hubert: Castellan of Dor Malvegil
Hogart: harbormaster of Dor Malvegil's port.
Karktan of Rivenwood, Master: Weapons Master for the Malvegils
Stoub of Rivenwood: Lord Malvegil's chief bodyguard; brother of Karktan
Torgrist, Brother: Dor Malvegil's high cleric.
Troopers Bern, Brant, Conger: Malvegillian soldiers

House Morfin
Baron Morfin: Patriarch of the House; a member of the High Council
Gallick Morfin: eldest son of the Baron.

House Tenzivel (the Royal House)
King Selrach Rothtonn Tenzivel III: His Royal Majesty: King of Lomion
Cartagian Tenzivel, Prince: Selrach's son; insane.
Dramadeens: royal bodyguards for House Tenzivel
— Korvalan of Courwood, Captain: Commander of the Dramadeens.
— Mavron: second in command of the Dramadeens; a hulking brute

Other Noble Houses of Lomion

House Tavermain
House Grondeer
House Dantrel

House Forndin
A minor House loyal to and located within Eotrus lands. Their major holding is known as Forndin

Manor.

Alana Forndin, Lady: matriarch of the House

Sir Erendin of Forndin Manor: eldest son of the House (deceased)

Sir Miden of Forndin Manor: younger brother of Erendin (deceased)

Sir Talbot of Forndin Manor: younger brother of Erendin (deceased)

House Hanok

A minor House loyal to and located within Eotrus lands. Their major holding is known as Hanok Keep.

Sir Bareddal of Hanok Keep: in service to the Eotrus (deceased)

OTHER HOUSES AND GROUPS

Clan Darendon of Darendor

Royal clan from the dwarven kingdom

Bornyth Trollsbane, High King of Clan Darendon.

Galibar the Great: the prince of Darendor, first son to Bornyth and heir to Clan Darendon

Jarn Yarspitter: councilor to Bornyth

The Black Hand

A brotherhood of Assassins

Brethren, The: term the assassins use for fellow members of The Hand.

Grandmistress, The: the leader of The Hand

Mallick Fern: an assassin; The Hand's second ranking agent (deceased)

Weater the Mouse: a Hand leader

Brood tet Montu of Svartleheim
The royal house of the svarts
Diresvarts: svart wizard-priests
Guyphoon Garumptuss tet Montu: high king of
Thoonbarrow, Patriarch of Brood tet Montu,
Master of the Seven Stratems, and Lord of all
Svartleheim, offspring of Guyphoon Pintalia of the
Windy Ways, Traymoor Garumptuss the Bold, and
Trantmain lin Backus tet Montu, great king of the
undermountains
Cardakeen rack Mortha: a svart seer
Orator, The: the spokesman for the svart king

The Lords of Nifleheim and Their Minions
Azathoth: god worshipped by the Lords of
Nifleheim and The Shadow League/The League of
Light; his followers call him the 'one true god'.
Arioch: a Lord of Nifleheim
Bhaal: a Lord of Nifleheim; came through the
gateway in the Vermion but was banished back by
Angle Theta
Hecate: a Lord of Nifleheim.
Korrgonn, Lord Gallis: son of Azathoth
Mortach: (aka Mikel): a Lord of Nifleheim; killed
by Angle Theta
— Reskalan: demonic foot soldiers in service to
the Lords of Nifleheim
— Zymog: a reskalan
— Brigandir: supernatural warrior(s) of Nifleheim
— Einheriar: supernatural warriors of Nifleheim

The Asgardian Gods
Odin (the All-father) (aka Wotan): king of the
gods

Thor (aka Donar): son of Odin
Tyr (aka Cyo):
Heimdall (aka Vindler):
Loki:
Baldr:
—Valkyries: sword maidens of the gods. They choose worthy heroes slain in battle and conduct them to Valhalla.

Other Gods
Dagon of the Deep: appears as a giant lizard; lives in caverns beneath an uncharted island deep in the Azure Sea.
— Dwellers of the Deep: very large, bipedal sea creatures that worship Dagon.
Thoth:
Donar: worshipped by the Jutens; akin to Thor; son of Wotan.
Wotan: worshipped by the Jutens; akin to Odin

Great Beasts, Monsters, Creatures, Animals
Barrow Wight
Blood Lord: legendary fiends that drink blood and eat humans.
Dire Wolves: extremely large breed of wolves
Duergar: mythical undead creatures
Dwellers of the Deep: worshippers of Dagon; huge, bipedal fishlike creatures
Fire Wyrm or "Wyrms": dragons
Giant (aka Jotun, pl. Jotnar):
Grond: a type of large monkey or ape native to Jutenheim
Jotnar: giants (plural of Jotun)
Jotun: a giant

Ogres:
Leviathan: a huge sea creature
Saber-cat: saber toothed tiger
Tranteers: the lithe, speedy horses bred in Dover
Trolls, Mountain: mythical creatures of the high mountains
Wendigo: monster of legend that eats people.

THE EOTRUS EXPEDITION

The Crew of The Black Falcon
Slaayde, Dylan: Captain of The Black Falcon
Bertha Smallbutt: ship's quartermaster
Bire Cabinboy: ship's cabin boy — was in league with Darg Tran
Chert: a young seaman
Darg Tran, son of Karn, of old House Elowine: ship's navigator
Eolge: a crewman (deceased)
Fizdar Firstbar "the corsair": former first mate (presumed dead)
Gurt, Seaman: (aka Gurt the Knife) a crewman; known for knife fighting skills
Guj: boatswain. A half-lugron.
N'Paag: First Mate
Old Mock: a crewman (deceased)
Ravel: ship's trader and medic
Tug, Little: Near 7 foot tall part-lugron seaman; Old Fogey — Tug's battle hammer

The Passengers of The Black Falcon
Sergeant Artol: 7 foot tall veteran warrior.
Claradon Eotrus, Brother: (Clara-don) eldest son of Aradon, Caradonian Knight; Patriarch of the

House; Lord of Dor Eotrus

Dolan Silk: Theta's manservant

Ganton, Sir (the Bull): a knight of House Eotrus

Kayla Kazeran: part Lindonaire elf, rescued from slavery in Tragoss Mor

Kelbor, Sir: a knight of House Eotrus

Lant, Sergeant: a soldier of House Eotrus

Lomerian Soldiers: a squadron of soldiers of House Harringgold, assigned to assist House Eotrus. Under the command of Seran Harringgold.

Malvegil, Sir Glimador: first cousin to Claradon; son of Lord Malvegil

Malvegillian Archers: a squad of soldiers assigned to assist House Eotrus by Lord Malvegil

Ob A. Faz III: (Ahb A. Fahzz) Castellan and Master Scout of Dor Eotrus; a gnome

Paldor Cragsmere, Sir: a young knight of House Eotrus, formerly, Sir Gabriel's squire

Seran Harringgold, Sir: nephew of Arch-Duke Harper Harringgold — assigned to assist House Eotrus

Tanch Trinagal, Par: (Trin-ah-ghaal) of the Blue Tower; Son of Sinch; House Wizard for the Eotrus. Aliases: Par Sinch; Par Sinch Malaban.

Theta, Lord Angle (aka Thetan): a knight-errant from a far-off land across the sea. Sometimes called the Harbinger of Doom

Thothian Monk, a: an elderly fellow; taken prisoner during the incident with Prior Finch at Tragoss Mor

Trelman, Sir: a knight of House Eotrus

Vid, Sergeant: a soldier of House Eotrus

THE ALDER EXPEDITION

The Crew/Passengers of The Gray Talon
Alder Marines: squadrons of soldiers from House Alder

Azura du Marnian, the Seer: Seer based in Tragoss Mor.

Bartol Alder: younger brother of Barusa; a Myrdonian Knight

Blain Alder: younger brother of Barusa

DeBoors, Milton: (The Duelist of Dyvers). A mercenary

Edwin Alder: son of Blain

Kaledon of the Gray Waste: a Pict mercenary

Kleig: Captain of The Grey Talon

Knights of Kalathen: elite mercenaries that work for DeBoors

Myrdonian Knights: squadron of knights assigned to House Alder

THE LEAGUE OF LIGHT EXPEDITION

The Crew/Passengers of The White Rose
Brackta Finbal, Par: an archmage of The League of Light

du Mace, Varak: Captain of The White Rose

Ezerhauten, Lord: Commander of Sithian Mercenary Company

Frem Sorlons: captain of the Sithians Pointmen Squadron

Ginalli, Father: High Priest of Azathoth, Arkon of The League of Light.

Glus Thorn, Par (Master): an archmage of the League of Light

Hablock, Par: an archmage of the League of Light (deceased)

Keld, Par of Kerth: a middle-aged wizard of the League of Light, short, stocky, balding, and nervous.

Landru, Par: a wizard (deceased); has several brothers

Lugron: a barbaric people from the northern mountains, on average, shorter and stockier than volsungs, and with higher voices.

Mason: a stone golem created by The Keeper of Tragoss Mor; companion to Stev Keevis.

Miles de Gant: a sithian soldier (deceased). Son of Count de Gant

Morsmun, Par: an archmage of the League of Light (deceased)

Mort Zag: a red-hued giant

Oris, Par: an elderly wizard of the League of Light; former mentor of Par Keld.

Ot, Par: an archmage of the League of Light (deceased)

Pointmen, The: an elite squadron of the Sithian Mercenary Company

Rascelon, Captain Rastinfan: former captain of The White Rose (deceased)

Rhund, Par: a wizard of the League of Light

Sevare Zendrack, Par: Squadron wizard for the Pointmen

Sithians: mercenaries under the command of Ezerhauten; some are soldiers, some are knights

Stev Keevis Arkguardt: an elven archwizard from the Emerald Forest allied with The League of Light; former apprentice of The Keeper

Teek: lugron guard/jailor

Tremont of Wyndum: a sithian knight (deceased)
Weldin, Par: a wizard of the League of Light
Thorn, Par (Master) Glus: an archwizard of the League of Light; a sorcerer
—Lasifer, Par: Glus Thorn's gnome assistant/apprentice.
—Nord: a stowron in Thorn's employ
Tribik: lugron guard/jailor

Sithian Mercenary Company
Ezerhauten, Lord: Commander
Frem Sorlons: Captain, Pointmen Squadron
Landru, Par: a squadron wizard (deceased)
Markus, Captain: 2nd Squadron's captain
Miles de Gant: a knight; son of Count de Gant
Rewes of Ravenhollow, Sir: a knight (deceased)
Tremont of Wyndum: a knight captain

The Pointmen (an elite squadron of the Sithian Mercenary Company)
Frem Sorlons: captain, Pointmen Squadron
Sevare Zendrack, Par: squadron wizard for the Pointmen
Putnam, Sergeant: Pointmen,1st Squad
Boatman: Pointmen (deceased)
Borrel: Pointmen; a lugron
Bryton: Pointmen (deceased)
Carroll, Sir: Pointmen; a knight
Clard: Pointmen; a lugron
Dirnel: Pointmen; a lugron (deceased)
Held: Pointmen (deceased)
Jorna: Pointmen (deceased)
Lex: Pointmen
Little Storrl: Pointmen,1st Squad; a young lugron

Maldin, Sergeant: Pointmen,2nd Squad, (Badly wounded, spear through chest)
Moag: Pointmen,1st squad; a lugron
Roard, Sir: Pointmen,1st Squad; a knight (deceased)
Royce, Sir: Pointmen; a knight
Torak: Pointmen; a lugron
Ward: Pointmen
Wikkle: Pointmen; a lugron

The Regent's Expeditionary Force
Alder, Brock (aka The Regent): 6th son of Mother Alder
Alder, Dirk: eldest son of Bartol Alder
Alder, Rom: brother of Mother Alder
Bald Boddrick: (aka 'The Backbreaker')
Bithel the Piper:
Black Grint:
Gar Pullman:
Kralan, Captain: a Myrdonian Knight in command of the Myrdonian cavalry squadron
Martrin, Captain: the Lomerian guard captain in command of the regulars
Sentry of Allendale:

Militant and Mystic Orders
Caradonian Knights: priestly order; patron—Odin
Churchmen: a generic term for the diverse group of priests and knights of various orders.
Freedom Guardsmen: soldiery of Tragoss Mor
Grontor's Bonebreakers: a mercenary company. The lugron, Teek and Tribik belonged to it.
Halsbad's Freeswords: a mercenary company that Pellan once worked for.

Kalathen, Knights of: mercenary knights that work for Milton DeBoors

Myrdonians: Royal Lomerian Knights

Odions, The: patron—Odin; Preceptor—Lord Jhensezil; Chapterhouse: in Lomion City

Orchallian Order, The: an Order of Seers; Mother Alder is one of them.

Order of the Arcane: the wizard members of the Tower of the Arcane

Rangers Guild, The: Chapterhouse — Doriath Hall in Lomion City; Preceptor: Sir Samwise Sluug; loyal to House Harringgold.

— Drydan, Captain: a guard captain

Sithian Knights, The: Preceptor—Lord Ezerhauten

Sundarian Knights: patron: Thor; Preceptor: Sir Hithron du Maris; Chapterhouse: hidden in Tragoss Mor

Tyr, Knights of (aka Tyrians): patron—Tyr

The Evermerians

Duchess Morgovia of House Falstad: ruler of Evermere

Moby and Toby: brothers; the "beloveds" of Penny.

Penny: a tiny wisp of a girl

Rasker: he guards the Duchess's warehouse

Rendon, Lord: a noble of Evermere

Slint: aka the "scarecrow"; the Duchess's henchman

Trern: he guards the Duchess's warehouse

People of Mindletown

A town of several hundred folks within Eotrus demesne. The Odinhall is their most secure building. All listed are missing, dead, or presumed dead, except for Pellan.

Alchemist, the: town council member of Mindletown

Baker, The and sons: townsfolk of Mindletown

Butcher, the: town council member of Mindletown

Cobbler: townsman of Mindletown; lives across the street from the alchemist

Constable Granger: constable of Mindletown

Farmer Smythe: a townsman of Mindletown (deceased)

Iceman: an ice merchant that sells his ice to Mindletown; hails from the northwest.

Innman: an innkeeper in Mindletown

Mikar Trapper: a trapper that sells his wares in Mindletown

Miller and his sons: townsmen of Mindletown

Old Cern: town elder of Mindletown

Old Marvik: a Mindletown merchant that lived across from the alchemist

Pellan: the "beardless dwarf"; a town council member of Mindletown and former Captain in Dor Eotrus's guard

Tanner, Mileson: a townsman of Mindletown

Thom Prichard: a townsman of Mindletown (deceased)

Wheelwright and his wife: townsfolk of Mindletown (both deceased)

People of Jutenheim

Angel of Death, The: a seer / "woman of the bones". Travels with a large boy and wolf.

Darmod Rikenguard: a guide. Works with his two sons.

Helda: Rothmar's wife; Ragnar's mother.

Kordan: a guide

Juten: a resident of Jutenheim

Old Fortis: proprietor of The Grasping Grond

Red Demon of Fozramgar, The: its coming was foretold by the Angel of Death.

Ragnar: Rothmar and Helda's son

Rothmar: owns Jutenheim's leading smithery; husband of Helda; father of Ragnar

Monastery of Ivald, The

Brother Abraxon: chief monk of the Ivald Monastery

Brother Bertold: the monastery's keeper of maps

Brother Rennis: man's a guard post in the seventh underhall

Old Brother Hordin: former keeper of maps (deceased)

Others of Note

Azura du Marnian, the Seer: Seer based in Tragoss Mor. Now travels with the Alders on The Gray Talon.

Gorb: Azura's bodyguard (deceased)

Rimel Stark: Azura's bodyguard and famed Freesword

Dirkben: Azura's bodyguard (deceased)

Brondel Cragsmere, Sire: father of Sir Paldor of Dor Eotrus

Coriana Sorlons: daughter of Frem Sorlons

Dark Sendarth: famed assassin in league with House Harringgold and House Tenzivel

Du Maris, Sir Hithron: Preceptor of the Sundarian Chapterhouse in Tragoss Mor; from Dor Caladrill

Graybeard, Captain: the captain of the schooner docked at Evermere

Halsbad: a mercenary leader

Harbinger of Doom, The: legendary, perhaps mythical being that led a rebellion against Azathoth

Jaros, the Blood Lord: foe of Sir Gabriel Garn

Keeper, The: elven "keeper" of the Orb of Wizard beneath Tragoss Mor

Krisona, Demon-Queen: foe of Sir Gabriel Garn

Kroth, Garon: newly appointed High Magister

Mardack, Grandmaster (Par) of Montrose: famed wizard; father of Par Talbon of Montrose

McDuff the Mighty: a dwarf of many talents

Pipkorn, Grandmaster: (aka Rascatlan) former Grand Master of the Tower of the Arcane. A wizard.

Prior Finch: a prior of Thoth in Tragoss Mor (deceased)

Sarq: a Thothian Monk. Known as the Champion of Tragoss Mor

Shadow League, The (aka The League of Shadows; aka The League of Light): alliance of individuals and groups collectively seeking to bring about the return of Azathoth to Midgaard

Sluug, Sir (Lord) Samwise: Preceptor of the Rangers Guild; Master of Doriath Hall

Snor Slipnet: Patriarch of Clan Rumbottle; a gnome

Spanzileers, The: attacked the Eotrus by way of the eastern hills.

Talidousen: Former Grand Master of the Tower of the Arcane; created the fabled Rings of the Magi.

Thothian monks: monks that rule Tragoss Mor and

worship Thoth

Throng-Baz : an ancient people that used runic script

Valas Tearn: an assassin said to have slain a thousand men; foe of Sir Gabriel Garn

Valkyries: sword maidens of the gods. They choose worthy heroes slain in battle and conduct them to Valhalla.

Vanyar Elves: legendary elven people

TITLES

Archmage / Archwizard: honorific title for a highly skilled wizard

Archseer: honorific title for a highly skilled seer

Arkon: a leader/general in service to certain gods and religious organizations

Freesword: an independent soldier or mercenary

Grandmaster: honorific title for a senior wizard of the Tower of the Arcane.

Hedge Wizard: a wizard specializing in potions and herbalism, and/or minor magics

High Magister: a member of Lomion's Tribunal.

Leren: (pronounced Lee-rhen) generic title for a physician

Magling: a young or inexperienced wizard; also, a derogatory term for a wizard

Master Oracle: a highly skilled seer

Par: honorific title for a wizard

Seer (sometimes, "Seeress"): women with supernatural powers to see past/present/future events.

Wizard (aka Mage, Sorcerer, etc.): practitioners of magic

Wizards of the Arcane Order

Gatwind, Par: a wizard originally from the Southron Isles; a member of the Freedom Council.

Pipkorn, Grandmaster (aka Rascatlan): former Grand Master of the Tower of the Arcane. Aka, "Old Pointy Hat"

Spugnoir, Grandmaster: a grandmaster of the Tower of the Arcane

Trask, Par: a member of the Freedom Council

Triman, Par: a member of the Freedom Council

Vizier, The (Rabrack Philistine): aka The Royal Wizard; High Councilor representing the Tower of the Arcane

The Freedom Council

Pipkorn; Mardack; Sluug; Mirtise; Harringgold; Par Trask; Tenzivel; Baron Morfin; Gallick Morfin; Spugnoir; Captain Korvalan; Par Triman; Par Gatwind; Lord Smirdoon of Lockely Bay; et.al.

THINGS

Miscellany

Alder Stone, The: a Seer Stone held by House Alder

Amulet of Escandell: a magical device that detects the presence of danger; gifted to Claradon by Pipkorn

Articles of the Republic: the Lomerian constitution

Asgardian Daggers: legendary weapons created in the first age of Midgaard. They can harm creatures of Nifleheim.

Axe of Bigby the Bold: made of Mithril; gifted to Ob by Pipkorn

Barsen's Reserve: a high quality brandy

Book of the Nobility: treatise containing the traditional Lomerian laws with respect to the nobility.

Cavindish Wine: a sweet white wine made in Lomion

Chapterhouse: base/manor/fortress of a knightly order

Dargus Dal: Asgardian dagger, previously Gabriel's, now Theta's

Dor: a generic Lomerian word meaning "fortress"

du Marnian Stone, The: a Seer Stone held by Azura du Marnian

Dyvers Blades: finely crafted steel swords

Ether, The: invisible medium that exists everywhere and within which the weave of magic travels/exists.

Ghost Ship Box: calls forth an illusory ship; created by Pipkorn and gifted to Claradon.

Granite Throne, The: the name of the king's throne in Lomion City. To "sit the granite throne" means to be the king.

Mages and Monsters: a popular, tactical war game that uses miniatures

Mearn: comes in a jar

Mithril: precious metal of great strength and relative lightness

Essence of Nightshade: a lethal, fast-acting poison; carried by Black Hand agents as suicide pills to thwart capture

Orb of Wisdom: mystical crystal spheres that can

be used to open portals between worlds.

Ragnarok: prophesied battle between the Aesir and the Nifleites.

Ranal: a black metal, hard as steel and half as heavy, weapons made of it can affect creatures of chaos

Rings of the Magi: amplify a wizard's power; twenty created by Talidousen

Seer Stones: magical "crystal balls" that can see far-off events.

Shards of Darkness: the remnants of the destroyed Orb of Wisdom from the Temple of Guymaog.

Spottle: a dice game that uses a live frog

Sventeran Stone, The: a Seer Stone loaned to the Malvegils by the Svarts.

Tribunal: the highest-ranking judiciary body in the Kingdom of Lomion; members of the tribunal are called "High Magisters."

Valusian steel: famed for its quality

Weave of Magic; aka the Magical Weave: the source of magic

Worfin Dal: "Lord's Dagger," Claradon's Asgardian dagger

Wotan Dal: "Odin's Dagger"; gifted to Theta by Pipkorn.

Yggdrasill: sacred tree that supports and/or connects the Nine Worlds

Sigils and Standards

Standard of the Lomerian Guard: a white tower on a field of green. Soldiers wear red helmets and red and gray tabards with the standard embossed on at the center of their chests

Lomion Colors: red and gray
Myrdonian Knight Colors: emerald greed armor and weapons

Languages of Midgaard
Lomerian: the common tongue of Lomion and much of the known world
Magus Mysterious: olden language of sorcery
Militus Mysterious: olden language of sorcery used by certain orders of knights
Old High Lomerian: an olden dialect of Lomerian
Throng Baz: a dead language
Svartish: language of the svarts
Trollspeak: language of the mountain trolls

Combat Maneuvers, Techniques, and Styles
Dyvers' thrusting maneuvers
Dwarvish overhand strikes
Cernian technique
Sarnack maneuvers
Lengian cut and thrust style
Valusian thrust

Military Units of Lomion
Squad: a unit of soldiers typically composed of 3 to 8 soldiers, but it can be as few as 2 or as many as 15 soldiers.
Squadron: a unit of soldiers typically composed of two to four squads, totaling about 30 soldiers.
Cavalry Squadron or Troop: same as "squadron" but often has additional support troops to tend to the horses and supplies.
Company: a military unit composed of 4 squadrons, totaling about 120 - 150 soldiers.

Mercenary Companies can be of any size, the word "company" in their title, notwithstanding.

Brigade: a military unit composed of 8 companies, totaling about 1,000 soldiers

Regiment: a military unit composed of 4 brigades, totaling about 4,000 — 5,000 soldiers

Corps or Army: a military unit composed of 4 regiments and support troops, totaling about 20,000 — 25,000 soldiers

Military Ranks of Lomion

(from junior to senior)
Trooper
Corporal
Sergeant
Lieutenant (a knight is considered equivalent in rank to a Lieutenant)
Captain
Knight Captain (for units with Knights)
Commander
Knight Commander (for units with Knights)
Lord Commander (if a noble)
General (for Regiment sized units or larger)

ABOUT GLENN G. THATER

For more than twenty-five years, Glenn G. Thater has written works of fiction and historical fiction that focus on the genres of epic fantasy and sword and sorcery. His published works of fiction include the first ten volumes of the Harbinger of Doom saga: *Gateway to Nifleheim*; *The Fallen Angle*; *Knight Eternal*; *Dwellers of the Deep*; *Blood, Fire, and Thorn*; *Gods of the Sword*; *The Shambling Dead*; *Master of the Dead*; *Shadow of Doom*; and *Wizard's Toll*; the novella, *The Gateway*; and the novelette, *The Hero and the Fiend*.

Mr. Thater holds a Bachelor of Science degree in Physics with concentrations in Astronomy and Religious Studies, and a Master of Science degree in Civil Engineering, specializing in Structural Engineering. He has undertaken advanced graduate study in Classical Physics, Quantum Mechanics, Statistical Mechanics, and Astrophysics, and is a practicing licensed professional engineer specializing in the multidisciplinary alteration and remediation of buildings, and the forensic investigation of building failures and other disasters.

Mr. Thater has investigated failures and collapses of numerous structures around the United States and internationally. Since 1998, he has served on the American Society of Civil Engineers' Technical Council on Forensic Engineering (TCFE), is the Chairman of that Council's Executive Committee, and is the past Chairman of TCFE's Committee on

Practices to Reduce Failures. Mr. Thater is a LEED (Leadership in Energy and Environmental Design) Accredited Professional and has testified as an expert witness in the field of structural engineering before the Supreme Court of the State of New York.

Mr. Thater is an author of numerous scientific papers, magazine articles, engineering textbook chapters, and countless engineering reports. He has lectured across the United States and internationally on such topics as the World Trade Center collapses, bridge collapses, and on the construction and analysis of the dome of the United States Capitol in Washington D.C.

BOOKS BY GLENN G. THATER

THE HARBINGER OF DOOM SAGA
GATEWAY TO NIFLEHEIM
THE FALLEN ANGLE
KNIGHT ETERNAL
DWELLERS OF THE DEEP
BLOOD, FIRE, AND THORN
GODS OF THE SWORD
THE SHAMBLING DEAD
MASTER OF THE DEAD
SHADOW OF DOOM
WIZARD'S TOLL ·
VOLUME 11+ (forthcoming)

HARBINGER OF DOOM
(Combines *Gateway to Nifleheim* and *The Fallen Angle* into a single volume)

THE HERO AND THE FIEND
(A novelette set in the Harbinger of Doom universe)

THE GATEWAY
(A novella length version of *Gateway to Nifleheim*)

THE DEMON KING OF BERGHER
(A short story set in the Harbinger of Doom universe)

To leave a review for any of Glenn G. Thater's books, please click here (http://www.glenngthater.com/thank-you.html).

To join Glenn G. Thater's Mailing List (to receive notifications about new book releases and special offers and discounts on my books), please go to: http://eepurl.com/vwubH.